TAWDRA KANDLE

The Only One

Cover by Laura Hidalgo at BookFabulous Design
Proofreading by Kelly Baker
Formatting by Stacey Blake, Champagne Formats

ISBN-978-1-68230-195-1

Dedication

To my first, my last, my only

Clint

With love always

Prologue

Mason

"HEY, SWEET CHEEKS." SOFT lips brushed against my face. "It's almost time to wake up."

"Mmmm." I groaned. "Don't wanna. Too early."

Her quiet laughter sent a thrill of desire down my middle. "Never did like getting up. I wish I could let you sleep longer, darlin' boy, but our daughter's about to call for you. She's going to want breakfast."

I rolled over and buried my face in the pillow. "Can't you get her? Just this one morning?"

"Would that I could, my love. I'd give just about anything . . . but I can't." Her voice was wistful, and even in the haze of half-sleep, a lump rose in my throat.

"Lu, don't leave me. Not today. Stay."

"I'm never far, love. And I'm so proud of you. What you're doing here . . . raising Piper, taking care of your mama . . . I always knew the kind of man you are, Mason. But even I never would've guessed you'd be able to handle all this." I felt her hand sweep over my hair, and I wanted to capture it in my own, but somehow I couldn't move.

"I don't want to handle it. I'm tired of doing it on my own. I want to stay here, with you."

Her sigh went deep into my soul. "I know. And that's going to change. But you've got to trust a little, and you're gonna have to give a little, too. It's all going to be wonderful, my love, trust me. But right now, you've got to . . ."

"Wake up! Wake up, Daddy!" A small hand pounded on my shoulder, and with no little difficulty, I dragged myself away from the tempting embrace of sleep.

"Okay, kiddo. I'm awake." I slung an arm over my eyes.

"No, you're not. Get up, Daddy. Tuneful Time!"

"Yeah, I know." I groped around the bed covers until my fingers closed on the TV remote. "Climb up here, princess. I'll turn it on."

As my daughter clamored over me, I managed to open my eyes just enough to push the right buttons, and seconds later, the way-too-damn-perky-for-seven-AM voice of Miss Debbie filled my bedroom.

"Good morning, chickens! Are your eyes awake? Stretch them open! Are your hands awake? Clap them loud! And is your voice awake? Sing out with me! Let's get tuneful!"

Piper bounced up and down and began to sing along with the crazy lady on the television, her voice climbing a rudimentary version of scales. "Me, me, me, me, me, me, me!"

I let my eyes drift shut again and reached back into sleep, trying desperately to hear my wife's voice again, to feel her touch or catch a whiff of her unique scent.

Nothing. She was gone, as she was every morning, as she had been every day for nearly three years. No matter how real the dream felt, it wasn't reality. At least, it wasn't mine.

Not anymore.

Chapter One

Rilla

THERE WAS NEVER MUCH traffic on Highway 72 this time of day, and that was a good thing, because by the time I got home from my job at the farm stand, I was so tired that I could barely keep my eyes open. I'd been zoning for the past ten minutes, driving on automatic pilot, so far out of it that I nearly missed my own driveway.

The dirt road was bumpy, dotted with potholes that probably pre-dated my own birth. This farm had been in my family for more generations than I could count. Gram told me that her mother-in-law, who would've been my great-grandmother, had claimed the land had originally been granted to our family by George I of England. According to Great-Grandma, our relative had been a marquess with a sense of adventure who'd wanted to try out the new world after he'd run afoul of a powerful duke. The king had taken pity on him and set him up with acres of land in the colony that bore his name.

Truth? I didn't know. It made for a good story, especially when I was getting bored during the history lessons Gram was teaching me. I had a good imagination, and I could just picture my many-times-over great-grandpa stepping off the boat, maybe in Savannah, and traveling out to the wilderness to begin a new life. Sometimes when I was on my way to the fields or working in the garden, I'd pretend that I was his daughter, helping my family survive. Later, when I was older, I'd wondered if he'd brought a wife from England or married a local girl. What had she looked like, my great-grandmother from so many generations back? Had she married the marquess because of his title and land? Or had her family forced her to do it? Perhaps they were desperately poor, and that marriage was their ticket out of poverty.

On particularly wistful days, I might wonder if she'd married him for love. I invented a beautiful story for them. He'd gone back into town to buy supplies, and she was the girl who waited on him at the general store. He took one look at her and was smitten. He stayed in town to court her, bringing her flowers and little gifts until she finally agreed to be his wife. Or maybe he'd fallen sick while in town, and she'd nursed him back to health, saving him from the jaws of death.

The old truck hit a particularly deep hole, one I knew how to avoid. I braced my hand on the cracked dashboard and sucked in a breath, gritting my teeth. That might've thrown off my alignment, and Dad would not be pleased. It would be just another piece of ammunition to be used against me keeping this job, even though it might've just as easily happened if I were driving home from the store or from running an errand for Gram. Or even church.

I maneuvered around to the back of the house at a snail's pace. I didn't know if my father was already inside or still out in the fields; he walked to and from each day, using the time for his personal prayers. But if he were inside and heard me driving over three miles per hour, he'd be unhappy. And I'd learned over my twenty-two years of life that keeping Dad happy was a good idea.

Not that my father had ever hurt me. Not physically, anyway. Oh, I was sure I'd had my bottom swatted when I was a toddler, or maybe my hand popped now and then if I went to touch a hot stove or something breakable. But from my earliest memories, I'd known that the emotional barometer in our household rose and fell with Dad's moods. If everything on the farm was running well, if the crops were growing, prices were good and all the machinery were in working order, and if I'd been behaving myself, finishing my homeschool lessons and my chores in a timely manner, Dad would be calm. He might give us one of his rare smiles and linger over coffee at the kitchen table while Gram and I did the dishes.

On the other hand, if we'd had too much or too little rain, or if something had broken down, or if I'd been mouthy or rebellious or sighed too much at church, Dad's forehead would furrow, and his eyes would go dark. He'd stare at me with thunder on his face, and Gram would tut-tut as she went about her work. I'd walk around with a perpetual lump in my stomach, afraid of my own shadow until everything eased again.

I turned off the truck and pulled the keys from the ignition, reached for my canvas handbag and slung the strap over my shoulder. I slid from the seat and closed the door behind me, careful not to slam it. I climbed the two steps to the back door and toed off my shoes as I stood on the mat.

"You can just come on in and relax. He's not back yet." Gram stood at the sink, her back to me as she rinsed off tomatoes.

I sighed and opened the screen door. "Thanks, Gram. Give me just a second to wash up, and I'll help you finish dinner."

"Take your time. The potatoes are done, and the chicken's keeping warm. It was too warm to keep on the oven, so I'm just slicing up a cold salad."

Smiling, I hurried through the kitchen and up the back stairs. Gram was old school. She'd come of age during the turbulent 1960's, but somehow, they'd never touched her. Instead, everything she did harkened back to what her own mother and mother-in-law had taught her. Supper was always meat, potatoes, vegetables and bread. She grew a full and varied garden, made fruit jams and canned vegetables and sewed her own curtains. She'd raised and homeschooled me, and I'd yet to find anything the woman couldn't tackle.

In my bedroom, I dropped my handbag onto a chair and tossed my sneakers into the closet. I glanced at my quilt-covered bed with longing; it'd been a crazy busy day, and crawling under the covers was more appealing than even eating at this point. But the last thing I needed was to give Dad another reason to argue against the job. So instead, I dragged myself into the bathroom across the hall, washed my hands and splashed water on my face before going back down to help get dinner on the table.

Dad had taken Gram's place at the sink, and he glanced at me over his shoulder as I came back into the kitchen. "You're late. Did you leave your grandmother to make dinner by herself? You know I expect better."

I steeled myself against wincing. That had been the story of my life. *He expected better.* I'd been disappointing my father as long as I remembered. I always wondered if those had been the first words I'd heard upon being born. And I wondered if my mother had felt the same way, which would explain why she'd gotten off the farm and as far away from Burton, Georgia as soon as she could.

"I got here as fast as possible, but—"

"Emmett, leave the child be. I started supper early today, and there wasn't a blessed thing Rilla could've done to help me. She would've been in my way." Gram shot me a wink and a smile.

Dad grunted. “Still. I told you this business with the farm stand is not what a young girl should be doing. It’s not right.”

“I’m twenty-two, Dad. I’m not sixteen. And I’m working at a family farm stand, with other people there. It’s not like I took a job at a bar serving beer.”

“Don’t sass me, Marilla Grace. You know what I mean. You might think you’re grown up, but you’re still living here under my roof. And my rules still apply to you.”

“I’m sorry, Dad.” I skirted around him to pick up the bowl of potatoes and carry it to the table. “I didn’t mean disrespect. I just meant, I need to do something, and working for the Reynolds is actually wonderful. They’re so good to me, and so nice, all of them—”

“That Sam marry the girl yet? The one who’s been living at their house for over a year now?” My father crossed his arms over his chest and stared me down, his eyebrows drawn together.

“No, I think they’re planning the wedding for next spring.” I avoided meeting his gaze. “But Ali and Flynn got married last month, you know, and they’re on their honeymoon.”

“Those are the two with the child they had out of wedlock, aren’t they? About time they did the right thing.” He shook his head. “When I remember their mother and father and what they’d think of those two . . .” His voice trailed off, but his tone left no doubt about the fact that Sam and Ali’s late parents would join him in disapproval. I felt a familiar stirring of anger in my chest.

“Dad, it’s not like that. When you consider how hard Sam and Ali worked to keep the farm in their family, and how hard they still work . . . they’re the nicest people. And Meghan and Flynn are awesome, too. I love being around them.”

Gram sucked in a breath through her nose, which I knew was her warning signal to me. *Don’t push him.* But sometimes

I was tired, just dog dead tired, of hearing my father run down good people simply because they didn't meet some impossible standard he held for the world. I knew disagreeing with him didn't do any good, but there came a point when I couldn't keep my mouth shut.

"Hard work or no, it doesn't excuse how they've conducted their personal lives. What do you think the Lord sees when He looks at them? He doesn't care about them keeping that farm. Better they'd given it up and worried more about their conduct and how it looks."

I swallowed back another argument that I knew wouldn't do any good. Instead, I found the salad tongs in a drawer and put them next to the salad bowl as Gram pulled out her chair to sit down. Dad took his place at the head of the table and waited for me to settle before he bowed his head.

"Lord, we thank you for the provision which you have so graciously placed on this table, and we ask you to remind us that all things come from you. Make us mindful of your blessings and of the many ways that we offend you daily. Give us hearts that seek your will and your way. Keep us from being a stubborn, stiff-necked people, and place us in your pathways. In the name of Jesus, Amen."

"Amen." Gram and I both echoed the word in murmurs, and she began passing the food. For a few minutes, there was no sound other than the metal spoons hitting the glass of bowls and then plates. I was last to serve myself, as I'd been my entire life, and once I'd finished putting food on my plate, I moved each bowl to the empty end of the table. Once upon a time, I knew, chairs had sat there, chairs that had been occupied by my grandfather and by my mother. Grampy had died when I was eight months old, and Mama—or whatever I'd called her—had left the farm six months later. Their chairs were pushed up against the wall, ready to be used in case we had company. Gram had once told me that my father had moved the chairs himself after my mother left. I wondered if the sight of her empty place had hurt him too much to bear.

"How was work today, Rilla?" Gram never set out to antagonize her son, but neither was she afraid of him. She smiled at me across the table, ignoring the frown on Dad's face.

"It was great." I cut into a piece of chicken. "Really busy. Oh, and Sam came by at the end of the day, and I went over the numbers so far on their promotional campaign. He was impressed. He asked if I might be interested in taking on a few more clients."

My father's exhale left no doubt about where he stood on the matter. "I thought your job was to sell vegetables at the stand. Sam Reynolds isn't paying you to mess with that other stuff. Computers and other nonsense."

"Actually, he is." I twisted my napkin in my lap. "Remember I told you he agreed to be my first client? I'm not charging him much, since he's sort of my guinea pig, but he's paying me for what I'm doing. I got a website up for the stand, and I started social media accounts, too."

"Ridiculous. What does a farmer need with advertising? That's not how we did things in my day." Dad's fork clattered against his plate.

"It's not the farm I'm promoting. It's the stand. And yeah, they've never done anything but road signs, but now people can see them on the Internet. They can look up what's in season, and people who're just driving through can find the stand if they look up a place to eat." I allowed a small smile to play on my lips. "Today a family stopped to buy peaches. The mom told me she'd found us on a restaurant app. It was so cool."

My father grumbled again, but Gram patted my hand. "That's wonderful. I'm sure Sam's real pleased."

"He seems to be." I took a bite of salad.

"I hope you're not working there with him by yourself. I don't want people saying things about my daughter being alone with man who isn't her husband or her relative."

"Dad." I tried to keep my voice respectful, even though my jaw ached with frustration. "First of all, it's a farm stand. I'm out in the open, not tucked back in some dark room. Second, no one cares what I do. There's no one around to judge me. And third, this is why I took classes, remember? I got my degree in business and marketing so I could get a job and start to make my own way."

He snorted and rolled his eyes. "Earn your own way. So I haven't been doing a good enough job all these years? Roof over your head, food on the table, clothes to wear . . . and now you need to chase after money?"

"I'm not chasing after money, Dad. I have a plan to grow my PR business."

"Then why're you working at a farm stand, selling vegetables?" My father might've been a farmer who never graduated high school, but he was still a master when it came to turning arguments in the direction he wanted. I'd never won one yet.

I sighed and shook my head. "Because I'm just starting out, and I wanted to earn some money to help build the company." I took a deep breath. "And so that I can make enough to get my own place and move out."

It was as though I'd uttered some kind of spell that halted movement at the table. Gram's hand, holding her fork, stopped halfway to her mouth. Dad had just taken a bite of chicken, and his jaw froze.

I pretended I didn't see anything, even though my hand shook a little as I reached for my glass of water. "It's going to take a few months, of course, but I've been keeping my eye open for some place in town that might work. You know, just a little apartment, something safe."

"No." My father spoke just one syllable, but it held such finality that my stomach plummeted.

"Dad, I don't mean any disrespect, but remember, I'm old

enough—"

"I said no. No daughter of mine is going to live off by herself, without her family or without a husband." He resumed eating and leveled a steel gaze at me. "Just what do you think Jonathan would think about you moving out?"

I stifled the urge to roll my eyes. "Jonathan really wouldn't have anything to say about it, would he? He's a friend. He doesn't have the right to express an opinion on what I do or don't do."

"Don't be flippant or stupid, Marilla. Jonathan's intentions toward you are clear. He's just waiting until he's established, with his own church, before he makes it official. If I didn't believe that, trust in him, I'd never let you spend as much time with him as you do."

I pushed away my plate, food only half-eaten. "I help out with the youth group. I see him at church. We're not exactly dating. I've never even been alone with him."

"No, and you won't be. Not until it's time for the both of you to make that commitment. Jonathan understands that. I've spoken to him."

"Dad, honestly." My face was flushed, I could feel it. "I'm not sure I'm interested in Jonathan that way. Please don't make promises that I'm not going to be able to keep."

"The child's right, Emmett." Gram wiped her mouth with her napkin. "This isn't the nineteenth century, and we're not part of some religious sect. She's old enough to make her own decisions about who she does and doesn't see." Her voice gentled as she laid a hand on his arm. "She's twenty-two. Most girls her age have been dating for six or seven years. Rilla's been a good girl, respectful of your rules. You've raised her right. Now you have to trust her—and what you've taught her—enough to let her try her wings a bit."

"Trying wings isn't safe in this day and age, Ma. Like you said, it's not the nineteenth century. Men have expectations.

They don't take no for an answer, and the first time she's alone with some idiot who thinks he's found easy pickings—"

"Dad! Enough." I swallowed hard. "Please. I'm not talking about running wild or going to bars—or anything like that. It's not like there's someone I want to date. Guys aren't exactly knocking down the doors to ask me out. And if Jonathan wants to talk about getting serious, I'll consider it. But for now, all I want to do is live on my own. Just have a little freedom." I pushed back from the table and picked up my plate.

"Mind your words, young lady." My father half-growled at me. "You may think you're all grown up, but you're still my daughter." He stood up, too, and stalked out of the kitchen, the screen door slamming behind him.

I turned on the faucet and let the hot water fill the sink, blinking back sudden tears that threatened. Gram stood next to me, sliding an arm around my waist.

"Don't be bothered, sweet girl. Your father . . . he's just worried, that's all. He sees you growing up, and it scares him. It was much easier for him when you were eight, and he could control your whole life." She nudged me with her elbow. "Or at least he thought he could."

"But I've never done anything to make Dad think I'd be . . . what he thinks I'll be. Why can't he trust me?"

Gram sighed. "It's not so much you, Rilla. You and I both know that. He looks at you, and he sees your mother."

"But I'm not her."

"No, you're not, but you look like her, and there's part of him that thinks if she'd been raised right, she wouldn't have left. He blames her family for not being stricter, and he blames himself for letting her leave. He's never yet gotten around to laying the blame where it belongs, which is on Joely herself. She's the one who decided to leave, not her mama and daddy. Not your dad. Not you. Just her, and yet that boy still can't see clearly enough to realize that."

I smiled through my tears at Gram referring to my father as 'that boy.' He frustrated both of us sometimes, it was true, but I knew that he acted out of love for me, and as Gram said, in reaction to my mother's abandonment of us all.

"What will he do if I move out, Gram? Am I wrong for wanting my own life? I don't mean to hurt him. But I don't want to stay here forever, either."

She patted my arm. "Honey, at some point, we all have to stand on our own two feet and make our own decisions. Your daddy'll be mad and sad when you move out, but he'll get over it. Nothing's going to change the fact that you're his baby girl. He loves you. And so do I."

I turned and hugged her, careful to keep my wet hands from touching her back. "Thanks, Gram. I appreciate it."

"Any time, sweet girl. Just remember your old Gram wouldn't mind seeing some great-grands before she shuffles off to the big vegetable garden in the sky. So don't let your father scare you into a becoming an old maid. Got it?"

I laughed. "Message received."

Chapter Two

Mason

"HEY, IS THIS PLACE open or what?"

The door banged open, and I straightened from where I'd been bending over behind the bar, checking the connection for the ice machine. Sam Reynolds grinned at me as he walked over, taking off his hat and running his hand over his short hair.

"Not open for reprobate farm boys who can't hold their whiskey." I held out a hand as I winked.

"You must be thinking of my brother-in-law. I can drink Flynn under the table any day." He shook my hand and paused as though considering. "Come to think of it, I'm pretty sure Ali can out-drink him, too. Have you ever seen my sister shoot whiskey?"

I nodded. "It's a scary thing. I don't mess with that one." I leaned against the oak bar. "So what's shaking, Sam, my man?"

He sat down on a stool across from me. "Not much. Just

happened to be coming home from town, and I thought I'd get a beer. You know, give you some business so this joint doesn't go under."

I unhooked a mug from the rack. "Thanks. It's just fellows like you keeping us afloat. Well, you and the hordes of women who come here to dance and drink just about every night. We had to turn people away this weekend. Hit capacity at nine o'clock."

Sam whistled under his breath. "That's great. You've got to be proud."

"I am." I propped one foot on the brass floor rail and leaned back again. "We're opening for lunch starting next month. Different crowd, different vibe, but I'm hoping it'll work." I stuck my hands in my front pockets and cocked my head at my friend. "So what're you really doing here? Why aren't you rushing home to that gorgeous woman of yours?"

He sighed. "Okay, you got me. Meghan's down in Florida this week. She wanted to get some wedding planning stuff done before school starts, plus you know her brother and sister-in-law just had a baby girl. I think she wanted to get her hands on that kid as much as she wanted to pick out her wedding gown."

"And you didn't go with?" I raised one eyebrow. Meghan and Sam were pretty much inseparable and had been for the last year. I'd had a front row seat to their developing love story; in fact, I liked to tease Sam that I'd seen his fiancée first, since she'd come into my bar with her best friend that night before the two of them broke down on the dark country road where Sam'd found them. He always retorted that it wasn't who saw her first that counted; it was who claimed her, and I couldn't argue with that one.

"Not this trip. Bad time of year, with the harvest and getting everything in, and then Ali and Flynn are gearing up to move up to New York, too. I just couldn't make it happen."

"Sorry. But you're welcome to hang out here as long as

you want."

"Thanks. I don't mind being alone. It's just the house is so damn quiet anyway since Ali and Bridget moved out. With Meghan away, I kind of wander around." He shook his head. "I'm pathetic, man."

Envy shot through me, a sensation so painful I almost bent over. "Nah. You're just . . . aware of what you've got. That's good. Too many people don't appreciate it until it's too late."

Sam held my gaze, his brown eyes steady. "I'm sorry, Mason. I didn't think . . . it's got to be tough on you all the time."

I shrugged. "It's been almost three years. And I'm luckier than some. I've got Piper. If I hadn't had her when . . . after the accident . . . I don't know. I might've done something crazy." I reached down into the small fridge under the bar and pulled out a bottle of my favorite craft beer. Using the opener built in beneath the lip of the wood, I popped the top and took a long swig. "I didn't mean to make you feel bad. I'm happy for you and Meghan. And for Flynn and Ali, too. Speaking of which . . ." I forced a grin. "When do they take off for the Big Apple?"

"Ten days. They're living in a short-term rental in town right now. But they're going to build a house out on our land to live in during the months of the year they're in Georgia. Broke ground on it last week."

"That's got to make you happy, knowing they'll be back. You're not really losing your sister and your niece."

Sam smiled. "Not really. Don't get me wrong. I'm not looking forward to them leaving, even just until spring. But I know it's the right thing for them. For all of them." He rubbed the back of his neck. "I've depended on Ali for too long. It's going to be tough, getting used to handling the farm and the stand on my own."

"I thought I heard you'd hired someone to take over the stand for her." I didn't miss much news from Burton, seeing that most everyone who sat at my bar was more than willing to talk.

"We brought on someone to help at the stand, yeah. Actually, we hired her to do PR for us, and then when Ali and Flynn decided they'd spend part of the year in New York and part of it down here, we asked Rilla if she might want to work at the stand, too. So far, she's been great."

"PR, huh? You guys hitting the big time?"

Sam laughed. "Honest to God, I never thought we'd advertise anywhere except on those old road signs, but Rilla made a good case. Plus, she's just starting out in this business, and she's working cheap in return for us spreading the word if we're happy."

"And are you?" I took another pull of my beer.

"Yeah, absolutely. I thought most of it was stupid, but I have to admit, she's brought in some customers we wouldn't have had otherwise. She's got good ideas, along with plain old common sense." Sam narrowed his eyes as he looked at me across the bar. "You should talk to her. See what she could do for you."

I shook my head. "Didn't you hear what I said before? Capacity. We don't need any more advertising."

Sam finished his beer and pushed the mug away. "What about your new lunch idea? Rilla could promote that for you. Spread the word. Maybe even pull in some tourist traffic. You're far enough out on the highway that you might be able to catch some of the folks leaving Savannah."

"Could, I guess. I figured mostly word of mouth would bring in traffic. It's not like I'm banking on the extra income to stay open. Just trying to pad the kid's college fund, you know." I winked, and Sam laughed.

"Right, I get that. Still, it couldn't hurt. I bet you'd at least make back in extra sales whatever you paid Rilla, which wouldn't be much."

I narrowed my eyes. "Just what are you up to, dude?

Why're you pushing this so hard?"

Sam blew out a long breath and sat back in the stool. "Okay, I promised Ali and Meghan that I'd talk up Rilla's business. I guess the girls are afraid she won't make it work, not without some help, anyway. And they like her."

"Why wouldn't she be okay without help, if she's as good as you say?"

"She's shy. Quiet. Smart, for sure, but until she gets to know you, she doesn't talk much. Remember Emmett Grant, lives off highway 72? Big farm? She's his daughter."

I frowned. "I don't remember him being married or having a family. Wasn't he part of the Guild?" My dad had been on the town's unofficial council for as long as I could remember, right up until the heart attack that ended his life. Those men met about once a month to discuss issues in Burton and what they could do to help make the town run better and prosper.

"He was. And he was married, too, I guess, a long while back. She ran off, though."

"I don't remember any Grants in school with us." Sam and I'd been in high school together, though it felt like a lifetime ago now.

"Rilla's younger. About Meghan's age, I guess. And she didn't go to the high school, she was homeschooled."

"Huh." I finished my beer and chucked the bottle into our recycling bin. "But she's good at this advertising stuff, you say? Did she go to college for it?"

"Went to school on-line and got her degree." Sam turned his empty mug in a circle on the oak bar. "She doesn't talk to me too much, except for farm stand stuff. She's polite and respectful and calls me 'Mr. Reynolds' even though I keep telling her I'm Sam. But I guess the girls have gotten her to open up some, and she told them that she wants to move out of her dad's house. So she's working real hard to make that happen."

I leaned back again. "Are we talking just a girl wanting to

spread her wings, or bad shit going down? Or don't you know?"

"Nah, I think it's just . . . over-protective father. Her grandmother helped raise her, too. And she's active in that community church off route 23. I get the sense she's feeling a little stifled. Meghan says once she relaxes and opens up, she's funny and really, really smart. I trust my girl's word. And like I said, Rilla's done good work for us."

I nodded. "You got a card or something? A number where I can set up to meet with her?"

Sam reached into his back pocket and dug out a small white rectangle. "Just so happens I do." He slapped it on the bar. "But don't let on you're doing this as a favor to me. You know how women are. I don't want her to get her back up and quit on me." He paused, and his eyes narrowed. "And don't go getting any ideas about hiring her to work here. You know, in the bar. She can do your PR, but we've got dibs on her at the stand."

I snorted. "A homeschooled church kid with an overbearing daddy? Yeah, I don't see her being a good candidate for waiting tables or manning the bar here. I don't think you have to worry, bro."

Sam cocked his head. "Stranger things, buddy. I didn't think the party-girl art student who came to stay with us was the right one for me." He spread his hands, his smile growing huge. "But look at me now."

"Whoa there, buddy. Just whoa. I meant it when I said this chick wouldn't be a good fit for my bar. But if you're talking about something more personal than that, I can tell you for damn sure I'm not interested. I don't have time for my life now. Hell if I can fit in a serious woman. Girl like that, she's gonna be serious trouble for sure."

Sam's eyes met mine, and his were filled with compassion. "Things getting rough, Mason?"

I blew out a sigh and reached for another beer, second-guessed it and grabbed a shot glass instead. "Nothing I can't handle." I tipped the Jack and filled the shot to the brim, set the bottle down and tossed back the liquor. "Doctors say Mom's got a good chance, but there's all this shit that has to happen first. She gets chemo, then her counts drop and she needs a transfusion, then that makes her sick . . ." I shook my head. "It's fucked-up, man. God, I know I sound selfish as hell, but I moved back here so my mother could help me raise my daughter. When the doctor told us my mom had leukemia, you know, it's crazy, but I wanted to laugh. Like, for real? First my wife, then my mother?" I rubbed my face.

"Sorry. Most of the time I'm okay. I just roll. But I didn't sleep very well last night." The memory of Lu's words whispered in my ear made me flinch, and I hoped Sam didn't notice.

If he did, he didn't say anything. Instead, in true Sam fashion, he only nodded, though the expression in his eyes spoke volumes. It wasn't pity, which I couldn't stand, or even sympathy, which I still kind of hated. It was understanding and compassion, making me remember that Sam and Ali had lost both of their parents in a horrific car accident when the two kids were only eighteen and fourteen respectively. Sam had been forced into adulthood and responsibility way too young. Of all the people I knew here in Burton, this guy understood what I was going through. Or at least he came closer than anyone else.

"I can't change any of that, dude. It sucks." He messed with the napkin under his empty mug. "Hope you know if you need anything, anything at all, I'm around." He glanced up at me, trepidation written all over his face. "I don't love babysitting, but I helped raise Bridget, so I can even do that, if you didn't have anyone else."

I laughed and clapped him on the shoulder. "Message received, Sam. You're on my last-resort list when I need someone to watch Piper. No worries right now. The woman I hired to help Mom and keep her eye on the rug rat was a good call."

"Awesome." Sam didn't try to hide the relief. "But if you

need someone to vent or talk or whatever, you know, I'm surrounded by women. I've got that sensitive sympathetic shit down."

I laughed. "Duly noted. How about when I need someone to get stupid wasted with, so I can forget all the crap?"

"Hey, I'm down for that, too. Though Ali might be a better choice. Like I said, my sister's scary good at holding her alcohol. But if she's not around, I'm willing to take one for the greater good." He frowned and rose up a little to reach into his back pocket again, this time pulling out his phone and glancing at the screen. The smile that spread over his lips had me feeling jealous all over again.

"Message from your woman?" I grabbed a rag and wiped at the condensation on the bar, just to have something to do with my hands.

"Yeah, she's just checking in." The smirk on his face told me Meghan was doing more than that, but I let it go. No way I needed any more information.

"Well, like I said, if you want to hang while she's gone, come in any time and I'll keep you set up." I pointed to his empty glass. "Sure you don't want another? For the road?"

"Nah, man, I'm good." He stood up and flipped open his wallet, digging for cash, but I waved him off.

"This one's on me, bro. Sympathy beer."

Sam raised one eyebrow. "You don't have to do that."

"I know I don't, but I did. Get on out of here. Go home to that empty house and call your girl. Have phone sex and don't tell me about it."

"Thanks, man. Hang in there, you hear? And don't forget to call Rilla." He pointed to the card that still lay between us.

I palmed it and stuck in my pocket. "Got it. See you around, Sam."

"Later, dude." Sam put his hat back on and stalked out of the bar. I noticed a few women's eyes linger on him, and I shook my head, grinning. Those chicks didn't have a shot in hell with Sam Reynolds. That guy was captured, hog-tied and strung-up for good by the red-headed art teacher who'd stormed into his life last year.

My smile faded as a thought darted into my mind.

I'd give anything to be strung-up like him still. Anything to go home and be greeted by my wife . . . to have her be pissed that I'd worked too late again . . . anything to call her up just to say, "Hey, baby. Whatcha doin'?"

"Hey, Mason, I need three Michelob drafts, a house red and a Bacardi and Coke." Darcy, our head waitress, slid her tray onto the bar and looked at me with narrowed eyes. "You okay, Mase?"

"Sure." I forced a smile and turned to the taps behind me. "Coming right up."

Chapter Three

Rilla

"YOU AWAKE THERE, YOUNG lady?"

I startled and glanced sideways at Gram. "Yeah, I'm awake." I kept my voice low as Pastor Shand droned on. "Just . . . absorbed."

"Uh huh." Gram wasn't fooled. She cast her eyes to the front of the church, where my father sat with three other men behind the pulpit. The elders of the church had begun this practice a few years ago, ostensibly to reinforce the idea that they stood behind the pastor's preaching—literally—but I had a hunch it was more likely a better way to keep an eye on the whole congregation during the sermon. It was annoying to me that I couldn't so much as fidget in my chair without hearing something about it later on.

"Sometimes this man just gets too fond of hearing his own voice." Gram's tone was dry, and her lips barely moved. "He made his point ten minutes ago. Roast beef's going to be burned today, for sure."

I bit the inside of my lip to keep from giggling. Years and years ago, before I was born, Gram was a young farm wife when a visiting preacher came to town. His sermon was record-breaking long, and my grandmother was in the habit of putting on the midday meal before her family went to church. That morning, she'd done up a succulent roast beef, apparently my grandfather's favorite. But thanks to the hour-long message, by the time they got home, the roast was burned to a crisp, overdone to the point of being inedible. Ever since, any time we had a long-winded speaker, we all said he burned the roast beef.

"You're going to get us in trouble." I kept my eyes on the pastor and murmured the words. "But is he ever going to finish? My stomach's growling."

"Let us pray." Pastor Shand finally said the words I'd been waiting to hear. I bowed my head and let out a long sigh. Next to me, I could feel Gram shaking with laughter.

The prayer went on for a few moments, and when he said, "Amen," there was a discernible rustle within the congregation as everyone began gathering their purses, sweaters and bags. The sermon was always at the end of the service, and today especially, the whole church was restless. One of the elders, Mr. Gavin, stood up to pronounce the final blessing and benediction, and then old Mrs. Roon began to pound out notes on the piano in the back.

"You know, my father used to say that since the good Lord made a whole world for us to worship Him in, he couldn't understand why people would want to waste an entire day in church, away from the beauty of nature." Gram shook her head as she looped her purse over her elbow. "Days like this, I think he was onto something."

I opened my mouth to agree, but before I could say anything, I felt a brief touch at my back. The man who stood just behind my chair was about a foot taller than me, with hair so light it was almost invisible. His pale blue eyes were fringed by lashes the same shade of his hair, which always gave him a slightly wide-eyed look.

"Hey, Jonathan." I turned, smiling. "How're you today?"

He ducked his head, a habit he'd had as long as I'd known him. "I'm just blessed! I don't know how anyone could be anything else after hearing that sermon and enjoying a worship time like we just had. Amen?"

I swallowed the lump of annoyance. I absolutely hated Jonathan's habit of ending any question with an amen. I knew he was a youth pastor, and so did everyone else. But he seemed convinced that if he didn't talk the talk all day every day, someone might forget. I heard Gram's sigh.

"Sure." I tugged down to adjust my skirt and stretched my back. "So did you have a good week? I haven't heard from you since last Sunday."

Jonathan's mouth pressed into a line. "Ah, yeah, it was a busy week. I went up to Charlotte with Pastor Shand for that meeting, and then I was with the Grays. Mr. Gray is getting close to passing." He wagged his head.

"Okay." I bit back the words I wanted to say. *You have a cell phone. You can have called. Just to check in. Just to make sure I was all right.* Instead, I amped up my smile and shrugged. "I know how much everyone needs you. I'm glad you could be there for the Grays."

Gram cleared her throat. "Jonathan, would you like to join us for supper? I have a pork roast in the slow cooker, and I'm fixing to pull it for barbecue. We have plenty if you're interested."

I wasn't sure if I was grateful or annoyed that Gram had extended the invitation without asking me about it first. Of course, she was free to have anyone to dinner she wanted; it was her house. But given the so-called understanding between Jonathan and me, I was surprised she hadn't checked with me.

"That's so nice of you, Mrs. Grant. It sounds mighty good if you're sure there's enough." His gaze didn't even slide to me, to see how I might feel about it. I felt as see-through as his hair.

"Rilla, why don't you ride with Jonathan? I'll just hustle on ahead to make sure everything's ready." Gram turned as though to leave.

"Oh, I don't think that's a good idea, do you?" Jonathan put on that expression of concern that went right down my spine. Privately, I called it his holier-than-thou look. "I mean, unless we can find someone to ride with us. It'll look funny if we're alone together in the car all the way out to the farm."

I bit my lip. Part of me understood what he said. It was how we'd both been raised: we had to be conscious of how circumstances looked, of any appearance of sin or, as I'd been taught, any occasion for sin to flourish. We kept ourselves tidy, as my Sunday school teacher used to say. Boys weren't alone with girls, unless they were siblings or married.

But a larger part that had been getting louder in the past few months rebelled against that idea. The ride between the church and the farm was about ten minutes, for cripes sake. What trouble could we possibly get into in speeding car during that time? Nothing that I could think of.

Gram's mouth pulled down, but she only nodded. "Whatever you say. Come on then, Rilla. We need to get home and finish up." She shot Jonathan a dark look. "We eat at one o'clock on Sundays, as you know."

"Yes, ma'am." Jonathan bobbed his head again and then turned in the direction of a cluster of youth who were chatting in the corner of the sanctuary. I wondered if any of them were standing too close together for his liking.

Gram and I made our way around the last lingering congregants who were gathered in small groups. She held up her hand in a wave here and there, but she didn't stop to talk with anyone. By the sharp click of her sensible heels on the tile floor,

I could tell she was unhappy. And I didn't think it was with me.

I climbed into the old gray sedan and shut the door behind me. Gram dropped her purse onto the floor at my feet and turned the key in the ignition. I was quiet as she backed out of the space and turned onto the empty highway.

"Gram, is there something wrong with me?"

She looked over at me swiftly, her brows drawn together and her mouth pursed. "Why on earth would you ask that? What do you mean?"

I crossed my legs on the seat, careful to cover them with my long skirt. "I don't know. Isn't it normal for a boy to want to be alone with a girl he likes? Maybe I'm some kind of freak, and that's why Jonathan never wants to be with me. I mean, I know he and Dad've talked about our future, and he's even told Dad that he plans for us to be together, but shouldn't he be . . . I don't know . . . more anxious to make it happen?"

Gram laughed, but there was no humor in it. "You'd think, wouldn't you?" Her fingers tightened on the steering wheel. "There's not a dang thing wrong with you, Rilla. You're a beautiful young woman, and any man with a lick of sense would be spending most of his time scheming to get you alone. If there's anyone who's a freak, it's that stick-in-the-mud who thinks he knows it all."

My mouth dropped open a little. "Gram. I thought you liked Jonathan."

"I've tried to be kind, for your sake and in the hopes that he's just exceptionally conscientious. Lord knows I don't want you with some wild boy who'll lead down the wrong path. But I don't necessarily agree with your father, either, who seems to think any kind of passion is a sin."

I flushed. We rarely talked about anything like this in my house. I didn't think I'd ever heard the word *passion* come out of my grandmother's mouth. "So you think maybe Jonathan doesn't really like me? Why would he say he wants to court me then?"

"Honey, I don't think it's that he doesn't like you. I think if he gave himself permission to feel that way about anyone, he'd like you fine. But he's been brainwashed by the whole lot of them that until he's married, he's not allowed to think that way." She rolled her eyes. "How they think any of us ever got to be married is a mystery."

It felt like my world was tilting just a little. "Gram, don't you—you don't believe what we're taught about courting and sin and everything?"

"I don't know, Rilla. It's not how I was raised. I met your grandpa, and . . ." She smiled, and her face softened. "I knew. He looked at me, and he was the first man who ever really saw me. He saw beyond the pretty girl to who I really was. And after the two of us got to know each other, why, we wanted to be together all the time. If we could work out to be alone, all the better."

"But weren't you tempted? Pastor Shand says boys and girls together alone face too much temptation. We did a whole year of study on it during youth group."

"I know." Gram slowed as we approached our driveway. "Were we tempted? Of course we were. We kissed, and we were . . . close to each other. But we waited to be intimate until after we were married. Sure, we wanted to be together before that. We were strong enough to wait, though." She parked the car in the back of the house and pulled out the keys, but she didn't make a move to open the car door.

"Rilla, the truth is that there's a happy medium. Your dad and Pastor Shand and a bunch of them at church see the awful things that happen in this world, and they want to protect all the young people from going astray. That's admirable. But I think they go too far. They've laid down these rules and taught y'all that feeling anything is wrong." She tapped her fingers on the steering wheel. "I guess Jonathan thinks that God's going to flip a switch on his wedding day and suddenly he'll feel okay about touching you. I just worry, that's all. I don't want you to make any mistakes, honey, but I also don't want you to have a marriage without love. Without passion."

I fiddled with the seatbelt. "My parents didn't have a marriage without love, did they?"

Gram blew out a breath and brushed several strands of gray hair out of her face. "Oh, honey. No. Well, they certainly had passion. And your father loved your mother more than anything in his life. She loved him, as best she could." She looked out the car window, over the vegetable garden. "Maybe your mom and dad were the opposite of what I'm talking about. They had the passion, but when it faded, as passion almost always will, your mama found out she didn't have the strength for lasting love. I'm not saying anything bad about her, mind you. My daddy used to say—" She smiled, and her eyes grew soft and vague. "I wish you'd known my father, Rilla. You remind me of him, sometimes. He used to tell me that I needed to find a man who could be a friend. He said, 'Love rises and falls, but friendship will keep you going during the times love feels far away.' He was right. I never stopped loving your grandfather, but there were times that if it wasn't for how much I liked him, I might've cheerfully shot him."

I couldn't help the bubble of laughter. "Gram! That's terrible."

She chuckled. "Might be, but it's true. And I bet he felt the same about me. But what saved us was how much we laughed together. How much we liked each other." Her smile faded as she touched the locket at her throat. "I miss that man. Every single day."

That look on her face, that wistful longing . . . that was what I wanted for myself. I thought about Jonathan, and instead of a swell of love, of desire or even of friendship, I felt irritation.

"When I think about Jonathan, sometimes I want to smack him. Is that passion?"

Gram reached for the door handle. "I'd like to say yes. But I'm afraid what you feel for Jonathan looks more like impatience and annoyance to me." She hesitated before climbing out. "I'm trying not to let my personal feelings interfere with my advice to you, Rilla. But the honest truth is that I don't like that boy. I gave him a chance today to spend a little time with you in place that no one would have to be any the wiser. And he not only turned it down, he managed to chastise me, his elder, in the process."

I closed my eyes and leaned back against the seat. "I know. I was mortified."

"Well, don't let it bother you, hon. I have broad shoulders. Takes more than a little upstart preacher to rattle me."

"I don't know what I'm going to do, Gram. Dad's set on me waiting for Jonathan to get a church and then marrying him."

She got out of the car and closed the door behind her while I did the same. "Rilla, I may not believe in everything that's preached at our church, but I know for sure there's a God who loves us and has a plan. Just bide a while and trust. It'll all work out. Might not be the way you think, but it will. Have a little faith."

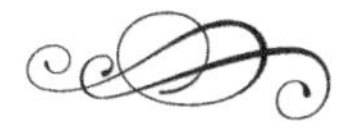

" . . . amen." My father finished blessing the food and reached for the barbecue. "Jonathan, help yourself. My mother makes a mean barbecue." He smiled at Gram and then glanced at me. "And she trained Rilla, of course, so you can bet she's a great cook, too."

I twisted my napkin around my fingers. Sometimes when Jonathan was around, I felt more like my father's prize heifer than his only daughter. He was always talking up my qualities.

On the other hand, I never heard so many compliments from him when we were alone, so I guessed I should be flattered.

"Yes sir, I've tasted Rilla's cakes and cookies at church. Delicious." Jonathan smiled at me and passed the coleslaw, careful to keep his fingers from accidentally brushing mine. "So I was wondering, Mr. Grant . . ." He cleared his throat, sounding a little nervous, and I jerked my eyes to his face. *Was he actually going to ask my father's permission for something involving me? Something to move our courtship along?* My stomach clenched. Whether it was in anticipation or dread, I wasn't quite sure yet.

"I was wondering if you might be willing to stand in agreement with me when I approach the elders about preaching. I know you all wanted me to wait until I had more experience as a pastor, and I appreciate that. But it's been a year, and I was thinking of beginning the process of planting my own church. I need some preaching time before I can do that."

I looked back down at my plate and scooped up a bite of barbecued pork and coleslaw. I should've known Jonathan wasn't going to ask for more time with me. He was too worried about messing up his chances for his own church. I understood that was his dream, but shouldn't I be part of that dream, too, if he wanted me to be his wife? He hadn't said anything to me in so many words, but he'd ask Dad if he might court me. At the time, I'd been excited at the prospect. I hadn't realized that in Jonathan's mind, courting me meant that I became his unpaid assistant with the youth group. Nothing else had changed, other than he always sought me out at church to speak a few words—in front of Gram or Dad, of course.

Dad hadn't answered Jonathan yet. He chewed his meat slowly, a thoughtful frown on his tanned face. I saw Gram close her eyes and shake her head, almost in disgust with the whole situation.

Finally, Dad nodded slowly. "I'll need to pray on it a bit

before our meeting on Wednesday, but unless the Lord gives me a clear sign to the contrary, I think I can stand with you on this. It's time you got some practice in the pulpit. After all, as you say, the sooner you do that, the sooner you can start up your own church. And I know you're anxious to get on with the rest of your life." My father nodded and smiled, turning his head to include me. "Both of you are. Rilla and I were just discussing that this week."

Jonathan looked pleased with my dad's answer, but when he glanced at me, I noticed his eyes dropped and skittered away. "Yes, sir, definitely. A lot to think about before we make any moves there, though. I mean, I think it would irresponsible to take on any other, uh, new situation while I was working on a church plant. Don't you think?"

Dad looked a little taken aback, but as always, he paused before answering. "That's one way to see it. Of course, a lot of people might say that it wouldn't be a bad thing to have a help-meet when you're doing God's work." He picked up a piece of cornbread and broke off a corner. "You're both old enough to be thinking seriously about the future."

I couldn't take it any more. Jonathan couldn't even meet my eyes, and here my father kept pushing me on him like he couldn't wait to be rid of me. I was beginning to wonder if Jonathan had ever really expressed interest in me, or if my dad had grossly misunderstood him. This was mortifying.

"Dad, there's plenty of time for thinking about the future." I smiled and kept my voice light. "I'm not in any hurry. My new job is going so well, and Sam said he thought I could expect a few more clients real soon. I like what I'm doing."

Jonathan turned to look at me in surprise, this time managing not to glance away. "What's this about a job? Are you working somewhere, Rilla?"

My father's forehead was drawn together; whether he was angry at me for spilling the beans about working off the farm or upset that Jonathan knew so little about my day-to-day life, I couldn't tell. I'd been working at the stand for almost two months now, and I'd been handling the publicity and ads for them even longer. The fact that I hadn't told Jonathan about my new job was more lack of opportunity than trying to hide anything from him.

I amped up my fake smile. "Yes, didn't I tell you? I guess I thought Dad might've. He talks to you more than I do." I shifted my eyes to my father and then back to Jonathan. "I'm working at The Colonel's Last Stand, the farm stand the Reynolds' family owns."

A series of different emotions passed over Jonathan's face. Pleasant surprise, the sort he might feel for any random stranger who'd just shared about a new job, was followed by concern as it dawned on him that my father wasn't happy about the situation and then finally a frown of disapproval as apparently all the reasons a twenty-two year old single woman shouldn't work outside the home occurred to him.

"Uh, no, I didn't know." He glanced around the table. "Well, Rilla, should you be leaving all the work here to your grandmother? Don't you think you should be helping her?"

"Bosh." Gram dropped her fork on her plate with a little more force than necessary, and we all jumped at the clatter. "I'm not some helpless old lady, Jonathan." She drilled him with the steely gaze that had made me quiver more often than I liked to remember. "I can run my own household. Besides, if I couldn't, what would you expect to happen when Rilla gets married? I'm sure no man wants his wife running back to her family home every day to lend a hand. Would you?"

He had the grace to blush a deep red. "Uh, no. No, ma'am, I guess not." He kept his eyes on his plate. "Not that I've been thinking about that yet, of course. You know, I have a long time yet before I'll be able to commit to being married. Pastor Shand says the Lord is calling me to single-minded focus on His work before I can think about the responsibility of a family." He looked up at my father. "That's why I'm so glad to know Rilla's part of a family who's keeping her safe and pure until that time. I appreciate it, sir."

My father's face remained unreadable, though I spied a small tic in his cheek. "There's no question about Rilla's purity. She's been carefully raised, as far from the world as we could manage in this day and age. But Jonathan, look, son, I don't want to contradict what the pastor's told you. He's got your best interest at heart. I'm not sure I agree that a wife would hinder you planting a church, though. Rilla's a smart girl, and she's a hard worker. Her grandmother taught her to run a home. She'd be an excellent right-hand for you."

"Dad, stop, please." I couldn't take it anymore. "I don't need you to sell Jonathan on me. If he doesn't want me, it's fine. You don't need to twist his arm." I stood up, pushing my chair back away from the table. "Gram, I'll come back and help you with the dishes, but I need a little air right now."

"Go right ahead, honey. Take a walk. I'm fine here." I heard the anger in her voice. I knew it wasn't directed my way.

As I stomped out the door, my father called my name, but for the first time in my life, I ignored his orders and just kept on walking. The screen slammed behind me as I headed for the woods that flanked our house. A small path led between trees and rotting logs, and I followed it, unseeing and unhearing for the first few minutes.

My hands were shaking with a rage I never remembered feeling before. *How could he do that?* My own father, trying to talk a reluctant man into taking me off his hands, like I was some piece of livestock. And right in front of me, like I wasn't even there and couldn't speak up for myself.

"I'm twenty-two years old, for the love of Pete." My voice echoed in the forest. "I can run my own life. I can make my own decisions." I reached the small brook that had been my favorite hiding spot since I was a little girl. Twisting my skirt with a fisted hand, I climbed onto a large flat rock hidden between two bowed trees and settled back, lying flat and looking up through the leaves.

Twenty-two. Lord in heaven, how had I gotten to be this old and still under my father's thumb? I arched my neck and closed my eyes, letting the tension in my shoulders run out. When I was little, I'd lay on this rock during hot summer afternoons, when Gram declared it was too hot to do anything but sit or play. My father had a strong belief in the benefits of keeping busy, but when he wasn't home, Gram gave me a little latitude. She herself had an equally powerful conviction about the importance of play for children.

I used to dream of growing up and leaving the farm, traveling the world. I wanted to see all the wonderful places Gram and I read about during our lessons, find some freedom from the house and farm where I'd spent all my life. And then in my teen years, the dreams had changed. In the youth group at church, we were taught the importance of perfect obedience, of listening to our parents and striving for holiness. Boys and girls could talk to each other, but only in the company of an adult. Even the older single people in church avoided being alone together; dating was done in groups, if it was done at all.

So when I began to entertain thoughts of romance, it was within that framework. I daydreamed about the day one of the boys from church would ask my dad if he could court me, and he'd sit with me during services, and he'd come to supper every Sunday at my house. After we ate, we'd sit out on the porch and talk about the future we were going to share. Then, when the time was right, there'd be a wedding and my life would really begin.

A leaf drifted down and landed on my face. I held it to the light, examining the tiny veins that ran through the green as my mind rambled. I never thought I'd get to be this old and not be married. Or at least about to be married. When Gram had finished homeschooling me, I'd been at loose ends, with no husband on the horizon and nothing but empty years stretching before me. Most of the kids from the youth group had ended up going away to college or leaving town to work, and none of them had met my father's strict criteria anyway. Dad wouldn't hear of me attending traditional college far from home, so when Gram told me that she'd read about classes on-line, I'd jumped at the opportunity.

Maybe Dad thought I was going to end up an old maid anyway, so I might as well have some sort of degree. He didn't necessarily approve of my education, but he didn't forbid it, either. We'd fallen into a rhythm of farm work, the classes I worked diligently to complete and church until two years ago, when Pastor Shand announced that he'd hired a young man fresh out of Bible college to see to our youth.

The group I'd been active with in my teens had dwindled to few kids in the church. But with a new crop of adolescents coming up, Pastor decided we needed someone who could devote himself fully to guiding them. So he'd brought on Jonathan Hunt.

When I'd met our new youth pastor, my first impression was intensity. He was zealous and single-minded. A few weeks after he started working at Burton Community, he stopped me after service one Sunday and asked if I'd consider helping him with the youth.

"The young women in the church need a godly role model. Someone who isn't running around with boys and taking up with the world. I think they'd really respond to you."

I'd agreed, mainly because my father encouraged me and there didn't seem to be any good reason to say no. Jonathan and I worked well together, in that he told me what he thought I should do and I made it happen. I gave him a few suggestions for activities the group could try and books we could read; a few he took, but most of the time, he nodded, smiled and said he'd pray over it. And then I'd never hear anything about it again.

About six months after Jonathan's arrival, my father came home from an elders' meeting with an unusual bounce in his step. Gram and I'd been in the kitchen, peeling apples for a pie, and Dad grinned as he closed the door.

"Well, Marilla Grace, I have some news that I think will make you happy."

I glanced at my father and then at Gram, who shrugged.

"Jonathan pulled me aside tonight and asked if I would consider letting him court you." He spoke as though I'd been waiting on tenterhooks for this announcement.

"Um . . ." I put down the knife and the apple. "Really? What did you tell him?"

Dad frowned. "I told him yes, of course. He's a good man, and he'll be a good husband for you." He paused, and his eyebrows drew together. "You seem surprised. You didn't know Jonathan was going to speak to me?"

I shook my head. "Dad, the most personal thing Jonathan Hunt has ever said to me was about the brownies I brought for the bake sale. We only talk about the youth group. I didn't have any idea he was thinking about this."

Gram hmphed just under her breath, but she didn't look at me.

Dad recovered, and though he didn't smile again, his forehead smoothed out. "That's because he respects you. He knew to approach me first. Now that I've given him permission, he'll probably be more comfortable with you."

Maybe Jonathan was more comfortable with me after his talk with my father, but it couldn't be proven by me. He continued to treat me with the same slightly detached deference he did every woman in church. I fell into an odd world where at home my father acted as though I were almost engaged, while the man he assumed I'd be marrying never gave me so much as a sideways glance. It was bizarre.

When I broached the subject with Gram, she only shook her head, shrugged her shoulders and growled, "Men."

The wind blew again, and tiny bits of pollen fell over me. I closed my eyes and tried to remember what it'd been like to dream. Somewhere along the way, I'd lost the belief that my life could ever be any different or any better than it was. Working with the Reynolds at the farm stand had been an eye-opening experience, and suddenly what I'd been willing to settle for a few months ago seemed lackluster and almost repulsive. There was so much more to the world than I'd imagined, and I wanted to see it all.

Even if it meant defying my father.

Mason

"READY, DADDY!"

I turned as my daughter clamored down the steps, her blonde curls bouncing around her small face. Her bright eyes met mine, and I saw the challenge only seconds before I had time to respond. She stopped on the fourth step from the bottom, crouched and leaped into the air.

My arms shot out of their own volition, and I caught her—barely. My heart thudded painfully against the walls of my chest as I clutched her tiny body to me.

"Piper Susannah, how many times have I told you? You can't just jump like that. Daddy wasn't ready for you. You could've been hurt."

She pulled away, and those hazel eyes that matched my own held not one ounce of contrition. "Daddy, I never get hurt." She wriggled until I put her down, and then stood before me, hands her hips. "Are we going? I want to go to the farm."

I bit back a sigh. This kid was out of control, and I honestly didn't know how I was going to change that. I offered her my hand. "Yeah, we're going. Let's go give Nan a kiss first, and make sure she's okay."

Piper tugged on my arm as she skipped toward the downstairs office that we'd transformed into my mother's room since her illness. She was sitting in the recliner today, with a book in her hand and an old black and white movie on the television. As we came in, she laid the paperback in her lap and smiled.

"Look at you, Miss Piper. Pretty as a picture!" She buried her face in the crook of my daughter's neck, closing her eyes and sniffing. "And you smell like springtime. Are you and your daddy going on an adventure?"

"Yes! We're going to Mr. Farmer Fred's farm and we're going to see the horses and I'm going to ride one and go so fast—"

"Whoa, there, princess." I stuck my thumbs in the front pockets of my jeans and rocked back on my heels. "I said we'd see the horses. You're not going to ride on them. Maybe when you get bigger, we can see about some riding lessons, but not today. Got it?"

Her lower lip jutted out in a pout I was all too familiar with, but I was standing my ground here. No way my little baby was going up on one of those big horses. Not this year.

"Piper, baby, I bet Mr. Fred and Miss Ellen will have apples for you to feed the horses. And maybe even some sugar cubes. How about that? Won't that be fun?" Mom smoothed her thin white hand over Piper's hair. I tried not to notice the slight tremor in her fingers.

"Okay." Piper's shoulders slumped. "I guess."

I ignored the display of despondency. "Mom, you okay? Can I get you anything before we go? Or while we're out?"

She shook her head. "I'm good, darlin.' Thanks. Mrs. Murphy'll be here any minute."

As if on cue, there was a rattle at the kitchen door and the telltale squeak of the screen door hinge. Piper disentangled herself from my mother's hands and took off in the direction of the noise.

"Mrs. Murphy! I'm gonna see horses!"

"That child never does anything slow, does she?" Mom closed her eyes and laid her head back against the chair. "Always in a hurry. What I wouldn't give to have a tenth of her energy."

I rubbed the back of my neck. "I know, Mom. But pretty soon you'll be feeling better." I turned my head, listening to Piper chatter away to the caregiver. "As for the pip squeak . . . Mom, I don't know what I'm going to do with her sometimes. I tell her stuff over and over, not to do something, what she should be doing, and she just looks at me with those big eyes and smiles, and does whatever the hell she wants anyway."

My mother's lips curled into a grin. "Why, son, where on earth would she get that kind of behavior? I can't even imagine."

"Yeah, I don't know either." I rolled my eyes, ignoring her sarcasm. "I mean, I was the best behaved, most obedient child ever known. Quiet, calm, serious—"

"I think the word you're looking for here is 'willful.' Maybe 'wild.' And as for how she charms you to get her way? Oh, honey, I remember you'd just look up at me with those huge hazel eyes, and I'd melt. So did Grandma, and every other female you ever came across. So maybe you need to keep that in mind. The apple, the tree—it never falls far."

"Thanks, Mom. That helps a lot."

"Anything I can do, honey, you know that." She opened her eyes. "I'm glad you're taking her out to Fred and Ellen's place. It was nice of them to invite y'all. Is that sweet-talking son of theirs going to be there?"

"Yeah, Alex is in town. That's why we're going today." I

worked my jaw back and forth.

"Son, it's okay to take a little time off work. The world won't come crashing down, I promise."

I lifted one shoulder. "Yeah, I guess, but it's a Saturday, and we got a new band playing tonight. They'll be coming in for sound check before opening."

"I thought you said Rocky was handling it." Mom leaned up a little to pull her sweater closer around her bony shoulders. She had trouble staying warm anymore.

"He is. It'll be fine. I'm just not used to not handling every part myself, you know?" I bent to help her draw the cardigan closer. "I hate that I can't be here with you all the time, helping you get well. And I hate that I'm not a better daddy to Piper. I wish I could be with her more. But at the same time, I know I have to make a living, and I get antsy when I'm away from the club too long."

"I know, honey. But you're doing good. I've got Mrs. Murphy taking care of me and watching Piper, and you couldn't have found anyone better. You're doing the best you can, and that's just fine. Try not to be so hard on yourself."

Footsteps sounded down the hall, and Piper skidded into the room. "Is it time now, Daddy?"

"Yes'm, it's time." I scooped her up and tickled her sides until she giggled. "I have my phone, Mom. We're going to stop at Sam Reynold's farm stand, too, while we're out there."

"Oh, really? Picking us up something fresh for dinner?"

"Maybe. But I'm mainly going to talk to that girl they hired to do their PR. Sam wants me to see about having her do some work for us at the bar. I'm thinking she could do something for the new lunch hours we're starting next week."

"A girl?" Mom raised one eyebrow.

"Yeah. Emmett Grant's daughter." When her other eyebrow went up, too, I shook my head and set Piper back on the floor. "Stop. She's just out of school, needs a job. That's it."

"I wasn't saying anything about you, silly. It's just that I didn't remember Emmett having a daughter. He used to be part of the Guild, when your father was on it. He must've kept the girl on a pretty short leash, because I don't think I've ever seen her."

"Sam said something about that—okay, Piper, okay." I let her pull me to the door. "Call me if anything comes up. We'll be back before dinner."

We went back through the kitchen, Piper chattering away about horses. Mrs. Murphy was putting together a tray, adding toast and a cup of tea to take to Mom.

"You all have a good time and don't worry about your mama. We're going to have us some tea and watch a movie. Enjoy the horses."

I grimaced and opened the door to go out. "Thanks, Mrs. Murphy. I appreciate it. Don't know what we'd do without you."

She waved us away, and I lifted Piper into the backseat of my truck, buckling her into her booster seat. After I climbed into the driver's seat, I hit the button to turn on the radio and turned it to my favorite satellite station, one that featured new acts and up-and-comers out of Nashville. Some old habits die hard.

I cruised until we got to the edge of town, then I opened her up and picked up speed. On the radio, a guy I'd never heard of before crooned a cover of Johnny Cash's *Ring of Fire,* and I grinned when I heard Piper's thin, clear voice singing along. She'd been raised on this music, and she probably knew more songs than people ten times her age.

The land out here was wide open, with large family farms separated by occasional sections of forest. I tried to imagine what it would be like growing up out here rather than in town. Back in high school, I'd had a few friends who lived on farms, but we usually hung out in Burton. Every now and then, someone would throw a big party in one of the fields, but that only happened once a year or so. I'd never thought about how it would feel to be bused to the school every day, or not to be able to walk over to the library or the pizza shop when the urge hit.

We turned down the dirt road that led to the Nelson farm, and Piper shrieked when she spotted horses. By the time we reached the house, she was bouncing up and down in her seat.

"Now listen." I pulled the keys from the ignition and turned around to give my daughter what I hoped was quelling and fatherly stare. "You need to be on your best behavior here. Mr. Fred and Miss Ellen invited us here, and I expect you to be respectful." I paused. "Do you know what that means?"

She frowned. "No."

"It means you need to not run around the house, not interrupt when adults are talking and wait until you're offered something to eat or drink. Don't ask for it. Oh, and we need to thank the Nelsons for asking us over. And be polite to Alex, too. He's one of my friends."

"Okay. I'll be 'spectful." She nodded, her face serious.

"Good." I opened the door and unbuckled Piper, swinging her down to the ground. She took my hand as we climbed the two steps to the porch. Before we reached the door to knock, the screen door creaked and Alex leaned out.

"Who is the ravishing creature approaching my house? Why, is that Cinderella? Or Sleeping Beauty? No, couldn't be her, since you're wide awake." Alex rubbed his chin, his eyes narrowing as he gazed down at my daughter.

"I'm not a princess today. I'm a cowgirl, 'cause I'm seeing the horses." She slid her eyes in my direction. "Was that 'spectful, Daddy?"

"Yep, it sure was." I stuck out my fist to my friend. "Dude."

"Bro." He pounded it, smirking. "Come on in. Mom made cookies, and I actually left a few for the company, as she calls you."

The Nelson home was very much what I expected. We walked into a large open living room with furniture that looked as though it might've belonged to Alex's great-grandparents. Family pictures filled the walls, including one huge section devoted solely to Alex himself. He caught me checking it out and nodded.

"Miracle baby, you know. They never thought they'd have a kid, then I came along. Surprise! So I'm pretty sure they snapped pics every time I sneezed."

"We weren't quite that bad." Mrs. Nelson wandered into the room and cuffed her son on his arm. "But you were a pretty cute baby, so maybe we got a little carried away." She bent to smile at Piper. "Hello, little lady. I hear you're going to visit with our horses."

"Uh-huh." Piper nodded with enthusiasm before she caught my eye. "I mean, please. And thank you."

"Well, I hope maybe you'll have a few treats before you go out to the pasture. I don't have any girls in my house, you know. So I made us some girly snacks to enjoy. Is that okay?"

Piper smiled. "Uh huh. I like cookies."

Mrs. Nelson beamed. "Then you're in luck. Now why don't you boys go out on the porch while us girls get the trays together, and then we'll bring them out to you?" Without waiting for an answer, she turned back toward what I assumed was the kitchen.

"We may as well go hang out. Once Mom's got an idea, there's no changing her mind. And don't worry. The cowgirl'll be fine. My mother's been so excited about you guys coming over."

I trailed Alex back to the porch and sat down in a wooden rocker. "Piper's been beside herself. She's on an animal kick right now, and horses are it. Last week it was rabbits. I'm just trying to keep up."

Alex smiled. "I can't even imagine. I look at you with the

pipsqueak and Ali with Bridget, and I think . . . thank you, sweet baby Jesus, that I don't have that responsibility yet."

"Yet?" I cocked my head. "Does that mean you think it'll happen one day?"

"I hope so." He pushed old swing to moving as he held onto the chain. "Things are moving slow with my friend in Savannah, but maybe someday. Who knows?"

"You're here to see him this weekend?" Alex, who lived in Atlanta, had been seeing an art dealer in Savannah for well over a year now. I didn't know any details, except what Alex had shared over drinks at my bar. The other guy had come out of a long-term relationship and nasty breakup and wasn't eager to jump back into the dating pool. It was proof of how much Alex liked him that he'd been willing to wait it out. Meanwhile, his visits to Burton, which was only about thirty miles outside Savannah, had become more frequent, which made his parents and his friends happy.

"Yeah, we've got a date tonight. I'm trying to talk him into coming down to The Road Block with me, but I don't think he's ready for that yet. Soon though. I hope."

"I hope so, too. I'd like to meet this mystery man. And I know Ali does, too." Sam's sister and Alex had been best friends for many years, and Alex was also close to Flynn, Ali's husband.

"Girlfriend's flying the coop to the big apple. So she just might miss out on my friend." Alex sniffed and pretended to look offended.

"Aww, you know you're happier for those two than anyone else. Pretty cool that they're making it work after all these years."

"Sure is. I'm thrilled. I had my doubts now and then, but deep down, I knew that boy couldn't stay away from my girl. They were meant to be. Soul mates. Just took them a while to see it through."

"That happens sometimes." We sat in silence for a few minutes before Alex stretched out his legs and yawned.

"I was surprised you could make it out here today. Aren't Saturdays your busiest nights?"

I nodded. "Yeah, but I don't have to be there until closer to opening. Rocky's handling set up for me. Shame you're going to be in Savannah tonight, though. We have a new group playing, and I think they're going to be big. They got a good sound."

"Maybe next time." Alex turned the chain of the swing between two fingers. "Meghan said you're stopping by the stand today to meet Rilla Grant. Thinking about hiring her?"

I rolled my neck. "Sometimes I forget how fast news moves out here. Yeah, I was planning to drop by and see if we can work something out. I never really thought about anymore advertising for the bar, but Sam had a good point when he said it wouldn't hurt to beef up the buzz on our new lunch hours. And I like to help someone just starting out."

Alex flicked his eyes up to me. "That's decent of you. The girl could use a break, I think. I've talked with her a time or two at the stand, but she's very quiet. Shy. My dad always said I could get a response from a brick wall, but I don't get very far with Rilla."

"Kind of strange to be in publicity if you're too shy to have conversation, don't you think?" I wondered if Sam might be off-base here, recommending her just out of his good heart. I felt bad for the girl, but I couldn't afford a pity-hire.

"You know, that's the weird thing. She's doing a terrific job at the stand, both with selling and with the advertising she's done. When she's talking about that or working with customers, she's a different person. It's just one-on-one when it's not business that she clams up. Ali said she gets the feeling from a few things Rilla's said that she hasn't been around many men outside her father."

"Maybe that's it. Maybe you make her nervous." I'd yet to meet the person who couldn't be comfortable around Alex, but if this chick didn't know guys, it was possible she didn't understand his easy charm.

"*I* make her nervous?" Alex hooted. "Oh, that's a good one. Well, buddy boy, let me tell you, if I give her anxiety, what's she going to do when she meets you?"

I shot him a dark look. "What's that supposed to mean?"

"Just that you're you, Mason. Larger than life, both literally and figuratively. You're taller than me by half a foot, you're seriously bulked up, and you ooze dangerous charm. Plus, you own a bar, whereas I'm just a downhome farm boy."

"Since when? You're citified now, Alex. You live in Atlanta and you've got a high-powered exec job."

Alex winked at me. "That might be true, but I still come off like plain old Alex Nelson, Fred and Ellen's baby boy." He paused, and before he could continue, his mother and Piper appeared with a large tray. Mrs. Nelson set down the food on the wooden table in front of us, and Piper climbed up to sit on my lap. Alex scooted over to offer his mother a seat, which she took with a sigh as she spoke.

"Gentlemen, it's tea time."

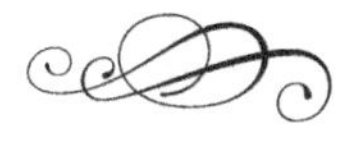

Fred Nelson's horses were mature, gentle animals, which was why I was okay with Piper climbing over the fence and into the pasture with them. As we drove back up the driveway toward the highway, she described every minute she'd spent in the field, even though I'd been there the whole time.

"Poker is my favorite. Or maybe Rummy. He tickled my hand when I gave him the carrot. Solitaire and Gin were funny."

I grinned. It was a well-known joke in Burton and the surrounding area that the Nelson horses' names were Fred's way of poking gentle fun at his wife's strict Baptist upbringing. Card games of all kinds had been forbidden in her youth. She still got flustered when anyone brought up gambling, liquor or dancing; I knew she pointedly ignored my occupation and refused to openly acknowledge that I owned an establishment that promoted both drinking and dancing.

On the other hand, Ellen hadn't blinked when her only son came out to his parents. Her love for him was steadfast and unwavering and trumped anything a church had tried to drill into her head. I had to respect that kind of character.

The Reynolds' farm was only a few miles down the road from the Nelsons. I knew they shared a boundary on one side, and Ali and Alex had grown up together, running back and forth from one property to the other. I envied that kind of long-running friendship. I was still friendly with some of the guys who'd graduated from high school with me, but these days, I didn't have time for more than a word or two at the bar. Truth was, Sam was the closest thing I had to a best friend.

The parking lot at The Colonel's Last Stand was almost full, but I found a spot between an SUV and another truck. I lifted Piper from her seat and carried her toward the small three-sided stand; with all the traffic here, the last thing I wanted was to chase my daughter around cars to keep her safe. She wound her small arms around my neck and laid her head on my shoulder, a sigh from her lips brushing over my neck. I tightened my arms around her, overwhelmed with my love for this kid all over again.

"Mason!" A pretty red head in shorts and a black T-shirt waved to me. "Hey. How're you doing?" She made her way through the customers wandering around the tables of fruits and veggies and reaching us, stood on tip-toe to kiss my cheek. "And this must be Piper. Hi there, sweet thing. I'm Meghan."

Piper barely lifted her head to respond. She yawned hugely, and I laughed. "We just came from the Nelsons' farm. Piper met the horses, and I think they wore her out. Well, them and Miss Ellen's tea and cookies."

"That'll do it. Bridge loves those horses, too. You should see the pictures she's painted of them. They pretty much cover the walls of her room." Meghan bit her lip and took a deep breath that I noticed was a little shaky. "Sorry. They left for New York the other day, and I miss her like crazy already."

"Yeah, Sam said they were getting ready to head up. Must be pretty quiet for y'all these days."

She nodded. "You know, when Ali and Bridget lived with us, seemed like I was always looking for some of the quiet. Now that I have it all the time, Sam and I look at each other and wonder what to do." Her face pinked a little as she looked away. "Well, I mean . . . you know."

I could imagine. When Sam and Meghan were together, the air between them practically crackled with the passion they shared. Yeah, they might be missing his sister and niece, but I was pretty sure filling the emptiness wasn't a real problem.

"Well, you can always come over to The Road Block if the two of you are so bored." I winked at her. "You know how Sam loves to get his boogie on."

Meghan groaned. "I wish I could get him out of the house and down there more. He's so tired after being in the fields all day, but maybe this winter, when things slow down." She turned to glance at the crowds milling around the stand. "Though when I see how busy we are these days, I wonder if it ever will slow down. I love what Rilla's done for us, but with Ali gone, we're all busting our—" She glanced at Piper and changed the shape of the word she'd been about to say. "Ourselves. Working really hard."

"Speaking of which, that's why I'm here. Sam says I need to meet this publicity guru and see about getting her to work for the bar, too."

"Yeah, he told me you were coming by." Meghan hesitated. "Mason, Rilla's really shy. She's not like Ali and me, you know?"

"You mean she's not a ball buster?" I smirked.

"Hey!" She swatted my arm. "And watch your language in front of the little one."

I shifted a little. "She's out. I felt her snoring against my shoulder a few minutes ago. And she looks little, but when she's asleep, she's dead weight. So can you point me in the direction of this shy little girl both you and Alex seem to think I'm going to overwhelm? I promise, I'll try to tone down my irresistible charm so she doesn't faint when she sees me."

Meghan rolled her eyes. "Yeah, irresistible charm. It's more that you're just larger than life, Mase. And sometimes you tend to forget it." She paused. "Alex said something to you about her, too?"

"Yeah. Actually, he said that exact thing. 'Larger than life.' Are y'all trying to say I need to lose weight?"

"God, no." Meghan's tone was fervent enough to make me grin again. "But you're tall, and you're built. And you just have this air, like you'd take someone over and . . . consume her."

I frowned. "Really? I always thought I was just, you know, folksy. Friendly."

"You are, Mason. Totally. You're a good guy and a good friend, and I'm glad to know you. I'd happily introduce you to any woman I know, but Rilla's so different. It's taken her weeks to open to me even a little, but when guys are around, she kind of freezes. She can handle herself with customers, and she seems to have gotten used to Sam and Flynn. But anyone else and she just stops talking and kind of shrinks."

"You're not making a good case for me hiring this chick, Meghan. An advertising expert who doesn't like people? Yeah, that doesn't sound like it's gonna fly."

"It's not like that, Mason. First of all, most of the work she does is online, so she's not even dealing with people. Second, like I said, she pulls it together for work. Rilla's good at what she does. And you know Sam. Even if he wanted to help her out, he'd never recommend her to you if she wasn't good."

"Okay." I nodded. "But the more important thing right now is letting me meet her, so I can get this kid back to the car and home. She's drooling, and it's going down my back."

Meghan threw back her head and laughed. "Oh, that's precious. C'mon, big guy. Follow me."

I walked behind her, careful to avoid bumping into people or produce. As we rounded the corner into the stand itself, I spotted a blonde in a pink shirt and long jean skirt. She was speaking with two older women, and she held a tomato in each hand. As I watched, she leaned forward a little, lifting one hand a little higher, as though she was making a point. When one of the ladies responded, she smiled just slightly, one side of her mouth lifting as she listened.

"Rilla." Meghan stopped next to the three women. "I'm sorry to interrupt, but when you're finished here, I'd like to introduce you to Mason. He stopped by to meet you."

Three pairs of eyes turned to look at me, and I realized I knew one of the women. She smiled and put a hand to her hip.

"Mason Wallace, what're you doing out here? Gettin' some food for your mama? And just who is that you're holdin'?"

I chuckled. "Afternoon, Miss Evelyn. I haven't seen you since I've been back in town. Where've you been hiding?"

"Oh, honey, we moved to the coast when Paul retired, 'bout five years back. I'm just here visiting my sister who lives out in Farleyville, and she said we had to come by the stand and get some fresh veggies for supper." She laid her hand on her sister's arm. "This is Ida. Ida, Mason was my star Sunday school pupil, once upon a time."

"Nice to meet you, ma'am. Sorry, I kind of got my hands full here." I patted Piper's back. "I had her over to the Nelsons and their horses just wore her out."

"Oh, Mason, how sweet she is!" Miss Evelyn came closer and peeked at my sleeping daughter. "I had no idea. I mean, I'd heard you were married, but you say you're living back in town now?"

"Yeah." This was always the awkward part of any conversation I had with people who didn't know what had happened in Tennessee. Awkward for them, painful for me. "Uh, my wife passed about three years ago. I moved back here a year after, and I opened up a place just outside town. Piper and I live with my mom in Burton."

There were the expected ohs of sympathy. "I'm so sorry, Mason. That's just heartbreaking. But thank the Lord He gave you this sweet baby. What's her name, did you say?"

"Piper Susannah. Yes, ma'am, she's a blessing."

"I'm sure she is. And how's your mama doing? I bet she loves having her grandbaby close."

"She does. Actually, she's doing okay now, but she's been pretty sick herself." I forced myself to say the word I hated. "Leukemia."

There were more gasps, and I let my gaze slide over to Rilla. I'd not spoken to her yet on purpose, thinking of what Alex and Meghan had said. Maybe if she saw I was harmless and loved by old ladies, she'd be more comfortable talking with me.

She was watching my interchange with Miss Evelyn and Miss Ida, her huge blue eyes moving back and forth between the three of us. When she heard what I said about my mother, the frown on her face deepened, and she brought her thumb to her lips to nibble on it. Fascinated, I watched as just the tip of her tongue darted out, touching the nail, and then vanished again inside her mouth.

"Miss Evelyn, can I finish up with you? Mason's here to talk some business with Rilla, and I don't want to hold him up anymore. You can see he needs to get home so his daughter can nap." Meghan stepped a little closer, insinuating herself between the two ladies and Rilla. The look she shot the blonde clearly said, *This is your cue to exit, stage left.*

Rilla dropped her hand away from her mouth, and her eyes grew wide. "Oh, thanks, Meghan. We were just talking about the beefsteak and Romas, and what might be their best choice for one of Miss Evelyn's recipes."

"I think we know what we want now, dear." Miss Ida beamed. "Evie, this is Meghan. She's Sam Reynolds' fiancée, and she teaches art in Burton now. She'll ring us up, won't you, honey?"

Meghan herded the women toward the register in the front of the stand. I pivoted a little, so that I was facing Rilla fully. God, she really was a little thing. The top of her head barely reached my chest. Her blonde hair was pulled back into a tight ponytail, making her look like she was barely in her teens.

But those blue eyes told a different story. They were wide, framed by dark lashes that didn't match her hair at all. She wasn't looking at me; instead, she stared down at the two tomatoes still in her hands. As I watched, she sucked in her lower lip and chewed on it. Yeah, nerves, just like Meghan had said. I could see it was going to be up to me to start this conversation.

"So. I'm Mason Wallace. Sam probably told you I own The Road Block. Have you been there?" I knew it was a long shot, but I had to begin somewhere.

"Me? Uh, no. Yes, Sam told me that you had uh, a bar. Owned it, I mean. And you're maybe looking for some publicity help?" Finally her eyes flickered up to me briefly before they dropped again to fasten somewhere behind me.

"Yeah, well . . . the bar part is doing fine. We're turning people away on weekends. So not so much there, but next week, I'm opening up for lunch hours. That was where I thought you might be able to help me." Even as I spoke them, the words sounded ludicrous to me. Honestly? I expected this little mouse of a girl to come in and promote my bar? It was never going to work.

But Rilla surprised me. She straightened up, her shoulders stiffening as though she were getting ready for a battle. The shirt she wore was too big, I noticed; it disguised any shape she might have beneath. Maybe that was the point, to hide her curves from evil-minded men like me who'd always be checking out any girl to see what she had.

"Can you give me just a minute?" She was speaking again, and this time her voice was stronger, more assured. "I did some research when Sam told me what you were thinking of, and I have the information for you, but it's in the back with my purse." She glanced at Piper head on my shoulder, and an expression I couldn't read passed over her face. "I'll only be a second, and you can take it with you. I know you need to get home."

"Sure."

As soon as I said it, Rilla was gone, maneuvering around the tables and boxes to a break in the partition. She disappeared behind the half-wall briefly and then came out with a manila folder in her hand. The bottom of her denim skirt flapped around her white Keds as she walked back toward me.

"Here you are." She thrust the folder into my hand. "Basically, I looked into how restaurants that add new hours most successfully capitalize on pulling their existing clientele into the additional times. And then I came up with some ideas to get the word out to an entirely new part of the population that you're offering a new and different kind of service." She shrugged. "See if any of it looks good, and then you can let me know. My card's stapled in there."

I frowned. "So you're giving me the work you already did. What's to stop me from just taking your ideas here and running with them by myself? Why would I need you?"

She tilted her head and finally looked at me for more than a nanosecond. "Because Sam says you're a good man, and I trust him. And if you're the kind of person who'd do that, I wouldn't want to work with you anyway." Her lips pressed together, and I thought I detected maybe the slightest tremor, but to her credit, she didn't look away.

"Sam may give me too much credit, but yeah, I wouldn't do that. I just—you need to be careful. Not all people would be that honest."

"And I wouldn't give all people the chance."

She was quick with the comeback, and that took me by surprise. It struck me that she might be shy, but she wasn't timid.

"Good to know." I nodded and with one hand, I flipped back the cover of the folder and glanced at the top sheet. The information looked like it was well-organized, printed on paper with a simple letterhead: *Marilla Grant.* "Marilla. That's not a name you hear often."

"It was my great-grandmother's. I'm named for her." She looked uncomfortable again, and I got another clue to this chick: like Meghan had said, when it came to business, she was confident and easy, but once the conversation shifted to anything more personal, anything about her, she was stiff and nervous.

"Huh. Okay." I twisted my wrist to close the file again and tapped the edge of it against my leg. "So if you're going to represent my business, I'd like you to come in and see it, get an idea of what you'll be promoting."

Pure, unadulterated panic filled her face. "Oh, no. No, I couldn't do that." She was shaking her head and backing away as though I were about to kidnap her and take her to The Road Block by force.

I didn't move, except to quirk an eyebrow. "Why not? This is business. You can't accurately promote what you don't know."

"I can't go to a bar. My father would—" She shook her head again. "He would be furious. And so upset."

A sudden and unreasonable anger toward her father shot

through me. There was something off about any girl her age—I remember Sam had said Rilla was about as old as Meghan—who was that tied up by what might make her father mad. I understood respecting a parent's wishes. I always tried to do that. But there was a limit, a time when I had to stand up for what I knew was right for me. My parents had respected that. That Rilla's father had her terrified to stop by a bar for something related to her work pissed me off.

"Look, I'm not asking you to come swig beer on a Saturday night. I'm saying, stop in during lunch hours next week. See what we're doing. Have a meal on the house." I shifted my weight onto the other foot. "Hell, bring your father with you if it'd make him feel better."

Rilla's mouth dropped open a little. "Oh, no, I don't think that's a good idea. But . . ." She looked down at the floor, and the thumb went back to the edge of her lip. I doubted she even realized she did it. "I do see your point. I think I could come over during lunch next week, if it's okay with Sam. And maybe then I could answer any questions you might have, and we could finalize the plans for your promotion." She raised her eyes again.

"That works. Lunch hours are eleven to three. Just let me—"

Piper moaned and lifted her head from my shoulder. Both the side of her face and my shirt were soaked with her sweat and drool. I grimaced. The bodily fluids stuff was one of my least favorite parts of fatherhood.

"Daddy—the horses were playing." She straightened, but her eyes were still closed. I smiled.

"Daddy's right here, princess. Shhhh. You're okay. I'm going to take you home to see Nan in a minute, and you can tell her and Mrs. Murphy all about the horses."

I looked back down at Rilla, prepared to finish up and make a quick exit in case Piper had one of her rough wake-ups and began throwing a fit. She had a bad habit of waking up from naps confused and disoriented, which often led to screaming and crying. It was always worse when she fell asleep away from home.

But the expression on Rilla's face gave me pause. She was looking at Piper with a mix of emotions that I couldn't figure out. Almost yearning, almost sympathy, but definitely the most open and genuine I'd seen her. Her hand reached out, and it occurred to me that she didn't quite realize what she was doing. Her fingertips brushed the side of Piper's arm, right where the tan skin met the blue of her shirt.

My daughter opened her eyes and looked down at the unfamiliar woman. I held my breath, waiting for the first scream, but instead, Piper only blinked and sat still.

"Do you want a blackberry? They're really good." Rilla spoke softly, but not in the high-pitched sing-songy voice some people used with kids. She glanced up at me from under those dark lashes. "If it's okay with your dad, I mean."

"Sure. She loves berries."

Rilla leaned around me and picked up a pint of berries in one of the green biodegradable containers. She nabbed a blackberry between her finger and thumb and offered it up to Piper, who studied it for just a minute before she leaned forward to take it into her mouth.

Rilla laughed. "Good thing I pulled back my fingers fast enough. You nearly took them off." She winked at Piper. "Are you sure you're not a shark?"

My daughter giggled. "No, I'm a cowgirl. But Gin almost bit my finger today when I gave him some sugar. But he didn't." She held up both hands, with all digits intact, and this time I laughed, too.

"Okay, cowgirl princess. Time to hit the road. Nan's going to be waiting to see you, and I need to get to the club before Rocky thinks I've deserted him." I moved her to the other arm and flexed the one that had been holding her for too long. It was stiff and tingling. "Rilla, it was good to meet you. I'll see you next week at The Road Block?"

She nodded. "Would Wednesday work? That'll give you time to look everything over."

"Yeah, it's great." I backed away and head for the truck. Meghan was still at the register, ringing up a man who looked like he'd bought out all their peaches. She shot me a wry look and a quick nod as I passed her.

Piper was quiet in the backseat of the truck until we were nearly back in town. Then she spoke up.

"That girl was pretty, Daddy."

"Who's that, princess?" My mind was already at the club, thinking about what I needed to accomplish before we opened the doors tonight.

"The berry lady. She had nice hair and big eyes."

"Oh, that's Miss Rilla, honey. Yeah, she seems cool."

"I liked her. Can we go see her again?"

"What? Oh, I don't know. Maybe. She might come work for Daddy, and then . . . I don't know. We'll see." I wasn't completely convinced the bar needed any PR, and even if it did, I wasn't sure that having the little blonde mouse work for me was a good move.

"You should. She could work for you and bring me berries all the time." There was a finality in my daughter's voice that I'd learned from hard experience not to argue against.

"Yeah, we'll see, honey. We'll see."

Chapter Five

Rilla

THERE WAS NO WAY on God's green earth that my father would've stood for me setting foot inside The Road Block. The very idea was laughable. I reminded myself of that fact for the rest of Saturday afternoon, as I smiled to customers, sold fruit and vegetables and helped Meghan close up. We were just turning the key in the lock that secured the rolling fourth wall when I heard a deep voice call out.

"Sell all my vegetables today, ladies?"

I glanced up at Sam, smiling as he came up behind Meghan and caught her in a tight hug. I tried not to stare at the two of them, but I couldn't miss the way his hand spread over her stomach as his arms wrapped around her, or the look on her face as she reached over her shoulder to caress the back of his neck. Seeing them together gave me a tight feeling in my chest, a kind of yearning for something I didn't even know I wanted.

"It was crazy busy today." Meghan slid the keys into the

pocket of her jeans shorts. "Rilla and I didn't have time to breathe."

"She has no one to blame but herself, for bringing in all those new customers." Sam grinned at me. "How you doing, Rilla?"

"I'm fine, thanks." It was an automatic, conditioned response, and I realized it came off a little brusque. I added, "A little tired. Meghan's right. We were swamped today."

"Rilla had a visitor." Meghan arched an eyebrow at her fiancé. "Mason and Piper stopped by."

"Oh, yeah? What do you think, Rilla? Did you pick up a new client?"

"Maybe." I dug into my purse and found my keys. "I'm not sure he liked me. And I'm not sure we'd be a good fit."

"Bull." Meghan spoke the word with a tinge of fond impatience. "Rilla, you're good at what you do. Sam, Ali and I are all impressed with what you've done at the stand. Why shouldn't you be able to do the same for Mason?"

"Because you guys have been patient with me. I know you let me do the promotion for the stand because you wanted to be nice, and I appreciate it. I think I've done a decent job. But this is a farm. A stand. It's not that far out of my experience. But a bar? I've never been inside one. I wouldn't even begin to know how to publicize it."

"I thought you already did some preliminary work. Didn't you have information to give Mason today? I saw that he had a folder when he left."

"I did." I twisted the strap to my purse between my hands. "I thought . . . but then I met him. I think his expectations might be beyond what I can do."

"I didn't get the impression that Mason had expectations." Sam rested his chin on top of Meghan's red hair.

"Which is probably because he doesn't really need my services. He's only thinking about it as a favor to you."

"Whoa." Sam stepped back from Meghan and held up one hand. "Yeah, I told Mason about you and said he should check out what you could do for his business. But I didn't twist his arm, and I wouldn't have suggested you if I didn't think you had it in you to do the job." He softened his words with a smile. "Rilla, I'm always willing to help, but I'm not going to lie about anyone to do it. When I gave your name to Mason, it was because I believed it would be a good fit for both of you."

I blew out a breath. "I'm sorry. I don't mean to be ungrateful. You don't know how much I appreciate everything you've done for me, both of you and Ali, too. Maybe I'm just scared." I didn't know I was going to say those words until I did, but as they tumbled from my mouth, I realized they were true.

"Oh, sweetie." Meghan stepped forward and hugged me tight. "It's okay to be scared. You're doing so many new things, it's only natural you'd be a little nervous. But you got this."

"Yeah, you do." Sam echoed her words and then paused. I sensed he wanted to say more. "Rilla, is everything all right at home? I don't want to pry, and it's none of my business, unless you need our help. Then I'll make it our business."

I swallowed over the lump that had suddenly risen in my throat. "Thank you. But no, everything's fine. I know . . ." I tried to think of the best way to explain my family to these two people who I truly liked. "My dad's a hard man in some ways. He's always been very strict with me, protective of me. I realize it must seem weird to you, like I'm some hick who doesn't know anything because of how I was raised. But he's really a good man. He just wants what's best for me."

"Of course he does." Meghan squeezed my shoulders. "Sam and I do, too. We want you to know that if you need anything, we're here for you. Sometimes it's hard for parents to know when to let go, and we don't want to disappoint them. But Rilla, you're twenty-two. You have a college degree, and now you have a job. Two of them, actually. It's okay for you to think about moving on with your life, leaving home even. It doesn't make you a bad daughter for thinking about it."

"I know. I mean, I try to tell myself that. When I'm here at the stand, I can think of all the possibilities. But when I'm at home, it feels like the only two choices are obedience or sin. There's no middle ground. I either do what my father wants, or I'm disrespectful."

Meghan nodded. "You're the only person who can make the decision about what's right for you, Rilla. Sam and I are here to help. But you've got to live with the consequences. You're the only one who can decide if having your own life is worth maybe not doing everything your father sees as necessary and right."

Her words echoed in my brain as I drove toward home. The sun was setting, and after the long and busy day, I should've been exhausted, but the restlessness in my spirit rebelled against going directly home.

I'm twenty-two. Is it so wrong to want just the freedom to go for a ride after work, without worrying that my father'll freak out?

When I pulled up to the stop sign where I had to make the turn for our farm, that restlessness took over, and instead of going left, I swung the steering wheel right and headed in the opposite direction. I had no idea where I was headed, only that it was some place that wasn't home.

The road was empty for the first few miles, and I relished the freedom of just driving. I rolled down the windows, grateful that Gram's sedan had electric controls instead of the manual cranks in the old farm truck I usually drove, and let the wind blow into my face and my hair.

I rounded a bend, taking it maybe just a little too fast. As I put on the brakes to get the car back under control, I saw a large building ahead on the left. Bright neon lights shone from the sign on the side, and the parking lot that surrounded it was filled with cars. In the opposite direction that I was going, a line of vehicles waited to get into the lot. When I drove a little closer, I could make out what the sign spelled out: The Road Block.

My heart pounded a little faster. So this was Mason Wallace's bar. I had to admit that it was not what I'd expected; in my mind, a bar was small and dark, where desperate men and loose women gathered to drink away their money. This place was huge and out in the middle of nowhere, though apparently that didn't stop everyone in three counties from showing up. Or so it seemed. I slowed a little more as I drew up next to the club. A man in an orange reflective vest was directing traffic, and when he spotted me, he pointed to my car and then into the driveway. I shook my head to tell him I wasn't going in, but whether he couldn't see me or didn't understand, he only pointed with more vigor.

I sighed in exasperation and followed his direction, thinking I'd just turn around once I got in. That was easier said than done: the car in front of me inched along, looking for a spot, and another one closed in behind me. I didn't have any choice but to keep going.

People wandered from their cars toward the front door of the building. I tried not to stare at the girls, some of whom were dressed in shorter, tighter skirts than I'd ever seen. Others wore jeans with rips in the knees and shirts that barely covered the essentials.

The men wore more clothes at least. I spotted quite a few in cowboy hats, and most of them were in jeans and T-shirts. I thought about Mason that afternoon, his shirt soaked from where his daughter had been sleeping on him. I wondered if he were somewhere in that building, serving drinks or supervising whatever else went on in there. Something with music, no doubt, since I could hear it all the way out here. It didn't sound anything like the praise music we sang in church or the hymns Grams and Dad played on the radio. Still, my foot began tapping to the rhythm as though it had a mind of its own.

A loud *thump* drew my attention back to the front of my car. A girl passing by had stumbled and caught herself by landing on my hood. She giggled as she laid there, her straw hat askew. The man behind her leaned over, grasping her by the shoulders. Before he pulled her up, I saw his hand wander down to her backside, which was only just covered by a denim skirt. His fingers flexed, and the girl rolled so that now she lay on her back. The car ahead of me had moved quite a bit, and behind me, a truck honked its horn.

The man glanced up, waved at whoever was in the truck and then hoisted the girl to her feet. He slung an arm around her shoulders and led her in the direction of the club.

I watched them go as I gave the car just enough gas to catch up with the line of traffic. The girl looked up at her boyfriend—well, I assumed he was her boyfriend—and he bent his head to kiss her forehead.

In the back of my mind, I heard my father's voice, mingled with that of Pastor Shand. *Sodom and Gomorrah. Sinners.* And yet . . . yeah, I wasn't thrilled that the girl had landed on the hood of my car and that I'd had to see her boyfriend grope her, but they didn't look like sinners. They looked like I'd always imagined two people in love. When I tried to picture myself in the girl's place, though, I didn't see Jonathan or any other guy from my church. Maybe it was the fact that I was driving through his parking lot, but all I could see was Mason walking with me, holding my hand, leaning to kiss the top of my head . . .

Giving myself a mental shake, I finally made my way back to the other side of the parking lot and maneuvered to the exit. No one else was trying to leave, so it didn't take long for me to turn onto the road toward home. I glanced at the club in my rearview mirror, surprised by the sudden sense of longing I felt. I had no desire to go into a bar. Did I? Why would I want to be in room full of loud music and drunken people? I didn't. Probably not. On the other hand, how I could I know until I tried it?

I shoved that thought away and focused on getting back to the farm. I was late. Seriously late, as in missing the start supper, and Dad was not going to be happy. My stomach began to turn, and I pressed down on the accelerator a little harder.

Once I made the turn onto the dirt driveway, I slowed down, letting the car bump along until I reached the back of the house. I took a deep breath, climbed out and hurried inside.

The kitchen was dark except for the light over the table, where Dad and Gram were sitting. My grandmother met my eyes over my father's head, and she shook her head just slightly.

I didn't say anything right away. Stopping only briefly to hang my purse on the hook just inside the door, I went right to the sink, washed my hands and slid into my seat.

"I'm sorry I'm late." I kept my voice even, although part of me was screaming a warning. *Apologize! Grovel! Beg for forgiveness!* For the first time in my life, I ignored that voice.

"Just where were you, Marilla?" My father was calm, which I knew from experience meant he was beyond furious.

I sighed and unfolded my napkin, dropping it into my lap. "We were super busy at the stand today, and I stayed a bit after we closed to talk to Meghan and Sam. And then, I don't know. I just felt like driving a little. I needed some air. It's a beautiful night."

"You went for a drive? When you knew that your grandmother was here making dinner and needing your help? Beyond that, you know that meals in this house are served on a schedule. You deliberately decided to neglect your responsibilities and just . . . go for a drive."

I served myself a piece of chicken. "Yes."

He brought his hand down on the table so hard the silverware rattled and Gram's glass turned over. I froze with my hand on the spoon in the vegetable bowl. Gram made a tsking noise and mopped up her water with a napkin. After a few seconds, I moved again, scooping up the green beans onto my plate. My face felt hot and my heart was racing, but I wasn't going to let him see it.

"I knew this was going to happen." He pushed back his chair and stood up. "I knew that letting you work at that stand was going to lead to disobedience and—and sinful ideas. I let you try it, and you see the results. Well, no more. You call Sam Reynolds tomorrow and tell him you won't be back."

"I will *not.*" I struggled to moderate my voice, to hold back the tears that threatened. "This is my job and my decision, and I'm not quitting. Not after I've just got the campaign for the stand running so well, and I'm good at working there, too. I like seeing people and talking to them. You can't keep me hidden here forever, Dad. I'm an adult."

"As long as you live under my roof, you'll speak to me with respect, and you'll obey my rules. You've disappointed your grandmother and me—"

"Oh, no, don't drag me into this." Gram stood up, too, picking up her plate. "This is between you two." She set the dish on the counter with a clatter and then turned and pointed at my father. "But Emmett, you need to stop and think about what you're saying. Some things can't be taken back, you know."

Before I could appreciate the idea that Gram was sticking up for me, she turned to me with her hands on her hips. "And you, young lady, if you're going to be an adult, which I agree you are, have the courtesy to let people know when you're going to be late. I expected you for dinner, and when you didn't come in on time, I worried. Along with the freedom of adulthood comes responsibility. And you were raised to know better."

"Yes, ma'am." I bowed my head. "I'm sorry, Gram. Time really just got away from me, and I didn't mean to be so late."

She patted my shoulder. "I appreciate that. I also appreciate that you're going to do clean up after you finish eating, since I cooked without you. That's not punishment, it's just consequences."

I nodded. "No problem."

"This doesn't solve anything." My father, still glowering, looked from Gram to me. "I stand by what I said. You need to stop working at the stand."

"I'm sorry, Dad." I broke off a piece of chicken, popped it into my mouth, chewed and swallowed. I was so anxious that it tasted like sawdust, but I couldn't let him see that. "I'm not going to stop working. As a matter of fact, I picked up another client today."

Gram had been on her way out of the kitchen, but she paused in the doorway. "Oh, really? Good for you, Rilla. Who is it? Another farmer?"

"Uh, no, actually. It's the owner of a-a restaurant. He's adding new hours, and he'd like some help promoting that. I gave him some information when he stopped by the stand today, and I'm going to meet with him this week."

"What restaurant is that? All I know in Burton is Kenny's Diner. Or is it out of town?" Gram smiled, and I quaked a little inside. My grandmother was trying to be supportive, but I wasn't sure even she would be able to get behind me promoting a bar.

"It's out of town a little. It's called The Road Block." I became very absorbed in getting the last few green beans on my fork, not daring to look up at my father or Gram.

"That's not a restaurant." Dad sat down in his chair, almost slumping. "It's a bar, Rilla. I've heard about it. They have loud music and wild dancing. And they serve alcohol. How can you even think about working for such a place, let alone advertising it?"

"It's a business, Dad. And I'm not really going to promoting that part of it. Mason's adding lunch hours next week, and that's what I'm going to be publicizing. Not the bar, just the restaurant." I stood up and carried my plate to the sink and began running the water over it.

"That's nitpicking, and you know it. What do you think the people at church are going to think if they find out? Will they assume you're only working for the non-alcohol part of the business, or will they think you're promoting the enemy's work?"

"I don't know, Dad. And you know what? I really don't care." I threw my fork into the water in the sink. "You're talking about people who've known me my whole life. If they're going to immediately jump to conclusions about what I'm doing and who I am, then maybe I don't want anything to do with them."

I heard my father's quick intake of breath. "You'd better take a minute and consider your words, Marilla Grace. You're skirting seriously close to blasphemy."

"No, Dad, I'm not." I rinsed my plate and slid it into the dishwasher. "If I were saying I didn't want anything to do with God or that I didn't care what He thinks, you'd have a case. But we're talking about people at church. They're hardly saints, any of them. Half of them don't pay any attention to what you and the other elders say. They might be pious on Sundays, but on the days between, they're off doing whatever they want."

"And just how would you know that?"

I dropped a pile of silverware into the basket of the dishwasher. "When I was in youth group, I heard the other kids talking about what happened at home. Very, very few of them live like we do, Dad. You've buried us out here to keep us away from the world and make us look better to all those church folks, but most of them could care less. They think we're weird."

"You don't know what you're talking about, Rilla. And . . ." He rose again. "I'm finished with this discussion. I've made it clear what I expect from you. You need to take my words into consideration and prayer." He stalked past Gram out of the kitchen, and I heard his heavy tread on the steps a moment later.

I finished the dishes in silence. Gram came back in, and her chair scraped against the linoleum as she sat down again.

"Well." She spoke slowly when I closed the dishwasher and dried my hands on a faded old tea towel. "You've stood up for yourself at last. I was waiting for this day. Feared it, because I knew by the time your father pushed you into finally speaking your piece, you'd have a lot to say. And you did." She sighed and leaned her head against her hand.

"I'm sorry, Gram." I sat down next to her and took her free hand. "I'm not trying to make Dad angry, and I don't want to disappoint either of you. But if I live my whole life trying not to do that, I'm never going to live." I touched her thin gold wedding band, the one piece of jewelry that my grandmother wore without fail. It hadn't left her finger in the last forty-six years, even though Gramps had been gone for almost half that time. "I don't think I want to marry Jonathan, Gram. Actually, I'm pretty sure he doesn't want to marry me, either."

"Is there someone else you want to marry, Rilla?"

I shook my head. "No. I just want to be able to make the choice myself. I don't want to get married just because it's convenient for Dad and for the church. And I know this probably sounds sinful, but I don't want to come second to a congregation. When I do find someone to marry, I want him to be so happy about the idea that he'd move heaven and earth to make it happen. You know?"

"I do, honey." She smiled at me. "I'm proud of you for realizing that. Just try not to be too hard on your father. Remember that no matter what he says, he loves you, and that's why he's so protective." She squeezed my hand. "He'll come around. Give him time. Just you wait."

I didn't want to disagree with my grandmother, but I had a feeling it was going to take more than time for my father to accept that I was ready to live life on my own terms.

Chapter Six

Mason

"HEY, BOSS, WE NEED to bring up another flat of bottled water and a case of shiraz."

I glanced up at Darcy from my tablet, where I was skimming a website. "Hmmm? Oh, okay. Yeah. I'll have Ryan grab it next time he goes past."

"Thanks." Darcy paused and leaned her hip against the bar. "Mason, you all right? You've been kind of out of it since you got here."

"I'm fine. Just a lot on my mind." I forced a smile. "I had a crappy morning."

"Anything I can do?"

I studied her, considering. Darcy had been my first hire after Rocky once I hit town and had the building for The Road Block mostly up. She'd worked in restaurants and bars in Savannah, Jacksonville and Hilton Head until she'd fallen in love with contractor who brought her to his tiny hometown in Georgia.

The two of them raised a family, but after her youngest started high school, Darcy had found herself bored and itching for something to do. It'd been around that time that I'd announced I was opening my bar. When she walked in that first day and I'd asked her why she wanted a job, she'd fixed me with a stare.

"I need something to keep me out of trouble. I'm the best damned waitress in the state of Georgia, maybe in the whole southeast. I've just been in temporary retirement for the last eighteen years. Now I'm ready to come back. If you don't hire me, I'll be forced to talk my husband into building me my own bar, and I'll be your competition. I figure if you let me work for you, it saves all of us a lot of time, energy and heartbreak."

Saying yes to Darcy was a decision I hadn't regretted. She was on time, responsible and professional. She'd also become a sort of mother hen to everyone else at the Block, keeping her eye on the younger wait staff and making sure everyone was behaving.

"No." I answered her at last. "I don't think so, Darce. Just keep doing what you're doing here, okay? It means a lot to me to know that if something happened and I couldn't be here all the time, you and Rocky could keep things running smooth. For a while, at least."

"Sure thing, Mason." She picked up her tray. "Just remember, if you need a shoulder or an ear, I'm around. And I give damn good advice. Just ask my kids."

I laughed as I turned back to the task at hand. Not that I was getting anywhere but frustrated. Not for the first time, I silently cursed leukemia and the health care system.

The door opened, and I glanced up out of habit and then did a double-take. I recognized the slim blonde who stood at the hostess stand, speaking to Niki.

Damn, I'd forgotten this was Wednesday. And that she'd promised to come by today to check out the restaurant.

Rilla Grant was more dressed up today. In the place of

the denim skirt, she wore a simple black dress that hit her just above the knees. The short sleeves skimmed the tops of her pale arms, and the neckline came all the way to her collarbones. I guessed it was about a size too big, as it was nearly as shapeless as the shirt she'd had on last weekend.

Niki pointed over to the bar, and Rilla's eyes followed the gesture. I knew the moment she spotted me, because her lips tightened into a line and her gaze dropped to the floor. When she stepped around the podium, I saw that her legs were covered with sheer black stockings and her shoes were plain black pumps.

Her hair was down today, though. No ponytail; instead, she'd caught the sides up, fastening them in the back with some sort of hair thingy. I didn't remember what it was called, but Lu used to wear them every once in a while. Loose curls danced over her shoulders, making me think of Piper's hair. It was almost exactly the same shade as my daughter's.

I watched her walk toward me, her face set and grim. I remembered her words about the bar, and I wondered if I should've just had Niki show her to a table in the lunch section. But it was too late now; she was almost to me.

I fully intended to greet her civilly and suggest that we talk at a table, but when I spoke, completely different words came out.

"Did you come from a funeral?"

She frowned, her light brows drawing together. "Excuse me?"

"You're all in black. In the middle of the day. I thought maybe someone died."

Rilla looked down at herself as though surprised. "No. I didn't come from a funeral. This is business attire. I'm here to discuss advertising and promotion, and I'm dressed as I should be when meeting a client."

I shook my head. "Darlin,' you're at a bar. Well—" I hurried to amend what I'd said before she turned tail and ran. "A restaurant. But a casual one. You could've worn jeans. I still would've taken you just as seriously. Maybe more so than looking like you're playing dress up in your mama's clothes."

Her mouth dropped open for a heartbeat before she shut it with a snap. Her eyes narrowed. "I'm not playing dress-up. I'm sorry if you're not used to dealing with people who know how to dress for the occasion, but I won't apologize for doing what I know is right." She glanced off to the side before she added, "Besides, I don't own a pair of jeans. Even if I did, I wouldn't have worn them here today. I understand you're more used to women who dress in micro-mini skirts and tight ripped jeans—"

"Whoa, whoa there, darlin.' I'm not used to women who dress that way. What the hell gave you that idea?"

Her face turned an intriguing shade of pink, and yep, there went the thumb to her lips. "I'm just making an assumption based on what people wear to bars like this. And please don't swear. I don't like it. A gentleman doesn't swear in front of a lady."

Holy shit, was this chick from some kind of time warp? I tried to remember the last time a woman other than my mother had scolded me for cursing in front of her. I couldn't. But here stood Miss Prim and Proper in my bar trying to tell me how to talk.

Darcy rounded the corner in time to hear her last words. The waitress glanced from Rilla to me, and a slow grin grew on her face. "She's right, Mason. A gentleman doesn't use those kinds of words in mixed company. If you were my son, I'd slap you upside the head."

My eyes widened. This from Darcy, who could out-swear the worst of us when challenged? I opened my mouth to say as much, but she folded her arms over her chest and stared me down, one eyebrow raised, until I finally shook my head and sighed.

"Okay, fine. No swearing." I ran my hand over my face. "Darcy, we're going to sit at number twelve. Can you tell Niki?"

"Sure." She pivoted to face Rilla. "I don't think we've met yet. I'm Darcy Hade, and I head up the wait staff here."

"Hi, Darcy, nice to meet you." Rilla stuck out her hand. "Rilla Grant. I'm going to be handling advertising and promotion for The Road Block."

"No sh—no kidding." Darcy didn't even blink at her near-slip, and neither did Rilla, I noticed. "That's cool."

"If I decide to hire you." I felt the need to reassert my control of this situation.

"Oh, you're going to hire me." Rilla turned her head and for the very first time, she smiled at me, full on, without a hint of shyness or self-doubt. My breath caught, and my stomach felt as though I'd just stepped off a rollercoaster. *What the hell . . .*

I didn't have any interest in a girl like her. When I needed a woman, she had to understand that I wasn't looking for more than a night. Not at this point in my life. Probably not ever again. This one didn't fit the bill by a long shot, but my body was reacting like it'd just met the answer to my prayers. *No way.*

I came out from behind the bar, and Rilla met me, pausing to see where I was leading her. Without really thinking about it, I pressed my hand to her lower back, just to guide her toward table twelve. She stiffened at my touch, but when I didn't move my hand, I felt her draw in a deep breath before she started walking.

I pulled out her chair for her and was rewarded with another slight blush and a murmured thanks. Going to the opposite side of the table, I spun the chair and straddled it, propping my elbows on the back and leaning my chin into my hands.

"Okay, darlin,' let's talk numbers here. I looked at the information you gave me the other day, and I'll be honest. I was impressed. You identified businesses that were very close to where I am, and you made interesting parallels. Your suggestions and ideas were things I wouldn't have thought of doing. Offering regular lunch tables to the Women's Club and the quilting circles, with special pricing? Brilliant. We're getting them to identify The Road Block as place they'd want to eat lunch, even beyond the regular meetings."

"Exactly." She folded her hands on the table in front of her, and I noticed how small they looked. Her nails were short and unpolished but still managed to look more feminine than the girls I'd seen with red-painted talons. "I had another suggestion, something that came to me . . . well, actually, it occurred to me in church on Sunday."

I chuckled. "Divine inspiration. I like it."

She smiled, and I was struck once again by how it transformed her whole face. Her big blue eyes danced, and those bow-lips curled up, making me want to lick—

God almighty, what the hell, Mason? I kicked myself mentally. Was I that hard up for a woman that this little slip of a thing looked good to me? I tried to concentrate on what she was saying.

"—so I know it might not be something you really want to do, but if you'll just think about it, you might change your mind."

"Um, sorry, what was that?" I shifted in my seat, dropping my hands to the table so they lay inches from hers. As I watched, her eyes followed the movement. All I would have had to do was extend my thumb the slightest bit, and it would stroke her pinkie finger. I waited, but she didn't draw her hands back. Instead she cleared her throat.

"Um, I was saying that for some people, the idea of going to a bar for lunch is—well, it's just not exactly what they're comfortable doing. And The Road Block does have a reputation as a hot night spot." Her tongue came out and ran over her lips. "So what if you gave your lunch time hours a different name? Called it . . . I don't know, The Road Block Café or something like that. Something less . . . threatening to some people's way of thinking."

"The Road Block is threatening to some people? Who?"

Rilla nodded. "Well, people who wouldn't usually frequent a bar. Church people. Maybe some professionals who don't want to be identified with a place that sells alcohol."

"We still sell alcohol at lunch, you know."

She stared at me for a minute and then closed her eyes and shook her head a little. "Yes, all right, but it's not your main focus. I knew you might not like the idea. It's fine, you don't have to do it. It was just a thought."

"I'll take it under consideration."

"Fine." She lifted her hands to fold them under her chin. "Do you have any other questions?"

One shorter strand of hair had escaped and curled near her forehead. I fought hard to keep from reaching across and brushing it away. "No, I don't think so. Not right now."

"Good. Then are we ready to move forward?"

I pursed my lips, looking at her. "I think so. If you're sure you can handle working for a big bad bartender, who sells alcohol."

She laughed and leaned back, crossing her arms over her chest. "I think that's a little redundant. Is there such a thing as a bartender who doesn't sell alcohol? Anyway, I don't think you're so big or bad."

I shrugged. "Even after the way I acted when you first got here?"

"Everyone has off days."

"Yeah." I gave a quick, humorless laugh. "Today's been one of those, for sure. Sorry I took it out on you."

She studied me. "Want to tell me about it?"

I was surprised that she asked, and even more so to find that I did want to tell her. "You don't want to hear about my problems."

"Maybe I do. I'm a good listener."

"Yeah, well . . . " I sat up a little straighter. "You heard me on Saturday, telling Miss Evelyn about my mom, right?"

Rilla nodded. "Yes, I'm sorry. Meghan had actually told me about the whole situation. She said after your wife—after you lost her, you came back to Burton so your mom could help you raise Piper, and then a few months ago, you found out your mom has leukemia. I'm so sorry."

"Yeah, that's pretty much the story. It sucks, but you know, we figured stuff out." I paused and glanced up at Rilla. "Is sucked considered swearing? I don't want to get into trouble again."

She cast her eyes up as though pretending to consider. "We'll pretend you meant it sucks eggs. That's only vulgar slang, not cursing."

I nodded, fighting to keep a straight face. "Of course that's what I meant."

"Suuuuure." Rilla's lips curved into a half-smile. "So what happened today?"

I rubbed my fingers over one of the chair's decorative dowels. "I hired this wonderful woman to come in and help with Mom and watch Piper, too. Mrs. Murphy's been a life saver. She works around my crazy hours, she has endless patience with both Mom and Piper . . . God, she even cooks for us. So this morning she came over as usual, right before I was ready to leave, and I could tell she'd been crying. Turns out her own mother was just diagnosed with Alzheimer's, and Mrs. Murphy has to move to Arizona to take care of her. She said she's been wracking her brain to find a solution, but time's run out. She has to leave Saturday."

Rilla leaned forward and laid her small hand on my arm.

"Oh, Mason, I'm sorry. That's got to be so hard on you. There's no one else? Family, friends?"

I shook my head. "Nah. My mom's from Mississippi, and she was the baby of the family. All her sisters are pretty old, and they don't leave their hometown except for funerals. I'm an only child. Mom has a lot of friends in town, but no one I could ask to do what we need." I rubbed my forehead. "I've been looking up caregiver referral sites, but in order to use those, I have to commit to steady hours. I need someone with flexibility. And I'd also have to hire one person to help Mom and another to watch Piper." I looked down at Rilla's hand, still on my arm, absently thinking how tiny and white it looked against my tanned skin.

She bit the side of her lip. "So you don't need someone with nursing experience? Really just a caregiver, right?"

"Yeah, Mrs. Murphy didn't have any background in medical care. The visiting nurses showed her how to do a few things, but it wasn't anything complicated."

Rilla stared at me for a long minute. She was leaning forward still, and the way she looked was a little unnerving. Her blue eyes drilled into me as though she could see my soul. I couldn't tell yet whether she found it wanting. I stayed very still, waiting for her to speak again. When she did, I nearly fell off my chair.

"I can help you."

This time, it was my mouth that fell open, and my eyes that stared. If Rilla Grant had just announced that she'd be willing to swim across the Atlantic naked and dance on the rooftops of Paris, I probably wouldn't have been any more shocked.

"Um, what?" It wasn't an inspired response, but it was the best I could manage at the moment.

"I could help you. Things are starting to slow down at the stand, and I think Sam would be willing to be flexible with my hours. I could work there when you don't need me."

I blinked and nodded. "Rilla, I appreciate the offer. You have no idea how much it means to me, actually. But . . ." How could I say this without insulting her? Or making her think her friends had been talking behind her back? "As I understood it, you still live at home. With your father. Your, uh, very overprotective father."

Rilla sighed. "Meghan?"

I didn't want to throw my friend under the bus, but I wasn't going to lie, either. "Yeah, she mentioned it to me. Not in a bad way," I hurried to add. "She wanted me to understand why you're a little different from girls I'm used to."

She tilted her head, and warning bells sounded in my brain. *Danger, danger! Abort, abort!*

"I'm . . . different? That's what Meghan told you?"

"No. Not really. She just said you hadn't had a lot of experience with new people until you started working at the stand, and that you're quieter. Maybe a little shy." When she didn't respond right away, I went on. "Meghan was afraid I might overwhelm you. She says sometimes I don't know my own loudness, I guess. Or whatever." There was nothing I could say that wouldn't make me sound stuck on myself.

To my relief, Rilla seemed to accept that. "I understand. I was really nervous when I came to work for Sam. I *have* lived on a farm my whole life, and my dad is really . . . careful with me. The only new people I've ever met were through church, or if we were doing a youth group project. So it took a little while to get used to them, especially Sam.

"But I think I do a good job now. I talk to customers all day long, and it doesn't bother me. I'm not a freak, just because I was sheltered."

"No one's saying you are, Rilla." I gentled my voice, and this time, I covered her fingers so that they disappeared beneath mine. "I think you'd be perfect to help my mom and Piper. But from what I hear about your dad, he might not like you working in town, in my house. It could make him uncomfortable, and I don't want to come between you and your family."

Her forehead wrinkled, and the corners of her lips turned down. "It's not any different than when I help out people at church. I volunteered one summer, taking care of an elderly lady who was living alone. It wasn't in town, but still. My father said it would be good for me."

"Yeah, but that's an old lady. This is my house. Remember me, the big bad bartender? I have a feeling your father'd have a different take on this idea."

Rilla pulled back to sit up straight in her chair, and she stared me down. "I'm twenty-two years old. I'm not a child. If I decide I want to work for you, in your house, taking care of your child and your sick mother, that's what I'm going to do." Her chin went up and her jaw clenched. "As a matter of fact, if I decide I want to come into the bar and pour beer for people, I'm going to do that. My father doesn't make my decisions. *I* do."

In that moment, I was honestly a little frightened of this girl—uh, woman—who sat before me. I'd assumed that she was all soft cotton, when she turned out to be steel. I'd thought of her as a timid mouse.

Today the mouse had roared.

Chapter Seven

Rilla

IN THEORY, MY FATHER knew that I was meeting Mason at The Road Block that afternoon to finalize the publicity I was going to do for him. I'd told Gram about it before breakfast, while she and I were at the sink. Dad was at the table, reading his Bible and waiting for his eggs and toast, and I didn't speak too loudly, not wanting to disturb him. Not that I would've known if I had; he hadn't said a word to me since Saturday night, when he'd left the kitchen.

But the point was that even if I hadn't gone out of my way to tell him directly, I'd said the words while we were both in the same room. In my heart, I knew he'd call that quibbling, which had usually resulted in a stiffer punishment when I was younger. All the same, given the circumstances, it was the best I could do.

Gram hadn't said anything when I'd told her about my appointment at the bar. Her mouth had pressed into a thin line before she nodded. I figured that was her way of staying out of the middle.

I'd worked the stand during the morning hours. Now that school was back in session, our weekdays were considerably slower. Sam hadn't even blinked when I'd told him that I needed to take off the afternoon to meet Mason.

"Maddy Weson asked me last week if she could pick up some hours at the stand, with Ali away now. She usually just helps out with the harvest, working in the barn and loading, but I guess now that her kid's in college, she wants to make a little more money. So if you need to pull back on some of your time, I can always have her fill in."

Mrs. Weson showed up at ten minutes to noon, greeting me with a smile. I ran a receipt on the register, just the way Ali'd taught me to do whenever there was a transfer of cashiers, and then I jumped into Gram's car and drove to the Reynolds' house. Meghan had suggested I get changed for my meeting there, rather than go all the way home. I figured she realized that if I went back and saw Gram and Dad, I might chicken out on going to The Road Block.

Once I was changed and back on the road, my nerves kicked in. *What did I think I was doing?* I didn't belong in bar, and there was no way I was qualified to handle advertising for one. I must've had a screw loose when I agreed to meet Mason there. There'd be drunk men, and they'd look at me in ways men shouldn't. I'd feel dirty and sinful.

But if I didn't go in, Mason wouldn't hire me, and I'd be stuck living on my father's farm until they carried me out feet first. Or the way I was feeling these days, possibly until the men from the loony bin came with the straitjacket. Neither of those sounded like a good option.

The parking lot had been empty compared to Saturday night. I'd taken a deep breath and forced my feet to make the walk to the door. Once inside, though, I was surprised by how bright and airy the place was. It was clean; there was no lingering odor of alcohol, no stains on the floor, as I'd expected. On the other side of the bar was a seating area, and I saw that some of the tables were occupied. The lunch hours had just gone into effect a few days before, and clearly they were going to need some time—and maybe even some of my hard work—to catch on.

The woman standing at the wooden podium smiled at me, and when I told her I was there to meet with Mr. Wallace, she pointed back to the huge oak bar that dominated the left side of the room. I glanced up, and suddenly I was having trouble breathing.

When I'd seen Mason at the stand a few days before, I'd been so flustered by all the customers milling around us, by the idea of pitching my work to him, that I hadn't had time to pay much attention to him. Plus, he'd been holding his little girl, and I'm sorry, no man can seem too intimidating when he's cradling a sleeping child.

But today was a different story. Mason Wallace stood behind the gorgeous polished oak of his bar, leaning over some kind of computer thing. His eyes were on me, and I had to concentrate on putting one foot in front of the other. I was so far outside my realm of experience that I didn't know which end was up. What was this naïve farm girl doing in a bar, of all places?

Breathe, I reminded myself. *And remember: this is all about work and being professional. It's my ticket off the farm and into my own life.* I had to keep all this in mind and try not to notice the way Mason's scrutiny made me feel warm and breathless. Or the way the muscles in his arms flexed as he leaned. A thought flittered across my mind: he looked as though he belonged there, behind the bar. As though he'd simply grown out of the solid oak, just as perfect and just as invincible.

No, I couldn't think about any of that. Not now.

I was ready with my formal greeting—*Hello, Mr. Wallace. Nice place you've got here. I'm looking forward to working with you*—when he spoke first.

"Did you just come from a funeral?"

I was confused at first, and then I was mad. He was making fun of me, making fun of my efforts, and that just got my goat, as Gram said. I was tempted to turn around and leave right there. But then I remembered my father's face. The idea of having to tell him I hadn't gotten this account because I'd been too scared to see it through and the thought of his smugness kept me from running.

Our discussion, surprisingly, had turned around and actually been positive and productive. I was shocked when Mason had apologized for his earlier behavior. He'd opened up, telling me about his mother's illness and his struggle to care for both her and his daughter. When I'd leaned forward without thinking to lay my hand on his arm, a spark zinged through me like I'd never felt, and something warm and intoxicating filled my head. The next thing I knew, I was offering to help him.

Temporary insanity. That was all I could figure. It had to be.

I wasn't going to back out, though. I'd driven half-way home in a daze, wondering what I'd just agreed to do, and then once I'd reached my decision—I was going to take care of Mrs. Wallace and Piper, no matter what anyone said—a strange strength and exhilaration filled me.

This was the perfect scenario. Mason had offered me a salary much higher than I'd expected, telling me it was the same he was paying Mrs. Murphy now. With that money, plus what I'd continue to earn at the stand, even with cutting back to part-time, and what I'd be making doing the advertising for both the stand and The Road Block, I could afford to move out. I could pay rent on the adorable little apartment I'd seen advertised in the newspaper.

I'd pumped myself up by the time I got back to the farm. There was plenty of time before dinner; I'd change out of my dress and tell Gram the news, and then maybe she could help me break the news gently to my father.

Not that it mattered. As I'd told Mason, my father wasn't going to stop me. I was taking this job.

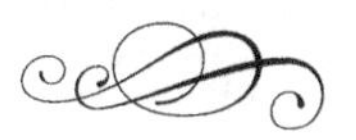

"So what did your father say about your news?" Meghan leaned against the side of the apple bin, looking at me with equal parts sympathy and amusement.

"I believe his exact words were, 'Absolutely not. Have you lost your mind? Working in the home of a single man, performing household chores for him . . . an unmarried young woman? No. I forbid it'."

She nodded. "Well, no surprise there, right? You didn't think he'd like the idea of you working for a guy who owns a club."

"No, I wasn't surprised. Disappointed that I was on target, I guess. Anyway, I told him I was doing it, and if anyone from church got squiffy, he could tell them I was doing God's work, caring for the sick and the young."

"And you're headed there now?" Meghan's green eyes sparkled. "Rilla Grant. I have to say, I didn't think you had it in you. You got spunk, gal."

I laughed. "Why, because I'm going to take care of sick woman and a little girl?"

"No. Because you're going to be working closely with Mason Wallace in not one job, but two. I honestly thought he'd scare you to death, but here you're going to be in his house."

"Why did you think Mason would frighten me?" I cocked my head. "Do you think I'm that much of a child? I'm as old as you, Meghan. Actually a few weeks older. And just because

I've been sheltered doesn't mean I'm scared of my own shadow. I just lack experience. I'm fixing that, starting now."

"I'd say you started fixing that this summer, when you stopped by and offered your PR services to Ali. That took gumption. I'm just surprised. Happily so."

"Thanks." I grinned at her. "I needed to hear that, because honestly, I'm a little terrified about this whole thing."

"Nah. You got this, Rilla." She gave me a quick hug. "Go knock 'em dead."

I tried to hold onto Meghan's encouragement as I pulled into the driveway next to the large brick house on a quiet street in Burton. A huge black truck sat further back down the drive. I smiled a little; it had to be Mason's. It looked like what I'd expect him to drive. I couldn't see him folding his huge frame into a little compact.

Before I could walk up the steps and ring the doorbell, the front door opened and a small blonde tornado flew out, heading straight for me. I braced myself as Piper launched herself at my legs.

"Hey, sweet pea!" I crouched and held her by the upper arms. "What're you doing outside by yourself?"

"She's not supposed to go out the front door without an adult." Mason stood in the doorway, his arms folded across his chest and a scowl on his face. "She knows the rules."

"I was watching for you, and I saw you. You're the berry lady."

"The berry . . . oh." I grinned down at her adorable face. Her blonde curls were in a ponytail, and her mouth was curved into an eager smile. But those eyes—they were what made her truly a gorgeous child. They were brown, but not quite; flecks of green and gold made them more hazel. Whatever the color, they sparkled with mischief.

I stood up and offered her my hand. "Why don't you bring me inside and tell me where everything is? I'm going to need you to show me the ropes, you know."

"Oh, we don't have any ropes." She shook her head. "Daddy says maybe I can get a jump rope for my birthday, but that's not for—how long, Daddy?"

"Five months, and that's not what Miss Rilla meant, princess. Showing someone the ropes means you're explaining a new job." Mason met my gaze as we neared him. "Hi, Rilla. Thanks again for doing this. I can't tell you how grateful I am."

"Thank you for giving me the chance. I'm glad to be able to help you, but remember, it's a good thing for me, too."

He nodded and glanced down at his daughter. "Piper, run and tell Nan that Miss Rilla's here. We'll be there in just a minute."

She took off down the hallway at top speed, and I wondered if the child ever did anything slowly.

"Hey." Mason touched my shoulder, and I jumped. He was standing much closer to me than I expected. I had to crane my neck to look up at him. "Did your dad . . . was everything okay?"

I could've fibbed and told Mason that everything was fine, that my father hadn't objected at all. But a liar I was not, and so I shook my head.

"He wasn't happy. But it's not just this. He's been upset at me for a while, since he didn't want me to take the job with Sam." I blew a lock of hair out of my eyes. "My father doesn't want to accept the fact that I'm grown up and he can't control me anymore. He'll get over it. Or so my grandmother says."

"I don't want to cause trouble for you." Mason rubbed the back of his neck. "Maybe I can put something together with one of the caregiver sites and a babysitter service . . ."

"No." The vehemence of my voice was unexpected, even to me. "Please, I mean. I really want this job. I meant what I said before. I'm happy to help you, but my salary here is going to make it possible for me to finally move off the farm."

He stared down at me for the space of several heartbeats, not speaking. His eyes were fastened on mine, and I realized that they were the exact same shade as Piper's. In Mason, though, they had an added intensity that made me shiver.

"Okay." He sighed and nodded. "We'll try it. But if things get too rough for you at home, promise you'll tell me right away. I can figure something else out."

"They won't." I spoke with assurance, but when Mason didn't budge, I added, "But I promise."

"Good. Okay, Mom's this way. Since you haven't met her before, you might not notice, but she's real thin. We try to find whatever sounds good for her to eat. She's not actively on chemo now, since she's between sessions, but she still has nausea sometimes." As he kept talking, Mason walked down the same hall Piper had run, and I followed.

We turned into a room that was lined with bookshelves. A single bed was set up in the corner, but I could tell it didn't really belong there; no doubt this had been an office or library before it was Mrs. Wallace's sick room.

She sat in a recliner near the center of the room. Her gray hair was cropped close; I guessed it was just growing back after chemo. A broad smile stretched across her thin face.

"So this is our angel of mercy!" Mrs. Wallace held out her hands to me. "Come here, darlin.' I'm so tickled to meet you."

There could be no doubt about this woman's origins. She may have left the great state of Mississippi, but it hadn't left her; it rang out through every word she spoke.

I took her hands gently within my own. "I'm not sure anyone would call me an angel, Mrs. Wallace, but I'm glad to meet you, too."

"Hogwash, darlin.' I can practically see your halo. And please, call me Naomi. We're gonna be friends, I just know it. I love your name, by the way. So pretty and timeless."

I laughed. "If that's a nice way of saying it's old-fashioned,

I appreciate your tact."

"Old-fashioned isn't a bad thing." She leveled a look at me that told me Mason had talked to her about my upbringing. "You be proud of that name and how you were raised. Nothing to be ashamed of."

"Yes, ma'am. Naomi, I mean."

"Mom mostly needs very basic help. Meals, getting up and down for the bathroom and help with dressing. There are a few simple medical procedures that have to be done now and then, but the visiting nurse can show you how to do that, if you're comfortable with it." Mason gripped the back of a chair and leaned his weight on that arm.

I glanced at him. "As long as it's not drawing blood, I think I'm okay."

Naomi laughed. "No, the vampire nurse does that. It's just a matter of hooking me up to IV drugs when they're needed. And I have a porta-cath, so as long as you can screw it in, we'll be golden."

"That I can do. What about doctor visits?"

"I take care of those." Mason's eyes lingered on his mother. "Rocky's great about covering things at the bar when we have appointments. But that's why I have to be out late some nights, too. You're sure you're going to be okay with that?"

"I told you I would be." I knelt down next to his mother's chair. "Naomi, if you'll be patient with me the first few days, I'll get up to speed as soon as I can. I'm sure it's been distressing to have Mrs. Murphy leave you, and I don't want you to have any more upset than necessary."

"Sweetie, we're going to do just fine." She beamed. "Mason, did you talk to Rilla about Piper's schedule yet?"

"No, we'll go over that now. You okay if we move to the kitchen?"

"Of course. Piper, honey, why don't you stay here with Nan for a bit so Daddy can talk to Miss Rilla?"

Piper scrambled up to sit next to her grandmother, and I noticed that she was careful not to lean on the older woman's legs or arm. She settled herself on the chair and rested her head on Naomi's chest.

Mason led me into the kitchen. It was open and sunny, with granite countertops and stainless steel appliances. He pulled out a chair for me at the wide oak-hewn table and then sat down across from me. A white dry erase board was propped against the sugar bowl.

It didn't take very long to review Piper's daily schedule, which was fairly loose.

"This was something Mrs. Murphy put together. To be honest with you, Piper doesn't really do well with schedules." He dropped his forehead onto his hand. "I probably should've told you this before you agreed, but my daughter can be kind of a brat."

I laughed. "Mason, she's three years old. That's pretty much a kid's job at that age."

"No, I know, but really she is. She doesn't listen, she's headstrong and wild . . . and how would you know about three-year olds? I thought you were an only child."

"I've been working in our church's nursery since I was ten years old. The kids who're just starting out in the youth group now? I changed their diapers. Sometimes we'd have ten or twenty babies under the age of four. Believe me, I can handle one willful three-year old."

Mason regarded me for a moment, one eyebrow raised. "Let's revisit that sentiment after you've been with Piper for a few days."

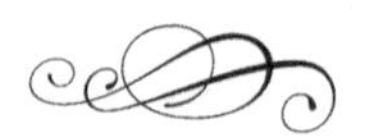

He wasn't wrong.

It wasn't that Piper was a bad kid. It wasn't even that she

was too active or disrespectful. She was smart and very, very busy. If I turned my back for a minute, helping Naomi to dress or in the bathroom, Piper would be in the kitchen, mixing cups of flour and sugar into a big pot. Or in her room, taking all the books off the shelves so that she could climb on them to reach the top of her closet. I caught her one afternoon about to cut her hair with scissors she'd gotten by pulling over a kitchen chair and emptying out a cabinet.

On the other hand, she was a kind child. Although she didn't fully grasp the concept of her grandmother's illness, she moved slowly around Naomi, careful not to jolt or jostle her. When we sat down to eat lunch or dinner together, she chattered away to me, holding conversation that was advanced beyond her age.

No matter how challenging Piper was, though, I loved being with her. She'd sit on my lap with her warm little arm around my neck, and when I put her to bed, she'd pull my face in to kiss my cheek.

"I love you, Rilla." Her sweet voice was high and clear, and every time she said it, I fell in a little more under her spell.

I'd been working at the Wallace house for five days. So far, everything was fairly smooth sailing; Mason was good about making sure I got in my hours at the stand, and I'd even been able to put some of our advertising plans for the bar into effect, since he let me use his laptop while Piper napped. I'd announced the new hours on all the social media sites, put together a newsletter list, and set up a frequent diner program. Mason seemed to be impressed, though it was hard to be sure; we didn't see each other except in passing when he came home.

Today had been a long day. I'd covered the morning and early afternoon at the stand before driving into Burton in time for Mason to leave for his evening shift at The Road Block. Piper was already up from her nap by the time I arrived at the house, so I didn't get any break: we were in perpetual motion from two in the afternoon until eight, when I finally got her to sleep.

I trudged down the steps and into Naomi's room, where I collapsed into the easy chair across from her recliner. I heard her soft laughter.

"Done in, are you, darlin'? Yes, I always say, nothing can wear a person out like a three-year old."

My head lolled to the side, and I opened one eye to regard the older woman. "She just never stops. How on earth did Mrs. Murphy do it? Mason said she was in her fifties. I can't imagine how she kept up with Piper."

"Well, there're a few differences. First of all, a child can tell how far she can get with an adult, and I think Piper knew Mrs. Murphy had her limits. She looks at you as younger and more energetic, and so her behavior has changed accordingly. And I think she's testing you, too. She's trying to see how far she can push before you break."

"We might've found out that limit today. I was about ready to hold her down until she fell asleep."

Naomi smiled. "I used to give Mason warm milk with a slug of brandy. I know it's frowned upon these days, but Lord, that boy wouldn't go to sleep for love or money. It was the brandy or my sanity."

I grinned. "I can see that. Gram told me once that she used to rub whiskey on my gums when I was teething." I paused, considering. "She probably had to hide it so my dad didn't know. He doesn't tolerate any form of alcohol in the house."

"Well, I respect that on principle. I was raised Baptist, and believe me, I grew up hearing more sermons railing against demon liquor than you can begin to imagine." She sighed, shaking her head. "Always bothered me, though. All that fuss about a beer or a shot of whiskey, yet there were people living in poverty two blocks away. Children who didn't have enough to eat. Seemed to me that was a bigger sin than tossing back a few on a Saturday night."

"Then you don't have a problem with Mason owning a bar?" I studied Naomi.

"Not a bit. He's responsible, my boy. If someone's had too much to drink, he cuts him off and makes sure he has a ride. He's been known to drive a tipsy customer home himself now and again."

I drew my legs up to cross them on the seat. "I heard Mason tell someone at the stand that he'd only been back in town for about two years. Meghan said he'd lived in Tennessee before then. Did he own a bar there, too?"

Naomi blinked at me, surprised. "Oh, honey, didn't you know? Mason was a talent scout for a huge record producer in Nashville. He left Burton right after high school, went out there hoping to get a job in the music industry, and he did. Hit it pretty big, too. He's got a real talent for seeing the potential in people." She smiled at me.

An unfamiliar warm tingle filled my chest. Was she saying Mason saw potential in *me?* The idea gave me a sort of glowy feeling. "He didn't go out there to become a star himself?"

"No. Oh, don't get me wrong, my boy's got talent. When I hear him sing, it gives me goosebumps. But I'm his mama, and I guess Mason realized he didn't have the heart to go to Nashville and get turned down over and over. Knowing your limits and your strength is very important, you know."

"Does he still sing?" Somehow, the image of Mason sitting with a guitar over his lap, strumming it with those huge hands, made that glowy feeling shine even brighter.

"Every now and again, for Piper and me. There's a tip for you, sweetheart—Piper's soft spot is music. I think she's probably got a fair amount of talent herself, given who her mama was. And then add what Mason can do . . . I'd be more surprised if Piper wasn't musical than if she is." Naomi shifted in her chair, wincing slightly.

"Do you need something?" I sat forward. "Are you in pain?" Mason had told me that his mother suffered with both the symptoms of the leukemia and the side effects of the chemotherapy.

"No, nothing more than usual. Sometimes I just need to change positions. Could you move that pillow a little farther down, honey?"

I fluffed up the pillow and wedged it against Naomi's lower back, tucking it until she leaned back and nodded. "That's exactly right, thank you."

"You're welcome. Can I get you anything else?" I leaned my hip onto the back of my chair.

"No, thanks, sweetie, I'm fine. Sit down and chat with me. It helps, you know—takes my mind off everything. Unless you have something else to do, that is."

"I'm good." I sank back into the chair. "I cleaned up the kitchen after dinner, and I don't have any PR work tonight." Fiddling with a thread on the hem of my skirt, I glanced up at Naomi again. "Could you tell me about Piper's mom? You said she had talent."

"Oh, she did. Lu had the voice of an angel. Mason found her singing in a little tiny bar an hour outside Nashville, and he brought her into his company. They signed her on the spot, and she had such a shining future." Naomi shook her head, her lips pulling into a frown. "Such a shame. I remember when Mason called Jack and me to tell me about meeting her. I think it was love at first sight, for both of them. They got married six months later, and then Lu's career was just exploding. Everyone wanted her. She went on tour with Faith Hill while she was pregnant with Piper."

My chest tightened. It sounded like a fairy tale, and yet instead of living her happily-ever-after, Lu was dead, and her husband was here alone, trying to raise their child. "What happened to Lu, if you don't mind me asking? I mean, if you don't feel comfortable talking about it, I understand."

"No, it's all right. You should know, seeing that you're taking care of Piper now. Lu was killed in a car accident. A drunk driver hit her late one night when she was on her way home from a recording session. It just about killed Mason."

"I'm so sorry." I whispered the words, as though speaking them louder might offend somebody. "That's terrible. And so sad. How old was Piper?"

"Just six months old. It was Lu's first night back at the studio."

Unexpected tears filled my eyes. "That poor child. She'll never know her mama. And Lu never got to be a mother to that baby." I sniffled and swallowed hard.

"I know." Naomi pressed her lips together, and I saw the glimmer of wet on her cheeks, too. "It about broke my heart, to see that baby looking for her mother for weeks after, and Mason barely holding it together. Jack and I went out there and stayed the entire month after the accident, just to help him. And then Jack passed, too, right after Piper's first birthday. Heart attack."

"Is that when Mason decided to move back?"

She nodded. "It just seemed right. We were both alone, and he was having trouble working and taking care of the baby, even with a full-time nanny. To tell you the truth, I think after Lu was gone, Mason just lost his heart for the music business."

"I'm surprised he'd open a bar, after what happened."

Naomi shrugged. "Mason is a practical man. I think he knows people are going to drink, and at least he could try to prevent them from driving after they'd had too much. Plus, it was a good fit. He still has contacts in the music industry, so he brings in new bands to play at the club." She laid back her head and closed her eyes. "Given everything that's happened, I believe Mason's as happy as he can be." Her eyelids rose just enough to gaze at me. "Of course, he's young. I hope he finds someone who can share the rest of his life with him."

"I'm sure he will." I thought of Mason, with his hypnotizing eyes, strong arms and that air of absolute confidence that surrounded him. I couldn't imagine that women didn't swarm around him. "Someone who'll love Piper, too. She needs a mother." I realized what I'd said and added hastily, "Not that you're not wonderful with her. She's so lucky to have a grandmother like you."

Naomi chuckled. "I know what you meant, honey." She watched me in silence for a minute. "I'm sure you know first-hand what it's like to be raised by a grandmother . . . and still miss your mama."

"I was very lucky, too." I bit my lip. "Gram is—she's just the best. I can't imagine my life without her. But I always wondered what it'd be like to have my mom around." I lifted one shoulder. "Of course, in Piper's case, her mother didn't choose to leave her, like mine did. Hers was taken away against her will. Mine ran as far from me as fast as she could."

"Oh, darlin' . . ." Naomi reached over to clutch at my hand. "Don't think that way. There's always more than one side to a story, and you don't know what your mama's was."

"I guess." I stretched out my legs and stood up. "I'm going to go make your tea and get your night time meds ready, okay? Mason said he was going to be a little late tonight."

"Saturday nights are always late." Naomi yawned. "Thank you, dear. I think I'll be ready for bed after my tea."

As I left the room, I heard her voice call out to me again. "And Rilla, no matter what anyone's told you, or what you fear in your own heart . . . you're not easy to leave. I didn't know your mother, but I bet anything it broke her heart to run away without you. And she wouldn't have done it unless she didn't have another choice."

I stood still for a minute, my hand tight on the door jam. "Maybe." I looked back over my shoulder at the older woman. "But if it were me, nothing short of death would pry me away from my child. I'd do anything to stay with her."

The lump in my throat stopped me from saying anything more. I fled to the safety of the kitchen before Naomi could respond.

Chapter Eight

Mason

IT HAD BEEN A long-ass night. I yawned big as I turned onto my silent side street, grateful that I'd managed to stay awake on the drive home. It wasn't unusual for me be home after midnight on Saturdays; Rocky and I shared the late nights at the club, and he preferred to take Fridays. Since our bigger acts tended to play on Saturdays, it made more sense for me to cover those days.

Tonight, though, had been insane. The band I'd booked had still been fairly obscure when we scheduled them, but ten days ago, their new single caught fire and headed straight for the top of the charts. That was great news for them, for sure, and pretty damn awesome for us too, except that dealing with all the extra fans was a fucking nightmare. We'd had lines out the door, and we'd had to call in more help with managing traffic and parking.

The set had started late, thanks to all the chaos, and the

band, riding high at their first show after hitting the big time, decided to play an extra hour. Again, it wasn't a bad thing, except it meant that I hadn't left the club until after two.

I felt a twinge of concern as I pulled into my driveway. The house was dark aside from the porch light, which didn't surprise me. But I hadn't been able to call home in the midst of all the bedlam at the club, and by the time I had a minute to breath, I was afraid that the ringing phone might disturb my mom or wake up Piper. I hoped Rilla wasn't freaking out.

I climbed out of the truck and closed the door as quietly as I could. My feet crunched over the leaves on the sidewalk, and my boots sounded too loud against the steps of the porch. I dug my keys out of my pocket and unlocked the front door.

The living room was mostly dark, except for the soft glow that came from the hallway light that was still on. I reached down to take off my boots, so I could walk through the house without waking everyone up.

I wondered where Rilla was, but given the hour, I assumed she'd found a place to sleep—maybe in with Piper, or in the guest room I'd told her she could use when she was here. Surely when I didn't get home by midnight, she'd realized I'd gotten held up and decided to just stay over. I hoped it didn't get her in trouble with her father.

I began to walk toward my mom's bedroom. I liked to peek in on both of my girls before I went to bed, just to set my mind at ease. As I stepped quietly through the dim room, a slight movement on the sofa caught my eye.

Rilla lay curled up on the couch. Her blonde hair was spread over the throw pillow, nearly hiding her face. She had her hands tucked under her chin, reminding me of the way Piper liked to sleep. Her green shirt was baggy, as her clothes always seemed to be, but the position of her arms had pulled the material tight over her breasts. To my shock, my mouth went dry and my cock stirred between my legs as I looked down at her.

I backed up a step, half stumbling, and knocked my leg against the coffee table. It scraped over the hardwood floor, and Rilla jerked awake.

She pushed herself to sit up, glancing around the room in confusion. Her hair curtained her face, and her long cotton skirt caught on her foot as she tried to swing her legs to the floor.

"Rilla, it's just me. It's okay." I struggled to keep my voice to a whisper. "It's late. I didn't know you were there. Sorry I woke you."

"What time is it?" She was still half-asleep, and her hands pushed the hair out of her face. The light from hall fell over her, and I watched her blink as her tongue came out to wet her lips.

Shit. I wasn't attracted to this girl. I couldn't be. She was too young, too innocent, and I wasn't looking for someone who was interested in anything serious. I'd just let myself go too long between casual hookups. That was all. Testosterone build-up could account for anything.

"It's uh . . . late. Almost three in the morning."

"Oh, no." She moaned the words and renewed the struggle to free her feet from the skirt. "I have to get home. Gram and Dad are going to be furious—and worried—where's my purse?"

"Whoa." I laid my hand on her shoulder, and she froze, stiffening the same way she had the other day at the bar, when I'd touched her back. "Rilla, you can't drive home now. You're half-asleep. Why don't you go on upstairs to the guest room, and then you can just go home in the morning?"

"I can't." She finally stuck one foot out of the material. "Tomorrow's Sunday. Gram needs her car, and if I don't go to church . . ." She wrapped her arms around her ribs, hugging herself. "I just need to go now. I'll be okay, I promise."

"No." I spoke more forcefully this time. "You're exhausted, you'd be driving out on those dark country roads, and you don't even have a cell phone. I can't let you do this. Go upstairs, sleep for a few hours, and then when the sun's up, you can head home. You'll be back in plenty of time for church. Your dad might be pissed, but he'd be a hell of a lot more upset if you ended up crashed into a ditch somewhere between here and there. Or broken down on the side of the road, with no way to call for help."

She muttered something under breath, but she'd stopped panicking, I could tell. For a moment, she sat still, staring at the floor, and then she nodded.

"You're right. I'll just sleep until the sun rises, then I'll get home. Gram'll understand." She rubbed at her eyes. "I meant to call, but then it was midnight, and I figured you'd be home soon anyway and I didn't want to wake her up. I was just going to sit here and wait, and it got harder and harder to keep my eyes open."

"I'm sorry." I sank down on my haunches so I could see her face better. "It was a crazy night. We had a new band and—well, I'll tell you more about it later. Come on upstairs and get settled in the guest room."

She pulled back away from me, her eyes wide open now. "Oh, no, I'll be fine here."

"Don't be ridiculous." I stood up, and putting my hands on my hips, I stared her down. "Why should you sleep on this uncomfortable sofa when there's a perfectly good bed upstairs?"

"Because . . ." Her face went rosy, and she bowed her head. "Because if my father asks me where I slept, and I say in a bedroom on the same floor as yours, he won't be happy." She laughed, but the sound was harsh and lacking in humor. "Not that he's going to be happy anyway. But if I say I slept outside your mom's bedroom, it'll be better."

"Okay." I hooked my thumb into my belt loops. "You do realize that's absolutely ridiculous, right? Whether you sleep here on the sofa or upstairs in the guest room, I'm not going to bother you." I shook my head. "Matter of fact, if it were my daughter, I'd be damned mad that there wasn't a door with a lock on it between my little girl and some guy I didn't know. But then that's just me."

For some reason, it made me unreasonably angry that Rilla's father's crazy rules made her so tense. I could see the anxiety on her face, and it pissed me off.

She winced, and then I was mad at myself for complicating an already shitty situation. Her arms circled her legs as though she were trying to make herself as small and inconspicuous as possible.

"Rilla." I sat down on the sofa, as far at the other end as I could. "I'm sorry. I'm not mad at you. I'm upset at the situation. Tonight was crazy at the club, and I should've thought to call you. I should've worked things out so that you weren't here so late. I'm sorry. I didn't mean to put you in a difficult position."

She peeked out at me from under her hair. "It's okay. I know it's all part of being an adult, and I told you I didn't care what my dad said. It's true. Or at least I'm trying to make it true. I guess I just panicked when I woke up."

I relaxed against the back of the couch. "Hey, you woke up in the dark, in a strange place with someone standing over you. Anyone would've been disoriented. I'm just lucky you didn't haul off and punch me."

My goal had been to make her smile, and it worked. Her lips curled up. "If I'd done that, I'd have broken my hand. Guess I'm lucky violence isn't my first instinct."

We both laughed, and then I sighed. "I gotta get some sleep. I better get upstairs, or I'm going to nod off right here on the sofa. Then your dad would have something to get upset over." I pushed up to stand. "You sure you don't want to sleep in the guest room? I could sleep down here on the couch, so it would be just you and Piper upstairs."

Rilla burst out laughing again, covering her mouth with one hand. I cocked my head at her. "What's funny?"

"The idea of you. Laying on this sofa." Her body shook, and she fisted her hand on her lips again. "I mean, it's a great couch, but you're huge."

I smirked. "Honey, let me assure you, I've crashed in tighter spots than this in my day. Compared to some of the places I've slept, this sofa would be a treat."

"Still . . ." She shook her head. "It's fine for me. Plus, I've got it all warmed up already."

"Speaking of which, let me grab you a blanket." Before she could protest, I stepped behind the rocking chair on the opposite wall and opened up a chest. Pulling out an afghan my grandmother had made when I was a little boy, I shook it open and stood next to the couch. "Lay down."

"Really, Mason. You don't have to—"

"Lay down." I gave her my no-nonsense voice and glare, and Rilla obeyed. I'd yet to meet the person who could stand up against my take-no-shit look. I draped the blanket over her, making sure she was covered from her feet up to her chin. "Okay. If you need anything else, come upstairs and knock on my door. Or help yourself, whatever you want." I turned to go upstairs and then paused. "Thanks for staying tonight, Rilla. Even in the midst of all the crap going down at The Road Block, I didn't worry about Mom or Piper once. I knew they were in good hands."

She ducked her head again, so that her face was hidden by the top of the blanket. "I'm glad. Do you need me tomorrow?"

"Nope." We'd agreed that Rilla would only work for us on Sundays in cases of emergency. They were quieter days at the bar anyway, and if I needed to run in for an hour or so during the day, I could take Piper with me. Mom was all right by herself for short periods. "Enjoy your day off. And Rilla, if there's a problem with your dad, call me. I'll be happy to talk with him, explain things."

She nodded. "Thanks, but it'll be fine. Good night."

"Night." I turned my back and went upstairs, where I fell into bed fully clothed. The last thing I remembered thinking about before sleep pulled me under was Rilla Grant's smile.

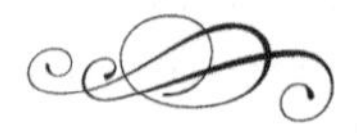

Piper woke me up in her usual gentle way . . . by jumping onto my back and sticking her fingers in my eyes until I opened them. Groaning, I grabbed her small body and tickled while she giggled.

"Hey, princess. Don't be too loud. Rilla stayed over last night, because I was so late, and she's sleeping on the sofa."

"No, she's not." Piper kicked at my sheets.

"What do you mean?" I frowned.

"She's not on the sofa. Just Nan is downstairs. I watched a funny show with her because she said to let you sleep, but then I got really hungry for pancakes. Can you make me pancakes? Please?"

"Sure, baby." I swung my legs off the bed and stood up, stretching my stiff body. I went to the window and pushed down a slat of the wooden blinds to look down at the driveway. I wasn't surprised to see that the gray sedan Rilla usually drove to my house was gone.

Downstairs, I found a note on the kitchen table:

Thank you for the use of your sofa last night. Call me if you need any help today – otherwise, I'll be over on Monday morning.

– Rilla

I held the paper in my hand for a moment, staring down at her loopy handwriting, wondering what time she'd left. The digital clock on the stove read 9:17, but I had a feeling Rilla had been gone for several hours.

"Pancakes, Daddy!" Piper tugged on my shorts.

"On it, princess. Run and ask Nan if she feels like she could eat some this morning, too."

Mom did in fact want some pancakes, which made me happy. Her appetite was so unpredictable these days that I was grateful whenever we found something she'd eat. I served breakfast in her room, so that we could enjoy it together.

I'd just forked another three pancakes onto my plate when my phone began to buzz. I leaned forward and slid it out of my back pocket, frowning when I looked at the readout.

"Hey, Sam. Everything okay?" I'd added his number to my contacts when we planned Flynn's bachelor party a few months back, but I couldn't remember the last time he'd called me.

"Uh, yeah, Mason. Sorry to bother you so early." I heard

the sound of birds singing in the background and realized he must be outside.

"No bother. I was just serving breakfast to my best girls. What can I do for you?"

He sighed. "I didn't know if I should've called you or not, but Meghan and I talked it over. We got a call this morning from Rilla. She asked us to come pick her up at her dad's house. Mason, he threw her out."

The bottom dropped out of my stomach. "Oh, shit." Across the room, my mother glared at me, one eyebrow raised. I mouthed an *I'm sorry* and stood up. "Hold on a minute, Sam." Carrying my plate into the kitchen, I set it on the counter and then continued outside onto the back stoop. "What the hell, Sam? What happened?"

"I didn't get all the details. Meghan and I drove over there to get her about two hours ago, and then Meghan told me to go out to the fields so they could talk. As near as I can tell, she drove home from your house first thing this morning, and her father had been waiting up all night. I guess they argued, and he told her if she couldn't follow his rules, she couldn't live in his house, either."

"Oh, God." I rubbed my forehead. "I was afraid of this when she came to work for me. I knew it was a bad idea."

"I don't know about that. This mess was just waiting to happen. If it hadn't been you, something else would've set him off. Don't beat yourself up."

"How can I not?" I scrubbed my hand over my face. "Was she really upset, Sam? When you picked her up?"

"You know, it was weird, but no. She was just quiet. She thanked us for giving her a ride, and Meghan told her she could stay with us for as long as she likes. We've got the room. And then she thanked us again, for the offer. Beyond that, she hasn't said much. At least, not in front of me."

"Thanks for getting her. I don't know what I should do.

Should I tell her I don't want her working for me, if it's tearing up her family?"

Sam cleared his throat. "I don't know, man. I kind of think that might push her over the edge, you know? Here she lost her family today, at least for a little while, and she's probably counting on the income from her job with you. I'm happy to have her at the stand, but that's not going to cover rent anywhere. Not by itself."

"Yeah, I—" A sound on the door behind me caught my attention. Piper's small face was contorted in fear as her fists pounded against the glass. "Wait a minute, Sam."

I opened the door and leaned in. "What's wrong, princess?"

"It's Nan. She—she made a funny sound and then she fell out of her chair and I can't wake her up."

Terror clutched at my heart. "Sam, something's wrong with my mom. I gotta go. I'll call you later."

Without waiting for his response, I shoved the phone into my pocket and ran into Mom's room. She was on the floor, slumped over, her head to one side.

"Mom!" I shouted and kneeling next to her, I gently laid her flat on the floor. Her chest rose and fell with reassuring regularity. *Good, she's breathing.*

"Daddy! Daddy. What's wrong with Nan?" Piper's hands clutched at the folds of her princess nightgown, and she was shaking.

"I don't know, honey. It's okay. We're going to take care of her." Without taking my eyes off my mother, I reached back for the phone and pushed 911. Choking out the words, I called for help.

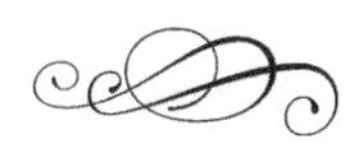

I never minded hospitals growing up. I'd had my share of broken limbs and cuts that required stitches, but the hospital was where they fixed me up and made me good as new, ready to take on the world again. Even when I got older, the hospital didn't scare me; Piper's birth had been my first adult experience there, and that day ranked with the best in my life.

But six months later, I was back in that same facility, on a different floor, in the trauma unit instead of the birthing center, and it was there I learned to hate hospitals. It was while sitting in the cold white waiting room that I heard the words that destroyed me.

I'm sorry, Mr. Wallace. We did everything we could. Ms. Briggs' injuries were too extensive for her to recover, and although we did our best, we were not able to revive her on the operating table, and she died.

I hated that they said it so baldly, but later, someone told me that medical personnel were taught to deliver bad news in that way. Apparently, breaking the news gently to a loved one could lead to denial. They had to say it plainly, no matter how much it hurt.

Since I'd moved back to Burton, I'd been in the local county hospital too often for my taste. This was where Mom was diagnosed, where she came to get her chemo treatments and where we ran whenever anything irregular happened.

Which was why we were here now, of course. I shifted in the hard plastic chair, ignoring the ache in my back. On my lap, Piper squirmed and then cuddled closer. I didn't like to have her with me here, but today there'd been no choice. I'd followed the ambulance over, and there was no one I could call to watch her. I texted Sam a terse sentence about what had happened and where we were; if need be, I was sure he and Meghan would come get Piper.

Mom had come back around briefly after the paramedics arrived, but she was confused, and her words were slurred. There was no question that she needed to be here, where the doctors could run tests and assess what had happened.

I let my head drop back against the plaster of the wall and closed my eyes. *Please, God. If you even exist, which I'm not sure I believe. But whatever and whoever is there . . . not my mom. Not yet. Help. Please.*

"Mason." A hand at my shoulder roused me, and Piper squealed.

"Rilla!" She slid off my lap and grabbed Rilla around the legs. "Nan got sick. I was so scared, but I went and got Daddy, and the doctors are going to make her better."

"Of course they are, sweetie pie." Rilla reached down to lift my daughter into her arms. "You were very brave and very smart. I'm proud of you."

Piper snuggled against her, and Rilla smoothed a hand over her tangled blonde curls. Their hair mingled together over Piper's back, and I couldn't tell where one began and the other ended. My daughter looked so comfortable and content with Rilla. Seeing them together gave me an odd feeling that I couldn't label. Rilla glanced at me.

"Are you okay?"

I realized I was staring at her and mentally shook myself. "Yeah. Yeah, I'm fine. Um, what're you doing here?"

She sat down next to me, turning Piper so that she sat across her lap with her back toward me. When she replied, it was in a low voice. "I thought you might need help. I can take Piper home and wait for you there." She gestured with her head toward the door of the waiting room, where I spotted a familiar couple. "Sam and Meghan are here, and they said they'd drive me to your house."

I exhaled long and pinched the bridge of my nose. "That would be great, but Rilla, we need to talk about what happened this morning. With your dad. Sam told me what he did."

She closed her eyes. "Actually, that's the last thing I want to think about right now. Let's concentrate on your mom. What happened?"

"I don't really know. We were eating breakfast in her room, and Sam called. I stepped outside to talk to him, and then next thing I knew, Piper was pounding on the door, telling me she couldn't wake up Nan. I found her in front of her chair, unconscious."

Worry filled her blue eyes, the same anxiety I'm sure she saw in mine. "Has this ever happened before?"

"No." I dropped my voice. "I'm just hoping it wasn't a stroke. Or . . ." I gripped the edge of the chair until my knuckles hurt. "The leukemia getting worse. She's supposed to go in for a bone marrow biopsy in two weeks, to see whether the chemo's worked enough to put her into remission. If it has, we can move ahead with the transplant."

Her brows knitted together. "Transplant?"

"Yeah. It's kind her get-out-of-jail-free card. Wipes out the cancer from her body, gives her a fresh start. They destroy her own marrow, and the donor stem cells grow new bone marrow."

"Oh. Well, we'll just pray it isn't anything bad. Maybe just a little hiccup, or maybe she has a virus or something. It might not be anything bad."

I managed to hold back on rolling my eyes, but I couldn't help the derisive tone in my voice. "Yeah, well, forgive me if I'm all out of hope right now. For the last few years, if anything could go wrong, it has. You've heard of Murphy's Law? Murphy's been living in my back pocket."

Rilla didn't argue with me. She laid her hand on my arm and squeezed; her fingers were too small to circle my bicep, so it felt more like a caress than a touch for comfort. I had an insane desire to cover her hand with my other one, but I held back. I couldn't afford to muddy the water when it came to my relationship with Rilla. I needed her help, and maybe she needed mine, but we had to keep it professional. All business.

"Rilla, can we go home?" Piper leaned back and reached her hands up to hold Rilla's face. "I didn't get to finish my pancakes."

"Sure we can, sweet pea, if your daddy says it's all right." She shot me an inquiring look, and I nodded. She stood up, adjusting Piper in her arms, and was about to leave when my daughter spoke up.

"Wait, I want to kiss Daddy good-bye."

Rilla smiled and turned around again. She leaned down low so that Piper's lips could reach my cheek, and as I kissed my little girl, I got a whiff of scent that was pure Rilla. I couldn't say what it was—not quite floral, not musky, but heady and intoxicating. It made me want to run my nose down the side of her throat until I found the source.

She straightened before I could do anything stupid, like lick her skin. "Can you call me when you hear something about Naomi?"

"I will." Looking up into her face, eyes filled with equal parts compassion and concern, I made a snap decision. "One of the first things we're going to do is get you a cell phone. It's just safer for you, and it'll make me feel better to know I can get in touch with you without ringing the house phone, if it's late at night or whatever."

She frowned. "What're you talking about?"

I let one side of my mouth curve up. "I'm talking about you moving in with us."

Chapter Nine

Rilla

I DON'T KNOW WHAT I said to Mason after his matter-of-fact statement that I was moving in with his family. I thought I nodded and then turned around to follow Meghan out of the waiting room and through the corridors of the hospital.

We'd just reached Sam's pickup truck when I heard running steps behind us and saw Sam himself trotting over. He held up his hand, and a key ring dangled from one finger.

"You need the booster seat for the car. Mason sent me out to unlock his truck for you." He pointed back to another section of the parking lot. "I'll grab it and bring it over to you."

"Why isn't Sam coming with us?" I let Piper slide down my body and sit on the passenger seat of the truck after Meghan unlocked the door.

"He's going to stay here with Mason while I drop you and Piper off, and then I'll drive back to get him. We didn't think

Mason should be alone at the hospital while he waits."

"That's really nice of you." I leaned against the side of the truck, making sure Piper didn't fall out as she jumped on the seat. "You and Sam are such great friends. To Mason. And to me. I don't know what I'd do without you, and you haven't even known me that long."

"It's not the length of the friendship, it's the breadth." Meghan dropped her arm around my shoulders and squeezed. "Sam and I love you, Rilla. So do Ali and Flynn. We want you to be happy, and we'll do whatever we can for you. You have a home with us for as long as you need it."

Sam returned with the seat and helped us get Piper buckled in before he dropped a quick kiss on Meghan's lips and went back inside. As we drove out of the lot, I glanced over at my friend and ran my tongue over my bottom lip.

"Meghan, about staying with you . . . just now, when I was leaving the waiting room, Mason said he wants me to move in with them. So I can watch Piper and help Naomi."

"Oh. Oh, wow." Meghan blinked, and her mouth drooped a little. "Um, I mean, yeah, that makes sense, doesn't it?" She turned her head to look at me as we stopped at the intersection. "Or not?"

"I—I think it does. I want to be able to keep this job. I love Piper and Naomi, and it feels right. I can still do my PR work, and since I'll be in town, I might even be able to get some more clients. And eventually, I can find my own place."

"As long as you're comfortable with it, Rilla. You're talking about going from living with your father and your grandmother, in a very protected environment, to moving in with people you haven't known very long."

"I know. But like you said, sometimes it's not about the length of time. It's scary, but at the same time, I finally feel like I'm moving forward. You know? I'm doing something that works for me. I'm being independent. An adult."

"After what you told me your dad said this morning, I'm not surprised you want to get away from home. Just make sure you're not jumping from the frying pan into the fire."

The memory of my father yelling the ugly, angry words as Gram cried at the kitchen table sliced through my heart. I'd never heard him say those things. *Whore. Slut.* And the phrase that had hurt the worst: *Just like your worthless mother.* I swallowed hard. It had almost been a relief when he'd told me to get out of his house. Despite Gram begging him to reconsider, I hadn't hesitated before going to the phone to call Meghan for help. I couldn't stay there any more than he could have me under his roof.

"I don't think I am. But it's good to know that if anything goes wrong, I can call you. I know I have other options, and that's something I haven't felt before. Ever."

Meghan nodded. "I'm happy for you, Rilla, if you're happy. If you're sure."

I wasn't sure about anything, especially about living in the same house with Mason Wallace, but the idea of taking care of Piper and Naomi felt right. With everything else in my life adrift, I clung to that one certainty.

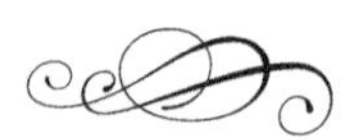

Meghan came inside with Piper and me for a few minutes, chatting with the little girl as I re-heated the pancakes and cleaned up the mess in Naomi's room. I found packaging paper that the EMTs had left on the floor, from syringes and tubing, and my hands shook a little as I crumpled it up and tossed it into the wastepaper basket. I whispered a prayer for the woman who had become dear to me in the short time I'd known her.

Once Meghan left, I played with Piper for a few minutes and then settled her down for a nap. She was exhausted from the morning's excitement and fell asleep almost immediately.

I wandered through the silent house, unable to sit still. It was odd to think that this was going to be my home, for a while, at least. I ran my hand over the counter, brushing crumbs into my other palm and dumping them into the sink. I remembered Meghan telling me that Mason had bought this house after he'd moved back to Burton. I wondered how many of the dishes and appliances were the same ones his wife had used in Tennessee. I couldn't imagine how difficult it would be to be reminded of her daily . . . although of course he had a living, breathing reminder in Piper. And maybe he didn't want to forget Lu. He'd never mentioned her to me by name, though he'd referred to "Piper's mom" now and then.

I heard a car in the drive and turned around in time to see Mason coming up the steps and into the kitchen. He was smiling, and relief flooded through me. Nothing could be that bad if he could grin like that.

"Sorry I didn't call. It was just going to be easier to come home and tell you in person." Mason dropped his truck keys into the bowl by the door. "Mom's fine. Turns out it was an issue with one of her medicines. They'd prescribed something for her blood pressure back when she was diagnosed and stressed out, and now she doesn't need it anymore. It made her pressure too low, and that's why she passed out."

"Oh, thank God." I pressed a hand to my heart. "I'm so glad, Mason."

"Yeah. They're keeping her overnight, just to keep an eye on things. And even better, they said her blood work looks so good, they're going to do the bone marrow biopsy tomorrow, while she's still in the hospital. We should know in a few days whether or not she's in remission."

"That's good, right?" I wasn't familiar with all the terminology of Naomi's disease, although I was learning.

"It's excellent." Mason looked about ten years younger than he had at the hospital. "If she's in remission, we can move forward. Don't get me wrong, she's still got a long, rough road ahead, but this transplant is her best shot at recovery."

I closed my eyes. "I was so worried."

Mason hesitated a beat and then reached toward me, drawing me against his body and wrapping his arms around me. It was innocent and friendly, and I knew he was offering me comfort, and maybe even drawing a little of the same from me. My heart went nuts, though, pounding against my ribs. In my memory, I'd never been hugged by any male other than my father, and that was when I was little. He'd stopped giving me any kind of affectionate touching once I hit my teen years.

I wasn't quite sure what to do. Did I just stand here and let Mason embrace me? Should I return the hug, wrap my arms around him? Before I could make a decision, he released me and stepped back, studying me with a frown on his face.

"Meghan and Sam went to get your stuff from their house. They're going to drop it off later this afternoon, and I think Meghan's bringing something over for dinner, too."

"That's . . . that's really great of them. I could've cooked, though." I swallowed and hoped my face wasn't bright red. I was sure Mason was used to girls for whom a quick hug like that was an everyday occurrence, not a reason to get flustered.

"You had a rough day, too." He stepped around the counter and scraped a kitchen chair against the tile before he sat down. "I want to talk to you about that. But first of all, I know I dropped that idea about you moving in here on you without any warning. It just seemed like a no-brainer, though. We need you. You need a place to live. I hope you don't feel like I'm forcing you into something that makes you uncomfortable."

I shook my head. "No. I was surprised, but you're right, it makes sense. I'm very grateful that you're willing to have me."

"You'll be helping us more than we're helping you." He rubbed the knee of his jeans with his thumb, smoothing out the cotton. "Why did your father kick you out?"

I needed to sit for this discussion. Pulling out a chair across the table from Mason, I sank down. "It's been a long time coming. My dad . . . he had a plan for my future. It wasn't a bad plan, but it didn't match mine. When I started working for Sam, starting up the advertising business, he was unhappy. In his mind, I was supposed to stay at home, help Gram, go to church on Sundays and be content until Jonathan was ready to marry me. I didn't agree with him."

"Who's Jonathan?" Mason frowned, and I bit my lip.

"He's the youth pastor at my church. My father thought he wanted to marry me."

"And he didn't?" His forehead was creased in confusion, and I didn't blame him.

"Apparently not. Or he didn't want to marry me any time soon. I'm still not sure if my dad just wanted it to happen, or if Jonathan actually ever said anything to him. Doesn't matter now."

"Wait a second. Why would this guy talk to your father and not to you?"

I felt the beginning fingers of embarrassment creeping over me. "Our church . . . it's pretty strict on dating. If a man's interested in a girl, he courts her, which means they go out in a group setting. They're never alone together. I think most of the time, a boy wants to court a girl because he likes her, but Jonathan never seemed to want to be with me. I have a sneaking suspicion he was only trying to please my father."

"By pretending to be in love with you?" Mason looked more angry than confused now.

"No, he never pretended to be anything with me. My dad's an elder in our church, and Jonathan wants approval to start up his own congregation. I think he felt that hinting he might be willing to marry me upped his standing with Dad. But he never followed through. He visited us a few times, and he asked me to help with the youth group, but that was it."

Mason shook his head. "I just can't understand it."

"What part?" I managed a smile. "I know it must sound really strange to you."

"Why would a church make rules about dating, and why would this jerk not be dying to be with you? I mean, you're beautiful, and smart, and funny. And you're one of the most genuinely decent people I've met."

Warmth swirled to fill my heart. "Thank you. That's really sweet of you to say. As far as the church, it wasn't so much a rule as a guideline, and not all the families followed it. I mean, we're not a cult. My dad has a tendency to take a suggestion and carry it through to an extreme. From what Gram said, he kind of shut down after my mom left, and he wanted to make sure I didn't turn out like her. So he was strict. He kept me at home as much as possible, and whatever the pastor said for everyone else went double for me. No dating, no being alone with any male outside my family . . . no life. Just sticking to the rules he made."

Mason nodded. "So the idea of you working for a guy like me, someone who owns a bar, would be bad enough, but when it meant you had to be in my house, that really toasted his biscuits, didn't it?"

I couldn't help laughing. "Toasted his biscuits? Yeah, I'd say. He was giving me the silent treatment, at least until this morning." *Had it really only been this morning? It felt more like years ago.* "He and Gram had been sitting up waiting for me all night. When I walked in the door—well, let's just say the silent treatment was over. He didn't hold back."

A tic twitched in Mason's cheek, and his jaw was clenched. I stood up, deciding we'd had enough of sharing time. No way did I want to get into the exact words my father had used. "Mason, are you sure you're comfortable with me moving in? I could live out with Sam and Meghan. They offered. And I could still come in and take care of your mom. Watch Piper."

He raised one eyebrow. "How're you going to get into town from the farm every day? Walk? I'm assuming your father didn't gift you a vehicle when he tossed your ass to the curb." Mason saw me wince and muttered something else under his breath. "Sorry. I'm just pissed." He held up one hand. "I know. You don't like the swearing. I'll try to keep it to a minimum, but if you're going to be living here, you're going to have to accept that I'm not a saint."

I giggled. "Mason, with all due respect and appreciation, I don't have any illusions about your sainthood."

He grinned. "Good. So to answer your other question, yes, I'm sure about you moving in. Honestly, I've wanted live-in help since Mom got sick. Mrs. Murphy lived so close, it didn't really make a difference, but knowing that I can run to The Road Block whenever they need me and not have to worry about everyone at home is going to be huge. I'm telling you, you're doing us as much of a favor as I'm doing you."

"Okay. Then can I use the guest room?" I leaned back, resting my hip against the countertop.

Mason cocked his head. "The guest room? But I thought the sofa was so comfortable." He winked at me.

"Very funny." I rolled my eyes. "It *was* plenty comfortable, thank you. But if I'm going to be here a long-term basis, I'd like a bed. And a door." I paused, gnawing on the side of my lip. "I realized something this morning while my dad was ranting. I stayed downstairs on your couch last night because I thought I was going to make my father happy. Or happier, at least, knowing I made the decision he'd want me to make, not sleeping on the same level of the house as a man who wasn't related to me. But it didn't matter, did it? He still thought the worst of me. So I may as well do whatever I want, right?"

Mason rubbed his chin. "As the father of a daughter, that statement sends chills down my spine. Rilla, I get that you're hurt and you're angry. But don't let what your father said or how he treated you change who you are. I respect your values. He might've been wrong about a lot, but I'm thinking he can't be all bad, since he raised a pretty cool daughter." He stood up and stretched, raising his arms so that his shirt rode up a few inches, revealing the taut skin on his stomach. Something new and unfamiliar tickled low in my belly.

"I'm going to check on Piper and then maybe grab a little nap myself. It was a long night and a longer morning, huh? You might want to do the same. Make yourself at home." He made it to the doorway of the kitchen before glancing back over his shoulder at me. "Because you are. At home, I mean. For as long as you want it to be."

Sam and Meghan arrived around six with my two bags and a picnic basket full of dinner that included fried chicken, potato salad, biscuits, coleslaw and green beans. When Meghan pulled out an apple pie, I wanted to cry. Bless her heart, she'd brought paper plates and plastic forks, so all I had to do was toss a tablecloth over the kitchen table. We sat down, passed the food, chatted, laughed and ate. It was just what we all needed after a stressful day.

After they left, Mason carried my bags upstairs, and I settled into the guest room. Piper was overjoyed by the idea that I'd be right down the hall from her all the time now; she tried to talk me into sharing her room, but when her father and I convinced her that wasn't going to happen, she amused herself by helping me unpack and put my clothes into the dresser drawers.

Mason came to the doorway, leaning against the jam and watching us. As I shook out a denim skirt and clipped it to a hanger, I caught the expression on his face.

"What?" I hung the skirt in the empty closet. "Why're you looking at me like that? It's okay that I use the dresser and the closet, right?"

"Of course it is." He hesitated. "What you told me this afternoon, about your dad and how he wanted to protect you—is that why you dress like you do? I've never seen you in anything but long skirts and shirts that don't fit you. Oh, and your funeral dress." He smirked.

"That was my professional outfit, buddy. Don't make fun." I pretended to be offended.

"Sorry." He held up both hands as though he were scared of me. "Your professional funeral outfit."

"Whatever." I shook my head. Piper handed me another shirt from deep inside my bag, and I kissed her silky head as I accepted it from her. When I looked back up at Mason, his eyes were clouded, and a crease appeared between his eyes.

"But yeah, you're right." I folded the top and put it away. "My father is . . . was very specific about what I was and was not allowed to wear. No jeans, no shorts, nothing tight or the least bit revealing. I can't show my shoulders or my knees."

"Huh." Mason straightened and slid the first two fingers of each hand into the front pockets of his jeans. "Did everyone at your church feel the same way?"

"Oh, no. Most people dressed like the rest of the world. But I was better than the rest of the world." There was more irony than bitterness in my tone. I dropped onto the end of the bed. "I guess there's nothing stopping me now from changing that, right?"

Mason lifted one shoulder. "That's up to you. If you're comfortable as you are, I don't think you need to be different unless you want to. You're in charge of you now, Rilla. No one else."

I studied him, thinking. "I think . . . I think I'd like to wear jeans sometimes." I reached down to pull a wriggling Piper into my lap. "But I don't want to go crazy. I mean, I saw some of the things people wore when I worked at the stand. Those really short shorts, where you could see the girls,' um—well, a lot more of them was out there for the world to see than what I'd ever be comfortable with."

"Got it. No Daisy Dukes."

"Is that what those're called? Hmm. Okay, no Daisy Dukes."

"Maybe Meghan could take you shopping. She'd probably love that." Mason came further into my room and snagged Piper from my arms. "Okay, princess. Time for bed. Let's give Rilla a few minutes to herself." He held his daughter upside down, her head dangling two feet from the floor as she squealed with delight. "You need anything, Rilla? Towels are the bathroom closet. Help yourself to anything else. Oh, and since tomorrow's Monday, I don't go in to the club until close to noon. So sleep in as late as you want. I'll be on rugrat patrol." He shot me a warm smile that lit up his eyes. "Good night."

"Good night," I echoed, not moving as the sound of Piper's laughter faded down the hallway. I hugged my arms around my ribs, looking around the unfamiliar room and trying to ignore the heady and equally foreign tingle that Mason's smile ignited in me.

I might've been innocent and more than a little naïve, but I wasn't stupid. Mason had come to my rescue at a time when I desperately needed someone, and it wouldn't be a surprise if I developed a big old crush on him. He was easily the best-looking guy I'd ever seen in my life, with those green-brown eyes, easy smile and his body . . . well, I'd been raised not to think this way, but when Mason had held me against him earlier today, I'd felt sparks in parts of my own body that I wasn't even supposed to think about.

But I had to remember who he was. Who *I* was. He was the kind of guy who could get any girl he wanted, and I had a feeling he'd had plenty. He was a bar-owner with enough charisma to charm the pants off any female, he'd been a big shot in Nashville—and he had a daughter. I was just the small-town girl who'd never been anywhere or known anyone outside my own tiny circle. My job was to keep his daughter safe and make his mother comfortable so that Mason didn't have to worry about them.

Between the two of us, there could only be friendship and respect. There wasn't room for anything else, and I was determined not to let any silly girlish idolizing get in the way of doing my work and moving forward. With a little luck, by the time Naomi had recovered enough to take over Piper's care again, I would've saved enough money to get my own place and be completely independent. I could live the life I wanted, on my own terms, with nobody telling me I was wrong. Or sinful. Or disobedient.

So as I slid between the cool sheets of the guest room bed that night—correction: it was my bed now, for as long as I lived here—I pushed aside thoughts of the man who was sleeping down the hall, thoughts of his eyes, his smile and his laugh. And I definitely didn't think about the way he made me feel when he teased, or when he said my name, or how my skin buzzed with energy whenever he touched me in even the slightest way. I convinced myself that I wasn't interested in the feel of his hard body against mine, the comfort of his arms wrapped around me or the scent of him when he was close and I breathed him in.

Nope. I was going to be smart and strong. And if I melted a little now and then when Mason winked at me, it didn't mean a thing. I could handle it. I was a big girl, an adult, not a giggling teen.

And if my dreams that night were more intense and sensual than any I'd ever had . . . and if they all centered around a certain man . . . well, I couldn't help that. I wasn't responsible for my subconscious.

Chapter Ten

Mason

WITHIN A FEW WEEKS of Rilla moving in with us, I couldn't imagine how we'd ever survived without her.

It was heaven for me to wake up each morning without worrying about how I was going to juggle my daughter, my mother and my business that day. Rilla made it all look easy, cooking meals, keeping the house neat and the laundry washed and folded, even as she amused Piper and made sure Mom had her meds and was kept comfortable.

Everything at The Road Block improved, too. I wasn't working longer hours, but because I wasn't distracted, worrying about what was happening at home, I was more efficient. We'd put Rilla's ideas for promoting our new lunch hours into effect, and volume was picking up, slowly but steadily.

"It's amazing how much difference one person can make in your life." I leaned my hip against the counter opposite the bar and popped open two beers, handing one to Rocky and taking a swig of my own. "I'm telling you, dude. I feel like a whole new man. Rilla keeps the house humming like a well-oiled machine."

"It's a beautiful thing, boss." Rocky tipped his bottle to me. "My wife's happier, too, since I'm not getting called in all the time to cover for you. Not that it was ever a problem," he hastened to add. "You know I love my job. I'm happy to help whenever you need me."

"Nah, it's all good. I'm glad your wife's happy, too. Happy wife, happy life, right?"

"You got it, man. And speaking of that, you ever think about . . . you know . . . having a happy life with Rilla? Damned good-looking woman. If I were you, I'd grab that before anyone else starts sniffin' around."

Unexpected and sudden irritation rose in my chest. "Shut the hell up, Rocky. It's not like that, and you know it. Rilla works for me. She's—she's a friend. Nothing else is going on." I finished my beer and tossed it into the recycle barrel with a little more force than necessary, and I heard it break against the other glass. "Besides, you know she's, like, seven years younger than me."

"Uh huh." Rocky nodded. "Say, isn't she actually a little older than Meghan, the girl Sam Reynolds is marrying? And aren't you and Sam the same age?"

"Drop it." I pointed at him. "Last thing I need is rumors starting up about Rilla. She's been through enough." I ran my hand over my buzzed hair. "And Rilla and Meghan might be close to the same age, but Meghan wasn't raised by an overprotective dad out on a farm. She's a lot more street-savvy than Rilla."

"True." Rocky finished his beer and slid the bottle to me. "She still hasn't heard anything from her family since she moved in with you?"

"Not a word. Rilla says it doesn't bother her, but I think it hurts that her grandmother hasn't even called. They were close." I picked up Rocky's bottle and stared at it a moment. "I wish I knew something about her mother's family. Rilla says her father wouldn't talk about them or let her grandmother tell Rilla anything about where her mom came from."

"Have you asked around? Small town like Burton, people are bound to remember who she was."

I shook my head. "No. I don't want to interfere more than I have, and I don't want people talking about her, either. My mother can't remember—she didn't know the families, I guess."

"Well, good luck, boss. If it's okay with you, I'm heading out." Rocky slid off the barstool. "See you tomorrow."

"Sounds good, Rocky. Thanks." I glanced around the dining area, making a mental note of how many tables were still active and how many needed to be bussed. We were in the slow period between the end of lunch hours and before things got busy on the bar side of the club, and only a few people lingered over late lunches.

I came out from behind the bar to make my final swing through, thanking the last diners for coming in and asking them to tell their friends. Rilla had had small cards made up that offered free dessert for returning customers and a discount for first-time lunchers. I handed out a few of each as I stopped at the tables.

A woman with light brown hair sat with her husband at the last booth. When I'd finished my spiel, she sat back, looking up at me with narrowed eyes. "You're Mason Wallace, the owner here, right?"

"Yes, ma'am, I am. I hope everything was all right today."

"Oh, the food was delicious, and the service was exemplary." She paused. "I've heard about you. We go to church out at Burton Community."

For a minute, I was lost, and then light dawned. "Ah. I

see."

"I've known Rilla Grant since she was a tiny thing. I heard she's living with you now. Left her father's house and moved in with you."

Shit. "Well, that's not exactly right, ma'am. Rilla works for me. I have a young daughter, and my mother has leukemia. I'm a widower, and I hired Rilla to help with my little girl and my mom. That's all." I felt compelled to add, "There's nothing wrong going on between us. And Rilla didn't leave the farm. She was thrown out."

If I'd expected shock from the woman over this revelation, I was disappointed. She only nodded. "Doesn't surprise me. Emmett Grant's a hard man, and I never did agree with the way he brought up Rilla. She was too good to play with my daughters when they were all young, because I let my girls wear jeans and watch television. Rilla had to sit still, wear dresses and keep quiet. That's no way to raise a child."

"I think I'd have to agree with you." I smiled. "I can't imagine telling my little girl that she couldn't play."

"It's a shame. There're people who take good teachings and twist them around to be something the good Lord never intended. My mother always said faith without fun wasn't going anywhere, because who wanted to take on a lifestyle filled with hateful people?" Across the booth, her husband laughed, and she smiled. "Anyway. I just wanted you to know that not everyone at the church is against Rilla. There's a lot of talk, I'm not going to lie. People who have too much time to spread gossip, which they justify by calling it prayer requests, and they're saying some ugly things. But not all of us listen. You tell Rilla, Carol Hampton said hey, and we miss her."

"I'll be sure to pass that on, ma'am. Thank you." I gave her a little head bow as I made my way back to the bar. It made me ill to think of people talking about Rilla, assuming what we were doing was sordid and wrong. I wanted to defend her, tell them the truth, but at the same time, I knew once a rumor was out there, it could be near impossible to make it go away.

"You hanging tonight, Mason, or you heading home?" Darcy came out of the back, tying on her apron. Her shift had just begun.

"I was going to stay, but you know, if you think you've got it handled, I might go home." I had a sudden urge to go home and make sure Rilla was all right.

"Sure thing. It's a Monday night. It's gonna be slow. You might as well have a night off." She jerked her head in the direction of the bar. "We've got plenty of staff on to serve, so I'll cover drinks."

"I appreciate it, Darcy."

"I know you do." She shot me a saucy grin. "How's your mom doing? Any word on when she goes in for the transplant?"

"Yeah, it's this week, actually. I'll take her in to the hospital early Wednesday, and then they start the chemo blast to kill off her immune system. If all goes according to their plan, she'll be ready for the new stem cells in about two weeks."

"I can't believe you were a match for her. That was a lucky break."

"Sure was." My mom's siblings and cousins had all been tested, as I had been. We were relieved when I was a match, since it was easier for me to donate, living here in Georgia. "Rilla says it wasn't luck, it was answered prayer."

Darcy smiled. "And she may be onto something. Whatever, I'm glad it happened that way." She hesitated. "Mason, everything going okay with Rilla living at your house? Is she adjusting all right?"

I frowned. "As far as I know. Why?"

She shrugged. "Just asking. You know I don't listen to gossip. But I hear things, and there's talk about Rilla living with you. People saying she's taking care of more than your mom and the kid. It pisses me off, because anyone who'd actually met Rilla could tell she's not that way. But I just thought you ought to know."

"Yeah." My hands curled into fists. "You're right, Rilla would never . . . and we're not. She works for me. She's amazing with Piper, and my mom loves her, too."

"I know." Darcy patted my arm. "Anyway, you know anything I can do to help while your mom's in the hospital, you only have to say the word. I can cover shifts for you, bring meals, even watch the ankle biter if you need me to."

"Thanks, Darce. I'll keep that in mind. Call me if anything comes up tonight, you hear?"

"Will do. Get out of here."

I mock saluted her and headed for the door.

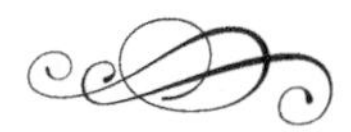

Everything I'd heard from Mrs. Hampton, the woman from Burton Community Church, churned around in my mind as I drove home. I thought of Rilla as a little girl, sober and serious, not allowed to dress like the other kids or run around and play. I didn't pity her, but part of me wished I could go back in time and save that child.

But I couldn't, and hearing that the gossip was flying about our living arrangements worried me. I'd wanted to help her, but was I actually making things worse? I pounded the heel of my hand against the steering wheel in frustration. *Dammit, when had things gotten so complicated?*

When I stepped into the kitchen at home, two blonde heads were bent over a coloring book at the table, a bucket of crayons between them. Rilla glanced up in surprise, blinking her blue eyes. For just a split second, I caught something else in her expression—pleasure? Gladness? Whatever it was, I wanted to see it again. No matter what the rest of the world might be saying, it felt somehow right, to come home and find Rilla here in my kitchen, with my daughter. She belonged here.

Suddenly aware that I was standing in the doorway staring at her, I cleared my throat and walked the rest of the way inside. "Hello, ladies. What're you up to?"

"We're coloring, Daddy." Piper spoke with a vague chiding, as if she were stating the obvious.

"I didn't expect you home for dinner. I thought you were working tonight." Rilla dropped her purple crayon into the bucket and stood up, looking around the kitchen. "We were just going to order pizza. But I can probably find something to cook."

I made a fast decision. "I have a better idea. Why don't I take my best girls out to dinner tonight?"

I watched several thoughts pass through her transparent eyes. First, she wasn't sure I was including her in the invitation. And when she realized that I did mean her, there was another flare of that same happiness I'd seen when I walked in the door.

"What about Naomi?" Rilla's eyebrows knit together. "Maybe you should take Piper, and I'll stay home with your mom."

"Nonsense." Mom's voice floated out from her room, strong and firm. "I'm fine here. I promise, I'll stay right in my chair and watch my shows. Y'all deserve a nice night out. Go on now. Rilla, if you don't go and enjoy yourself, I'm going to be very cross with you, darlin'."

"Yes, ma'am!" She grinned and turned to me. "Give me just a minute to change, and I'll be down, okay?"

She looked fine to me, but I'd known enough women not to say that. "Sure. I'll get Piper's shoes on her. C'mon, princess. Let's wash your hands, too."

Ten minutes later, Rilla was back in the kitchen. I sat at the table with Piper on my lap, and the island counter between us meant I only saw Rilla's upper half. She'd pulled her hair back in a low ponytail, which made her eyes look even bigger. But what caught my attention was her shirt. It was deep blue and sleeveless, showing her toned arms. The top few buttons were undone; there was nothing revealing about the blouse at all, but it actually fit her, molding to her curves just enough that I wanted to investigate closer.

And then she stepped closer to us, and I couldn't hide my grin. "Rilla Grant, are you wearing jeans?"

She flushed, but I could tell by the way her eyes shone that she was pleased I'd noticed. "Yes. I thought tonight would be a good time to give them a try."

Rilla and Meghan had gone shopping together just the weekend past, and while I hadn't seen any of her new clothes until now, I knew she was excited about what she'd bought.

"Come in here and let me see!" Mom called from her room. "Dang, I always miss out on the good stuff."

Rilla grinned and turned toward my mother's room, giving me a tantalizing view of the way the denim hugged her ass. *God almighty.* Who knew shy little Rilla Grant was rocking a body like this under all that material?

I knew I had to rein myself in. I hadn't been blowing smoke when I'd told Rocky that Rilla and I were only friends, that she worked for me, that she was far too young for me. I meant it all. But just for now, just for tonight, it was fun to let my mind down paths of possibilities. It felt right to pretend that we were a little family, that I was going to enjoy a night out with my girl and my daughter.

Mom ooohed and ahhhed, and once Rilla was satisfied that she was settled for the evening and would be all right while we were out, the three of us got into my truck. I buckled Piper into the backseat and then stood back to help Rilla climb in, clasping her small hand tight in mine for a little longer than necessary and holding back from giving her a boost. My fingers itched to cup her backside, just to cop a feel over the jeans. I lectured myself sternly as I walked around to the driver's side.

Cool it, buddy.

Other than my own establishment, Kenny's Diner was the only place to get a decent dinner in Burton. Consequently, it was almost always busy. Mondays were a bit slower, but I saw the lot was nearly full when we pulled in. Rilla carried Piper, and I held the door for the two of them as we went inside.

It was a seat-yourself place, and we found a booth not too far from the door. I handed out the laminated menus, and Rilla helped Piper decide what she wanted to eat.

Our waitress had just taken our drink order and left when a shadow fell over the table. I glanced up, expecting to see her returning with a tray. Instead, a tall man with black hair and heavy brows that were drawn together stood next to us, staring down at Rilla.

She didn't notice him at first. She and Piper were giggling over a picture they were drawing on the kids' menu, and her attention was fully on my daughter.

"Rilla." His voice was deep and full of shocked censure. At first, I assumed he was her father, but then I noticed the woman standing alongside him. She was nearly as tall, though much slimmer. Her hair was graying, and her lips were pursed as though she'd sucked a bowl of lemons. This was definitely not Rilla's grandmother, and I doubted Mr. Grant frequented restaurants with women.

Rilla looked up, the smile on her face fading as she took in the man and his wife. Her eyes darted between them, and the color left her cheeks. For a moment, I thought she might try to run.

Then she drew herself up to sit straight. Her thumb went to the edge of her lips for a second before she dropped it and curled her mouth into a smile that didn't quite reach her eyes.

"Pastor Shand. Mrs. Shand. So good to see you."

They didn't answer, and Rilla's eyes flew to me. "Uh, this is Mason. Mason Wallace, and this is Piper. His daughter." She shot me a look of pleading. "Mason, this is Pastor Shand. And his wife. They, um, they're from church."

I slid out of the booth and offered my hand to the man. I had a dual purpose: first of all, no matter how sour this woman was, she was a lady I was meeting for the first time, and my mother had taught me that a gentleman stood when meeting a lady. Second, I had the good pastor by several inches, and I wasn't above a little height intimidation.

Pastor Shand looked at my hand as though it might bite him, but finally he took it, shaking half-heartedly.

"Nice to meet you, sir. And ma'am." I glanced at the woman. "Did you have a good dinner?"

"We did, and then we were just leaving when we spotted you. Rilla, I don't have any desire to make a scene, but . . ." He shook his head. "What's happened to you? You leave your father's house, run off to live in sin with this man who's not a believer. I just can't believe this of you."

"Pastor, it isn't quite like that. And with all due respect, this is between my father and me. Not you. Not the church."

"There's where you're wrong." The pastor stabbed a finger at Rilla. "First of all, what you did affects the entire body. And your father is an elder. You've caused him shame and embarrassment. He may be forced to step down. Did you stop and think of anyone but yourself?"

Rilla's face flushed. "Pastor, I didn't do anything to shame my father. I took a job, working to help a man whose wife has passed, whose child needs tending and whose mother is ill. What he does for a living doesn't matter. Not to me, and it shouldn't to you, either. And did my father share with you the fact that he made me leave? I didn't just up and go. He threw me out."

"It was his only option, given the level of your disobedience." Pastor Shand nodded, emphasizing his own point.

"How could you, Rilla?" This time it was Mrs. Shand who

spoke. "The girls in the church look up to you. What kind of example are you, living in sin with this man?" She glanced at me, distaste filling her eyes.

"I really don't care what anyone else thinks. If you want to know the truth, I'm happy to tell you that I haven't done anything wrong. If you don't believe me, well . . ." Rilla spread her hands. "That's your problem. That's between you and God, because I know sure as—as heck that everything between God and me is A-okay."

"As long as you continue to live in sin and in defiance of your father and the church, you will be estranged from God, no matter what you think." He folded his hands over his stomach and pressed his lips together. "When you are ready to repent, Rilla, your brothers and sisters in the Lord will be ready to receive you in love and forgiveness." He turned to look down at his wife. "Come on, dear."

They swept away from us, hurrying out. The bell over the door jangled in their wake.

I was almost afraid to look at Rilla, for fear I'd see devastation and pain. Instead, though, her eyebrows were raised and her mouth arranged in a slight smile. Only her hands, fisted as they rested on the table, gave me a hint about what she was really feeling.

"Do you want to leave?" I leaned forward to murmur across the table. "We can order our food to go."

Rilla shook her head. "No. I'm not going to let him force me into hiding. I haven't done anything wrong, Mason, and I'm tired of people making me feel like I have."

I gazed down at her face, still flushed, her eyes bright and certain. She was making a stand, I realized. It was almost killing her, but she wasn't going to let the assholes get to her. I admired the hell out of her.

Whether it was what Rocky had said, or Mrs. Hampton telling me a little more about Rilla's childhood, the sight of her in my kitchen with Piper when I came home or the way she'd stood up to the pastor just now, I wasn't sure. I wanted to protect her from anyone who'd hurt her. I wanted to stand between this girl and the world. Suddenly, nothing was more important than protecting her, making her happy, and there wasn't a damn thing I wouldn't do to make it happen.

Something shifted deep inside me, and I heard myself speaking words I'd never expected to say again in this lifetime.

"Rilla, let's get married."

"You're crazy. Just flat-out, no-holds-barred insane."

Rilla didn't wait for me to open her door this time when I pulled the truck into the driveway. She jumped out and then leaned back to unbuckle Piper. "Come on, sweet pea. Let's get you ready for a bath and bed."

"Rilla, come on. We need to talk about this." I followed her into the house. "Just wait a second."

"No, thanks. I'm going to put Piper to bed, and then I'm going to help Naomi with her medicine and help her get changed for bed. And then I'm going to my room and going to bed myself. I suggest you do the same. Clearly you got too much sun today, and it fried your brain."

"It didn't go above seventy-two degrees today, Rilla. I don't have heat stroke. I just—"

"No." She stopped and spun on her heel, shooting me a stern, shut-your-mouth look that halted me in my tracks. "Not another word." She turned around again, pausing only at the doorway to my mother's room. "Naomi, as soon as I get the little one down, I'll come help you, okay? You all right 'til then?"

I heard my mom speak, cautious and curious. "I'm fine, darlin.' The bigger question is, are *you* okay?"

"I'm peachy. Be right back. Piper, say good-night to Nan."

Rilla bent to set my daughter on the floor, and Piper scampered to hug her grandmother. She ran back to grab Rilla's hand and marched up the steps.

I went into Mom's room and dropped into the easy chair, rubbing the back of my neck.

"I'm nearly afraid to ask, but what happened? Here I was happy, thinking the three of you were off having yourselves a time, and instead Rilla comes home in a snit and you're trailing her around, begging her to give you a minute of time."

I sighed. "You're not going to like it, and I'm not sure I can deal with another pissed female tonight. So let's just say I said something that made perfect sense to me, but apparently was the last thing Rilla wanted to hear."

Mom laid her head back against the chair. "Oh, son. 'Fess up, now. Tell me what you did."

I steepled my fingers and stared down at them. "I asked Rilla to marry me."

There was silence for a long moment, and then she spoke, her voice even. "Oh."

"It didn't come out of the blue. Or maybe it did. We ran into the pastor from her church, and he and his wife were horrible to her. They accused her of being a sinner and disobeying her father . . . it was ugly."

The lines of confusion on Mom's face smoothed out. "Ah. And then after that, you proposed."

"Well, yeah. It made sense to me. The way the people from her church see it, as long as Rilla's living here with me, she's committing some sin. The truth doesn't matter to these people. So if we get married, we'll no longer be sinners in their eyes." I paused, considering. "Well, probably I would still be a sinner, since I don't go to church. But Rilla would be okay."

"And has Rilla said anything to you, about how she's worried that people are talking about her?"

I shrugged. "Not in so many words, but I know it bothers her. She might not believe in everything they taught at that church, but it's still the way she was raised. You can't just turn your back on that all at once. And what if she decides she wants to go back to church there one day? If we're married, she can do that."

Mom nodded. "Right. And what was your angle on this proposal?"

I frowned. "What do you mean, angle?"

"What do you stand to get out of marrying Rilla? What's in it for you?"

I didn't have a good answer to that. "I don't know. I guess the satisfaction of knowing it's the right thing to do, for Rilla."

"Is she in love with you?" Mom's voice was gentle.

I drew my brows together. "No. I don't think so."

"And are you in love with her?"

"Of course I'm not."

"Then how can you think getting married is a good choice? Mason, we're not living in the dark ages. People don't jump into marriages of convenience anymore. All of this talk will blow over, eventually. And you know that. So I have to think that you have another reason for wanting to marry Rilla, something you might not be admitting even to yourself."

I didn't know how to explain my thought process to my mother. "Sometimes marriage doesn't start with love. Maybe it can begin with . . . respect. And like."

"Maybe." My mother regarded me, her eyes steady. "But I think that's risky."

"Well, you don't have to worry, because not only did Rilla turn me down flat, she thinks I'm crazy. I thought girls were supposed to be flattered when a man proposes, but she acted like I'd insulted her."

"Possibly because she thinks you proposed out of pity. Think about it, Mason. Rilla just got out of her father's house, where her life was planned out for her. She's finally getting a sense of standing on her own two feet. And then you sweep in and tell her you'll marry her out of the goodness of your heart. That's not something that's going to send a girl into swoons."

I pushed myself to stand up. "Thanks for the pep talk, Mom. I appreciate the support for your only child. Remember the dude who's giving you his stem cells? That's me. At least you could've told me my heart was in the right place."

Mom laughed. "Oh, all right, darlin.' Your heart's in the right place. You mean well."

"Thanks." I leaned over to kiss her cheek.

Before I straightened, she added in a whisper, "You know what they say about good intentions and the road to hell."

"I heard that. Good night, Mother dearest." I winked at her as I left the room, just to be sure she knew I was teasing. Exhaling a long breath, I trudged up the steps, where Rilla ran smack into me at the top.

"Sorry." I grasped her by the top of her arms, and I couldn't stop my fingers from rubbing against the bare skin there.

"My fault. I should've watched where I'm going." She took one step backwards and crossed her arms over her chest.

"Is Piper asleep?" I lowered my voice.

Rilla nodded. "Or close to it. I'm going to down to give Naomi her medicine."

"Can you wait just a minute?" I caught her arm again before she could slip past me. Emotion warred across her face before she closed her eyes and sighed.

"Okay."

I followed her into her room and watched her hesitate before she closed the door behind us. She leaned her back against it and crossed her arms again.

"Before you say anything, I guess I need to apologize." I held up my hands as she began to speak. "Hold on. I want to say I'm sorry for how I asked you . . . that question. It was insensitive."

Rilla rolled her eyes. "I'm not mad because you didn't have flowers and a ring, Mason. I'm upset because you felt like you had to do it. You told me that me living here helped you as much as it did me. I believed you. But when you proposed tonight, it was because you felt sorry for me. Not because it's a situation that would benefit both of us."

"How do you know that? I told you before, Rilla, I'm no saint. If I asked you to marry me, you can bet I expect to get something out of it." Even as I said them, the words were news to me. But I realized they were true.

"Oh, really? And just what benefit do you get from marrying me?" She raised one eyebrow in challenge.

I began counting off on my fingers. "I know I'd be giving my daughter a mother who'll love her forever. I see you with Piper, Rilla. You're amazing with her, and she loves you with all her heart."

Rilla blinked, and I bit back a smile when her thumb rose toward her face. I was getting to her.

"I love Piper, too. But I'd stay with her as long as you want me, whether I was married to you or not."

Damn. "Okay, but there's a difference. If we got married, you'd really be her mother."

She quirked her brow and rolled her hand in a go-on gesture. I took a deep breath.

"I like you, Rilla. I like you a lot. I'm comfortable with you. We laugh together . . ." I swallowed hard. "I came home tonight and thought how much I like coming home and finding you in my house. In my kitchen. It feels right."

Something I couldn't identify passed swiftly over her face and then was gone. She rubbed her thumb over her bottom lip before she dropped her hand back to her side. "I appreciate that you thought you were doing the right thing, Mason. But I've thought about marriage a lot. When my father told me Jonathan wanted to marry me, I was thrilled on one level—because

I've always wanted to be someone's wife. And then someone's mother. But I was worried because I didn't understand how Jonathan knew he wanted to marry *me.* I convinced myself that he'd noticed more about me than I'd thought. Eventually, I realized the truth.

"If I'd stayed at home, Mason, I think I would've ended up married up to Jonathan. Not this year, maybe not for five more years, but it would've happened. And the only reason he would've done it would be to please my father, and because a pastor needs a wife. I might've gone along with that. That might've been my life. Do you know how that makes me feel, when I think about it now? It horrifies me."

My gut began to churn as what she said sunk in. Was I guilty of doing the same thing as her father and that jackass Jonathan?

"Rilla . . ." I clenched my jaw. "I don't want to control you. I want to set you free. That's why I asked you to marry me. I thought if you and I got married, you'd be free to be whoever and whatever you want. You want to make your PR business grow? I'll support you, a hundred percent. You want to stay home and be a mom to Piper? I'm cool with that, too. I just . . . I want you to be part of my life."

"You want that now." She glanced up at me through her lashes. "What happens when you meet someone else? Someone who you love? I don't want to be divorced, Mason. I'd rather take my chances on 'living in sin'"—she gave the words air quotes—"than end up divorced."

"Rilla." I risked stepping toward her and taking one of her hands in mine. "I have to be upfront about something. My wife . . ." I swallowed back a surge of emotion. "Lu was it for me. I'm never going to fall in love again. She was everything, and I'm never going to experience that again." I lifted her hand so that it was closer to my face, stroking the smooth skin on the back of her fingers. "You asked me what I'd get out of marrying you. I'd get to not be alone. I'd have a friend who I can share my daughter with. I'd have . . . comfort."

Rilla stared into my eyes, and I didn't blink. The silence that surrounded us was so complete that I thought I could hear the beating of her heart.

Finally, she closed her eyes and nodded.

"Okay."

Chapter Eleven

Rilla

I DIDN'T KNOW WHAT I was thinking. I'd steeled myself to argue against Mason until I was blue in the face, until he finally gave up and accepted that marriage to me was the single worst idea he'd ever had.

And then I'd heard his words about Lu, telling me that he was never going to love anyone like he had loved her ever again, that she was his only true love and there would never be anyone else like her in his life.

Naturally, it was after that I'd said yes.

I was a moron. A stupid, masochistic idiot. I'd just set myself up to marry a man who I was pretty sure I had a crush on, who'd admitted freely he only wanted me for companionship and to be a mother to his daughter. Only a person who had no other options or very low self-esteem would agree to a plan like that.

Or me, apparently.

I'd tossed and turned that night, until I calmed down enough to realize that I had time. Naomi was going into the hospital in two days for her stem cell transplant. There was no way Mason would want to do anything like get married while his mother was in the middle of a medical procedure like this. I'd have weeks to think about everything and decide how I really felt. Mason would have weeks to realize he'd made a huge mistake in asking me.

I'd been a little worried about seeing Mason the next morning, but nothing had changed. Naomi felt well enough to join us at the breakfast table, and we talked about what special meal I could make that evening, since it was the last night she'd be home for a long time. Mason lingered at the table as Piper helped me wash the dishes. And by helped me, I mean she stood on a stool next to me and played in the bubbles as she passed me the dirty silverware.

I felt his eyes on us as we worked and played, but he didn't say much until it was almost time for him to leave for the club. He kissed Piper good-bye and called to his mom before laying a hand on my back. I tried not to hold my breath at his touch.

"Rilla, can you walk me out?"

I nodded and patted Piper's head. "Run and see Nan for a minute, sweet pea. I'll be right back."

Mason opened the door for me and then followed me out. He slid his hand down my spine, to my lower back, rubbing just enough to send shivers over my skin.

"I wanted to say something in private." He licked his lips and turned me so that I faced him. Running his fingers down my arms, he took my hands. "Thank you for saying yes last night. I want you to know, I heard what you said, about your worries. Your doubts. I promise, I'll do anything in my power to make sure you never have reason to regret agreeing to marry me."

"Thank you." I wasn't sure about the proper response in

this situation.

"I was thinking that maybe we could drive into Savannah Thursday to get married. What do you think?"

My mouth dropped open, and my eyes widened. "Thursday? As in the day after tomorrow?"

"That's what I was thinking. I figured we want to do it as soon as possible, so that no one can harass you anymore about living here."

"But what about your mom? She'll be in the hospital."

"I know, but the first few days, they're just running tests. The chemo blast won't begin until Friday. That's why Thursday's perfect."

I couldn't think of a good reason to say no. "Okay. But what about Piper?"

"The schools are closed on Thursday and Friday this week for fall break. Meghan said she'd watch Piper for us."

I frowned. "When did you ask her?"

"This morning. We texted."

"Did you tell her why we were going to Savannah?"

Mason shook his head. "I just asked if she'd mind helping. I figured you'd want to tell her."

"Yeah." I nodded. "Okay. That sounds good."

"Great." He hesitated and then bent to kiss the top of my head. "I better get to work. I'll be late tonight, since Rocky's covering for me tomorrow while I'm at the hospital with Mom. I'll have my phone if you need me."

I nodded again before I went back inside, feeling that my life had spun rapidly out of the control I'd held for a few weeks. I was going to marry Mason Wallace. It was the craziest idea in the world. I had to talk him—and myself—out of it before Thursday.

It didn't happen. No matter what I said, Mason had an answer, and on Thursday morning, I found myself in Mason's truck, sitting next to him as we pulled out of the driveway, on our way to Savannah. To get married. I definitely felt as though I'd fallen down the rabbit hole.

"Meghan thinks we're crazy, doesn't she?" Mason glanced at me.

"You know, it's kind of weird, but no. When I told her, she just laughed."

"Huh. I'd have thought she'd be yelling at me for pushing you into it. Did you tell her I had to twist your arm?"

"No." I toyed with my seatbelt. "I just said, you know, it seemed like the right thing to do. And Meghan said she wasn't surprised, because . . ." I let my voice trail off.

"Because . . . ?" Mason prompted.

"I don't want to say."

"Come on, Rilla. We're about to get married. No secrets, and complete honesty. Right? That's how marriage works. Tell me what Meghan said."

I sighed. "She said she could tell from the day we met at the stand that we'd end up together." I held my breath waiting for Mason's response.

To my surprise, he laughed. "Only Meghan would see two people having a civil conversation and instantly think they'd end up madly in love."

I forced myself to join his laughter. "I know. Crazy." I stared out my window so Mason couldn't see my face.

"Do you mind if we stop real fast on the way out of town? The front blinker's out on the truck, and I don't want to drive all the way into the city without fixing it. I want to see if Boomer has a replacement."

"Boomer?" I crinkled my forehead.

"Yeah. He owns the auto repair shop." He looked at me sideways. "I forget sometimes that even though you grew up around here, you don't really know the town."

"I know. When I go to the grocery store with Piper, people ask me when I moved here." I shrugged. "I just go along with it."

Boomer's Auto Repair was on the main street leading into town. Mason turned into the parking lot and opened his door. "I'll just be a minute, but why don't you come in? I'll introduce you to Boomer."

I climbed down from the truck and followed Mason into the small shot. I could hear country music and the sound of machines and pounding coming from the adjacent garage. A man shouted out something, and another one responded.

A short, rotund balding man in a blue coverall with the name BOOMER embroidered on the chest stood behind the desk in the corner of the room. He was on the phone but turned when the bell on the door announced our arrival. He nodded at Mason and then his eyes dropped to me and he froze.

His stare was so intense that I looked behind me to see what this guy might be looking at. Mason frowned and draped his arm around my shoulder, drawing me closer to him.

"Let me call you back." Without waiting for an answer, Boomer hung up the phone. He didn't look away from me.

"Hey, Boomer. I just needed a replacement bulb for my blinker."

The man behind the desk nodded. "Yeah, okay, Mason. Uh, who's this?"

Mason tightened his hand on my upper arm. "This is Rilla. She's, um, well . . ." Mason glanced down at me as though he'd forgotten who I was. "She's been helping me with Piper and my mom."

"Rilla Grant?" Boomer shifted, folding his arms across his broad chest.

"Yeah." Mason's eyebrows were drawn together. "What's going on here, Boomer? Y'all look like you're seeing a ghost."

Boomer rubbed his hand over his eyes. "I think in a way I am." He blinked and shot me a tentative smile. "Guess you don't know who I am?"

"Should I?" I tried to return the smile, but my heart was thumping erratically. I had a sudden premonition about what Boomer was going to say.

"Guess not. But I know you." He came out from behind the desk. "Your mama was my baby sister."

I closed my eyes. "Yeah, I figured it was something like that when you looked at me like I'd risen from the dead." I paused. "She's not, though, is she? Dead, I mean?" I'd always pictured my mother living some place glamorous, living an exciting life. Finding out she wasn't even on this earth anymore would be harder than I'd expected.

But Boomer was shaking his head. "Naw, honey, she's alive. Far as I know, anyway. She lives way out in Texas, last I heard." He pointed to the hard fiberglass chairs in the tiny waiting area. "Will you sit for a minute?"

Mason stayed close to me, and I was grateful for his nearness. "So you've lived here in Burton all this time, knowing where I was, and you never came to visit?"

Boomer perched on the edge of a chair and braced his hands on his knees. "Yes and no. Yeah, I always lived here, and I knew where you were. But I did try to see you. When you were a baby, Millie and I came out to visit you and your mama all the time. Your cousins just loved you to bits."

"My cousins?" I'd always wanted a big family and kids my own age to play with. Cousins had been a dream as long as I could remember.

"Oh, yeah. Millie and I got four girls, and then my other sister Tammie has two boys and a girl. She lives over toward Macon, though."

Seven cousins. I had seven cousins. I pushed aside that thought to ask Boomer another question. "Why didn't you keep coming after my mom left?"

He shook his head. "We wanted to, honey. But your father wouldn't let us. He said he didn't want any reminders of your mom at the farm, and he didn't want us to, uh, influence you as you grew up." He exhaled heavily. "He blamed my parents and me for spoiling your mother. He said what we'd done was part of the reason she'd run off. He couldn't ever forgive us, and he stuck to his guns. It about broke my parents' hearts."

"Do they still live here in Burton?" Another set of grandparents . . . cousins . . . and an uncle and aunt. It made my head spin.

"I'm sorry, honey, they both passed. Daddy first, about sixteen years ago, and then Mama went ten years back."

I fought tears over the grandparents I'd never know. "Why didn't you fight my dad? You had rights. Or at least my grandparents did."

"Your dad threatened to hire an attorney to keep us away. My parents didn't have money for a lawyer, and even if they did, well, we all thought given the circumstances, we had to respect what your father wanted. He was the one raising you. I think we all felt a little guilty for your mama running off like she did." Boomer scratched the sparse hair on his head.

I nodded, though I didn't agree. There wasn't any argument to be made, really; I couldn't go back and change the past, no matter how much I might regret what my father had done. And, come to think of it, what my mother had done.

"Why did my mother leave me?" I didn't mean the question to come out so plaintively.

"I wish I could tell you. She was real young when she married your dad, and I think once the novelty of being married and having a baby wore off, she didn't have enough in her to stick. She did love you, though. When she calls me . . . which isn't often, but once or twice a year . . . she always asks if I've heard anything about you and how you're doing."

"Does she ever come back here?" I wanted the answer to be no. I wasn't sure I could take knowing she'd come to town and not demanded to see me.

"No. Not since she left." He hesitated. "So you're living in town now?" Boomer glanced at Mason. "If you wouldn't mind, I'd like to see you again. Maybe have you come over, meet Millie and the girls. I could even have Tammie drive in for a day."

"I'd like that." I leaned into Mason a little more. "Actually, Mason and I are driving into Savannah today to get married. So I'll be living at his house."

"Is that right?" Boomer's face split into a huge smile. "Well, that's just great, honey. Mason." He stuck his hand out, and when Mason grasped it, he pumped it up and down. "Congratulations."

"Thanks." Mason stood up and offered me his hand. "Rilla, are you sure you still want to go today? I mean, if you wanted to stay and catch up with Boomer some more, we could wait."

I shook my head. "No, I don't want to wait." Suddenly, it was true. I wanted to go to Savannah with Mason and connect my life with his. Meeting my uncle, realizing I'd had family so close for so long without knowing it—I wanted to be linked to someone. To a family. I didn't want anyone to be able to tear me away from Piper, and if marrying Mason took care of that, it was just one more good reason.

"Naw, y'all go off and make it official. We have time." Boomer patted my shoulder a little awkwardly. "I promise, honey, you're going to have more family than you know what to do with."

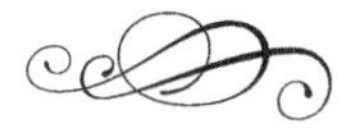

I never would've guessed that getting married would end up to be the anti-climatic portion of that day. But as it happened, the ceremony in the courthouse in Savannah was so fast and quiet that it didn't even feel real.

Mason and I hadn't said much more on the drive into the city. All of my thoughts were consumed with what I'd learned that morning: I had a family. There were people related to me who'd lived mere miles from me my entire life. They loved me, even when loving me meant doing what was painful for them, because they assumed it was best for me. I was sad that I'd never known my mother's parents, but I couldn't wait to meet my cousins. After a lifetime of only my dad and Gram, suddenly I had people. Not only my newly-discovered blood relations, but Piper, Naomi . . . and of course, Mason.

I glanced sideways at him. He was paying attention to the road, but his face was relaxed, a slight smile playing over his lips.

"What did your mom say when you told her we were—what we were doing today?"

The smile vanished, and I saw his Adam's apple bob as he swallowed. "I didn't actually tell her yet. I thought we'd go into the hospital to see her, maybe tomorrow, and we could tell her together."

"Okay." I smoothed my gray skirt over my knees. I was wearing another of my new outfits today, though when I'd bought it, I'd thought it would be something pretty to wear when I met new clients, not my wedding dress. Or skirt. My mind wandered back to Naomi. "Will she be upset?"

Mason smiled, this time full and bright. "Not a bit. She loves you, Rilla."

I nodded. "Did she love Lu, too?"

His hands tightened on the steering wheel. "She did. Everyone loved Lu."

"Can you tell me about her?"

"Seriously? We're on our way to get married, and you want to hear about my wife?"

I shrugged, trying not to let it bother me that he'd said "wife," as though Lu might pop back into town any minute. "Mason, neither of us is pretending this is a love match, right? I'd like to know more about Piper's mother."

He nodded. "Okay. Well, Lu was . . . she was beautiful. And bright, and funny and so talented. She saw the best in people, and she laughed every single day I knew her. She always said life was too short to take it seriously." His sigh was deep. "Turned out she was right."

"Did you ever fight? Or was your marriage perfect, too?"

If Mason heard the archness in my tone, he ignored it. "We fought, but never for long. Mostly over how hard she worked. Lu loved to sing, and she was a really brilliant songwriter. When she started writing, though, she'd ignore everything and everyone else, and it was hard to feel like I was coming in second. She'd go deep into her head for a week or two, and then she'd come out with all these songs . . . and begging me to forgive her for being so absent."

"And you did."

"Of course. I couldn't stay mad at her for that. She had so much talent." His thumbs rubbed the steering wheel. "Lu was amazing."

I looked out the window at the passing scenery, and I didn't ask any more questions until we arrived in the city.

Mason parked the truck in a garage a few blocks away from the courthouse. When he came around to open my door, he offered me his hand and helped me down, and then stood in front of me, so that I was trapped between his body and the truck. My heart began to thud at his nearness.

"Rilla, I just want to say, if you've changed your mind, I understand. We can just go have lunch and walk around the city, and then drive home. It's okay."

I looked up into his eyes, and for a moment, I couldn't speak. Did he want me to say I'd had a change of heart? Or mind?

"Now that you know you have family in town, maybe you're thinking you don't need us anymore. You could easily move in with Boomer, and all the talk would die down. You have options."

I ran my tongue over my lips without dropping my gaze from Mason's, and inhaling deep, I reached forward to take his hand between both of mine. It was large and warm, and I wanted nothing more than to hold it to my face. Turn my lips and kiss his palm. I swallowed hard.

"Mason, I haven't changed my mind. I love Piper, and I love Naomi. And I . . ." I wanted to say something about how I felt about him, but I chickened out. After all, I didn't know how I felt. Not really. A crush, probably. Something that might melt into contented like over the years. "I don't want any options. I'm ready to get married. But if you're not sure—"

"No, I am. I just wanted you to feel like you have a choice."

I ventured a smile. "Maybe we should stop offering each other a way out and just go do it."

Mason grinned and lifted his hand to my face, just I'd wished he would. He brushed the backs of his fingers over my cheek and then stepped back and took my hand. "Okay. I should probably tell you that I called a friend and asked him to stand as witness for us today. Do you know Alex Nelson?"

"I've met him a few times at the stand, with Meghan and Ali."

"Good." Mason nodded. "He happened to be in town today for work, so I asked if he'd take a few minutes and stand up for us. I thought we'd go out to lunch afterward, if that's okay."

"Sure. That sounds good."

"All right then." Mason squeezed my hand. "Let's go get married."

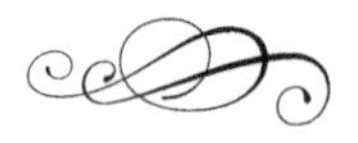

When I'd pictured my wedding while I was growing up, I'd always imagined walking down the aisle of our church on my father's arm, wearing a dress that was glaringly white to assure the world of my intact virginity, while music rolled off the piano in the front of the sanctuary. Gram would be standing in the front pew, dabbing at her eyes. And the man who waited at the end of the aisle would be the embodiment of my every wish and dream.

Instead, I stood up in a small book-lined room, in front of a cluttered desk, while a harried judge in a rumpled suit spoke words that sounded more like a business deal than a sacred covenant. The man who stood beside me, holding my suddenly-clammy hand in his, was nearly a stranger to me. And our witness, while he said nothing, was clearly concerned and skeptical about the whole situation.

It was over within minutes. When the judge pronounced us man and wife, Mason touched his lips to mine briefly. The judge wished us the best of luck, and I followed Mason and Alex out of his office, into a corridor teeming with people.

"Well. Congratulations." Alex shook Mason's hand and bent to kiss my cheek. I thought distractedly that he smelled better than any man I'd ever known.

"You'll have lunch with us, Alex, right? Where's the best place to go?"

Alex nodded. "I know a place." He glanced at me, his eyebrows drawn together and spoke hesitantly. "I'd like to—would it be all right—well, I thought maybe Cal could join us. If you two don't mind."

Mason's eyes got big. "Wait a minute. You're going to let us meet him? The elusive new boyfriend?"

Alex grinned. "Yeah, I guess I am. Meghan and Ali are both going to howl at me about it, and probably yell at you, too, so get ready. But I think it's time." He let his gaze skim over me. "Uh, not to be rude, Rilla, but are you going to be okay with this?"

I forced a smile on my face. "Well, of course. The more, the merrier. It'll be fun."

A hint of relief glimmered in Alex's eyes. "Great. I'll text him to meet us. There's this fabulous little bistro just around the corner. It's actually in a basement, but the food is to die for. C'mon."

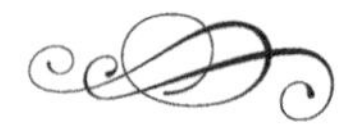

"I don't think I'll ever eat again." I leaned back against the car seat, closing my eyes. "That was delicious."

Mason laughed. "Trust Alex to find the best restaurant in Savannah. That was one of the most incredible meals I've ever eaten." He slid a glance at me as he backed out of the parking space. "What did you think of Cal?"

I considered. I could pretend that there hadn't been anything at all startling about eating lunch with two men whom I knew were in love with each other. I could give Mason a standard trite answer. Or I could be honest. Since I'd just made vows promising the rest of my life to him, I decided honesty was the way to go.

"He seemed really nice. I . . . you can imagine what I was taught growing up in the church. When I met Alex, I had no idea he was gay. But I heard Meghan teasing him about his new boyfriend, and I figured it out."

"Did it bother you?" Mason's voice was carefully neutral.

"Actually, no. Alex is so friendly and just who he is. I like him." I drew in a long breath. "But I was nervous when he asked about Cal. I thought it would be weird. But it honestly wasn't. I had a good time."

Mason's shoulders relaxed, and he smiled. "I didn't know Alex very well growing up. He was a lot younger than me. But he hangs out at The Road Block when he comes through town, and I've enjoyed talking with him. He's become a friend. It would've been harder if you were uncomfortable with who he is."

I shrugged. "I think I'm beginning to learn that a lot of what I was taught growing up wasn't necessarily what I believe now. I don't want to throw away my beliefs, but I need to make sure they're really mine and not what I've been told to accept. Does that make sense?"

"It does." Mason was quiet for a beat. "Do you think you'll want to go back to church at some point?"

I nodded. "Probably, but I doubt it'll be Burton Community. There're plenty of other churches in town." I glanced at him. "Do you go to church?"

His jaw tightened. "Not since Lu died. God and I . . . well, let's just say I don't see eye-to-eye with him. I have to question the existence of a deity that would take a mother away from her baby."

There was so much I wanted to say to Mason in response, but it wasn't the time. Instead, I tackled another question that had been worrying me.

"Mason, can I ask you something?"

He smiled, though I noticed it didn't quite reach his eyes. "Sure."

"I probably should've talked to you about this before . . . well, before. But we're married now. What is that going to mean? Between us." My face was hot, and I was positive it was flaming red.

"I'm not sure I get what you're asking." He frowned.

"I mean . . . do you . . . want me to stay in the guest room?"

Understanding dawned on his face. "Oh. I, uh . . ." He kept his eyes on the road ahead of us. "I figured we'd see what happened. I . . ." He exhaled. "There're a few things you should know about me, Rilla. You're right, we should've discussed this before." He rubbed his forehead, and dread pierced me. He was going to say he didn't find me attractive. He didn't want me that way.

"I'm not the kind of guy who cheats on his wife. Or his

girlfriend. We're married now, and even though it happened fast and maybe not for the reasons most people do it, I don't take it any less seriously. I'm just saying, I don't intend to sleep with anyone else."

"Good." I was a little more emphatic than I intended, and Mason grinned.

"But I know you haven't had any kind of experience. I don't expect go home and jump into bed with you. I think we should take things slowly. We'll see what happens." He reached across and took my hand. "I'm not going to rush you into anything. You can trust me."

"Okay." I understood that Mason was trying to be considerate of me. Part of me wanted him not to be. Part of me wanted him to be so eager to get home for our wedding night that he'd break every speed limit. I couldn't make myself say that, though I had to ask one more question. "But you don't find me repulsive, right?"

"God, no." His answer was fast and fervent, and I couldn't help smiling.

"Oh, good. That's a relief."

He traced circles on the back of my hand with his thumb. "Rilla, I'm going to be honest with you. I told you I'm no saint. I never would've suggested we get married if I wasn't attracted to you. You're beautiful. I should've said that to you today, all day, probably, but I'm out of practice. And I don't want to make you uncomfortable. But you are beautiful. Please don't think that because I'm willing to take things slow, I don't want you. Because I do."

A peculiar heat pooled low in my abdomen, and I could feel the pounding of my blood in different parts of my body. This must be desire, I decided. It made me want to unbuckle my seatbelt, crawl over to Mason and climb into his lap. What I'd do once I got there, I wasn't quite sure, but I thought it might involve kissing. And touching.

I didn't do any of that. Instead, I contented myself with holding his hand a little tighter, enjoying the feel of his palm pressed against mine and his fingers threaded through my own. Staring out the window at the passing scenery, for the first time in quite a while, I let myself daydream about the future.

Mason

AS IT TURNED OUT, Piper came down with a cold the day after Rilla and I got married, so Rilla stayed home with her while I went to the hospital to visit Mom. When I told my mother what we'd done, she only nodded.

"I knew you were going to marry that girl, Mason. It was just a matter of time."

I took her hand, so thin and frail in my bigger grip. "Are you upset? Mad at me?"

She shook her head. "Not a bit. Just . . ." She hesitated. "Remember Rilla's young, son. She looks at you with stars in her eyes, even though she might not realize it yet. Don't break her heart."

"As if I would." I frowned. "How can you even think that?"

Mom sighed and closed her eyes. "Because you're stubborn and you're a man. You don't see what's in front of you sometimes. You've managed to convince yourself that you married Rilla out of some sense of obligation or duty. Riding in on your white horse to save the day. But you may be surprised to learn one day that in the end, it's going to be Rilla who saves you."

I thought about her words the next day as I worked at The Road Block. It was Saturday night, and we were busier than normal. People thronged the bar, shouting out drink orders faster than Rocky and I could fill them. The band was hot, the dance floor was filled, and we were turning people away before nine. Still, I stole a minute before the live music began to step outside in the back and call home.

I'd gotten Rilla a cell phone as I'd promised, but she was still getting the hang of texting. At least, that was what I told myself to justify calling her instead of sending a text. I wasn't ready to admit to myself that I really just needed to hear her voice.

She answered after the second ring. Her "hello" was quiet, which told me Piper was already asleep.

"Hey, darlin.' It's me. Just checking in on you."

She laughed, soft and low, and an arrow of need rocketed down my spine to land between my legs. I pictured her curled up on her bed, reading, her blonde hair messy as it lay over the pillow.

"We're good. I gave Piper the new cold meds the doctor recommended, and she seems to be sleeping better. No cough, so that's a relief."

I smiled. This was Rilla's first real experience with a sick kid, and she'd worried over this mild cold like any new mama. "Great."

"And I called over to the hospital and spoke to your mom. She says she's feeling some better after the transfusion. I told her you'd be by to visit tomorrow, and Piper and I'll go over once she's not contagious anymore."

"Uh huh." I shifted the phone to the other ear and leaned

back against the building. The wall fairly vibrated with the noise of all the people inside. “I didn’t call to take report, Rilla. I wanted to hear your voice. I miss you.”

There was silence on the other end of the phone for a minute. “You do? You just saw me this afternoon, Mason.” She sounded cautious and a little confused.

“Yeah, I know, but it’s crazy here at the bar. And I’m looking out at all these people dancing and having fun . . . and I miss my wife. Is that so wrong?”

She was quiet for another beat. “No.” She spoke so softly that I pressed my ear closer to pick up her words. “That’s the first time you’ve called me your wife.”

“Then I’ve been an idiot.” There was a shout from inside, and I realized the band must be ready to go on. “Listen, Rilla, I need to go introduce the band. I’ll be late tonight, so I’ll see you in the morning, okay?”

“Okay. Good night, Mason.” She sounded wistful, and I wanted to keep talking to her. Say more. But there wasn’t any time right now. I ended the call and slid my phone back into my pocket before I went inside to do my job.

As I’d predicted, I didn’t leave the club until nearly three. The house was silent when I went inside and climbed the steps. I opened the door to Piper’s room and glanced inside, smiling when I saw her spread out over the bed, arms wide and head thrown back as she snored. Drawing the door closed softly, I headed down the hall to my own room, pausing as I passed Rilla’s door.

Nothing had really changed in the few days since we’d become husband and wife. Rilla still slept in the guest room, and between Piper’s cold and my work, we hadn’t had more than a few passing minutes here and there.

I eased open her door and leaned inside, hoping that maybe she was still awake. No light burned in her room, though; I could just barely make out her curled form under the covers.

Her hair shone, and I had to fight the urge to go inside, pull her against me and run my fingers through the tangles.

I closed the door and went into my own lonely room. And although I was tired to the point of exhaustion, I took a cold shower before I slid between the sheets.

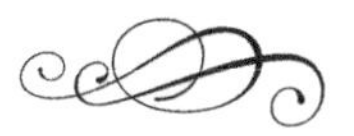

I woke the next morning as I did most Sundays: with Piper pulling at my eyes and whispering into my ear. I groaned as I rolled over, grabbing blindly at her small body to make sure I didn't knock her off the bed.

"Wake up, Daddy! Rilla and I made waffles. They're gonna get cold."

I pushed to sit up a little, blinking as I tried to clear my head. "Okay, princess. Give me a minute here."

"Piper Susannah." A voice in the doorway startled me into alertness. "Didn't I tell you not to bother Daddy yet? He worked late last night. He needs his sleep."

I laughed. "You might as well give that up, darlin.' Piper just can't help herself when it comes to my sleep."

"Hmmm." Rilla leaned against the door jam and crossed her arms. I narrowed my eyes a little more, taking her in.

"Well, lookit who's wearing shorts today. Lookin' good, honey." And I wasn't lying. Who knew such a petite little thing could have such long legs? I had a sudden flash of those legs wrapped my body, and I had to adjust the sheet to cover my obvious interest.

Rilla flushed. "Thanks. They don't look too short, do they?" She glanced down at her own legs as though surprised they were there.

"Not a bit. Don't worry, sweetness, those aren't Daisy Dukes." I winked at her, and Rilla laughed.

"Daddy, what're Daisy Dukes?" Piper held my face in her

hands to get my attention.

"Nothing you'll ever wear, baby girl." Rilla pushed away from the door and came into my room to scoop my daughter from the bed. "C'mon. Let's go downstairs and set the table for breakfast so Daddy can get dressed."

She'd just turned her back to me when I snagged her hand. She looked down at me, one eyebrow raised.

"You really do look good, Rilla. You look pretty." I rubbed my thumb over the back of her hand, and she shivered.

"Thank you, Mason." She stood still for a minute before easing her hand away as my two girls headed downstairs.

Sundays were usually pretty laid-back for me. I went into the club about midday, just to check on things, but I was home in time for dinner, even with a quick stop at the hospital to visit with Mom.

Rilla had made spaghetti, and the three of us devoured it, sitting around the table. I watched Rilla as she moved deftly around my kitchen, and again I had the sense of her belonging. I might've thought that meant I only appreciated her cooking, but the truth was, I'd had that same feeling this morning as she stood next to my bed, holding my child. Rilla was part of my life. I wanted her to stay that way.

I took over Piper bathing duty so Rilla could clean up from dinner. I read my daughter two stories, tucked her in and said good night. I'd just clicked off the overhead lamp when she called to me.

"Daddy."

"Yeah, princess. What do you need?"

"Is Rilla my mama now?"

I hesitated, frozen in the doorway. "Uh, why are you asking, honey?"

"She lives with us, and she loves us, and she takes care of me. Doesn't that make her my mama?"

"Princess, you know who your mother is. You have her picture right on your dresser." I glanced over to where the frame sat, but the dark obscured Lu's laughing face.

"Yeah, but she's my in-heaven-mama. I need a mama down here, too. Someone like Rilla. So I think she should be my here mama. Is that okay?"

I swallowed over the lump in my throat. It had been three years, and I'd thought I was done losing pieces of Lu. I thought that pain was over. But our daughter had just let go of another piece, something I hadn't even realized we'd both been clutching. Piper was releasing the idea of a mother she'd never known, so that she could embrace the woman who loved her here and now. I needed to let her do that.

"Of course it's okay, princess." I whispered the words. "Your mama—she'd want you to do that. I think she'd love Rilla, too."

"She does." Piper spoke with the calm assurance of her three years. "She asked God to send Rilla to us, so she can love us and we can love her."

"Oh, really?" I frowned. "Who told you that?"

I saw my daughter's small shoulders lift and fall. "Nobody. I just know. That's how it works, Daddy."

"Okay. You go to sleep now, you hear?"

"Yup." She yawned wide and snuggled back down under the blanket as I closed the door.

Downstairs, Rilla was folding a tea towel over the oven door handle. She looked up with a smile as I can into the room. "She's in bed?"

"Yeah, all set." I hooked my thumbs through my belt loops. "You need any help in here?"

"No, thanks. Everything's cleaned up, and the dishwasher's running." She pointed to the machine, as though I didn't know where it was. We both stood for a minute, neither of us sure what came next.

"Well, I guess I should—"

"Do you want to—"

We spoke simultaneously, and I laughed. "What were you saying?"

"No, nothing. What were you asking me?"

I leaned my hand on the counter. "Do you want to come sit with me in the living room? Watch some television?"

Rilla's eyes sparked interest, but I couldn't be sure if she were more interested in my company or the idea of watching TV. She'd been denied access to it growing up, and I'd found she was fascinated with the variety of shows on air. She was a little cautious about what she watched, but I'd caught her enjoying the cooking channel and public television.

"That sounds like fun. What do you want to watch?"

I bit back a grin as I followed her out of the kitchen. If everything went according to my plan, we weren't going to be really watching anything. But I answered as innocently as I could. "I like history documentaries, and there's one on tonight about the moon landing."

"Oh, cool!" Rilla dropped onto the love seat. "I love history."

I picked up the remote and sat down next to her, just close enough that I could feel the warmth of her body. Flipping around the channels until I came to the right station, I propped my feet onto the ottoman in front of us.

For the first ten minutes of the show, we were quiet, and I didn't move. When the first commercial came on, I decided it was time for one of my signature moves, one I hadn't used since I was in high school. I hoped I wasn't too rusty. This was a classic for a reason, but without finesse, I could screw it up.

Yawning, I stretched my arm over my head and then slowly . . . slowly draped it over the back of the love seat. I felt Rilla's silky hair against the crook of my elbow, but if she noticed, she didn't give any indication, except for the slightest twitch of her lips. I relaxed until my arm circled her shoulders and my fingers rested on her upper arm.

"You know, we didn't have a love seat like this growing up." I kept my voice light, just making small talk.

Rilla turned her head enough to glance at me out of the corner of her eye. "Oh, no?"

"Nah, we had this great big sofa. I loved it. It was the perfect make-out couch."

Now I had her attention. She shifted, not away from me but so that she could see me better. "You made out on your family sofa?"

"Oh, yeah. From about seventh grade on. I had moves, baby."

"Did you? Tell me about it. How would you get a girl on the famous make-out couch with you?"

I smirked. "It didn't take much. I'd just invite her to come over and watch TV with me."

Realization dawned in those gorgeous blue eyes. "Like maybe a history documentary?"

"Nah, in those days, it'd be music videos. And she'd get here . . . sit down with me . . . and I'd lead with my signature move. The old arm-stretch and side hold deal."

Rilla turned her head to deliberately look at my hand where it rested on her shoulder. "Uh huh. And then what?"

"Well, mostly, I'd just hold her this way for maybe a song or two. And then when I couldn't wait any longer, I'd go like this . . ." With my free hand, I reached to touch Rilla's chin, guiding her face to turn toward me. "And then . . . like . . . this."

With the slightest move, I closed the distance between our mouths and sealed mine to hers. Her lips were soft, warm, and oh thank God, welcoming. She made a small noise in the back of her throat and it went through me, igniting such want that I had to tense, hold myself back from forcing her down onto the sofa here and now.

Slow, dude. Take it slow. This is her first kiss. Make it worth remembering.

I slid my other hand, the one not holding her chin, to cup the back of her neck and ease her head to a better angle. She acquiesced, following my lead. I kissed the corners of her mouth and then put the slightest pressure on her chin, tugging it downward and coaxing her lips open. My tongue teased the seam of her lips, tracing and then darting forward to press insistently against small opening until she relaxed a little, letting me in.

I wanted to sweep my tongue into her mouth, but I held back, careful not to scare her. Instead, I touched the very tip to the inside of her lips, making a slow and sensuous line.

When Rilla lifted her hand to lay it alongside my cheek, I slid my fingers from her chin to cover her hand, threading our fingers together so that we could feel our mouths moving against each other. I let my tongue surge forward and stroke the inside of her mouth. She moaned a little and pressed closer to me.

The hand that wasn't linked with mine against her face moved tentatively to my back, rubbing languorous circles over my shirt. I itched for her slide her fingers underneath and touch my skin, but I wouldn't push. Not yet.

We kissed until neither of us could catch our breaths, but I never touched her anywhere else other than her neck and her face. My lips and my tongue explored every crevice of her mouth, and after a bit, her tongue ventured into my mouth. I sucked on it, and she startled, making me smile when she didn't pull back but stroked her tongue into my mouth again.

I didn't know how long we made out. I hadn't done anything like this—just necking with a girl, with no plan to move things along—in too many years for me to remember. There was something sweet and almost erotic about knowing we weren't going to take it any further than kissing.

Still, my body was beginning to rebel. I wasn't a fifteen-year old kid who'd never had sex; my cock had been trained to expect more after the hot and heavy kissing. I eased my lips away from Rilla's, dropping small caresses along her jaw and then leaning my forehead against hers.

"So," I whispered, staring into her luminous eyes. "Do I still have the moves or what?"

Rilla grinned. "I'm thinking yes. But then again, what do I know? That was my first kiss." Her breath fanned over my skin. "I think I might need a little more convincing."

I chuckled. "Sweetheart, I'd love to lay here all night convincing you, but I think we both need some sleep."

"Hmmmm." She let her eyes slide shut and laid her head against my shoulder. "I guess you're right. I might not agree with you tonight, but tomorrow when Piper wakes me up at six, I'll be thanking you."

"Oh, that reminds me." I brushed her hair over her shoulder, rubbing a few soft strands between my two fingers. "Piper asked me tonight if you were going to be her mama. She said her in-heaven mama asked God to send you to us."

Rilla pushed against my chest and sat up. "I didn't say anything to her, Mason. I promise. I would never, ever do that."

"Oh, darlin,' I know. She told me that's just the way things work. I wanted to give you a head's up in case she says something to you."

"Did it . . . did it upset you?"

I leaned back and blew out a long breath. "It's another tie cut with Lu. Logically, I know she's gone, but it feels like each time I move ahead, I'm letting her go all over again. As though I'm making the decision to do it."

"I'm sorry." Rilla touched my face. "I can't imagine what it must be like for you, to have someone you loved like you did her ripped away from you. But what I can relate to is how Piper feels. At least to a certain extent. It's true that Lu didn't choose to leave her baby, like my mom did, but neither of us remembers having a mother. I look at her little face, and I just want to give her all the love I wanted when I was her age."

I lifted Rilla's hand from where it lay on my arm and brought it my lips. "That's why you're perfect for her. I'm not upset at all, Rilla. If anything, it just makes me more grateful that you're in her life." I turned over her hand and pressed my mouth to her palm. "In our lives."

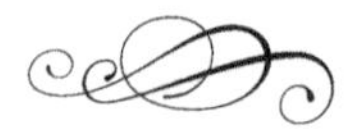

After that night, Rilla and I fell into a routine. Every night that I was home before midnight, she waited up for me, and we'd sit on the love seat, watching TV. I found a channel with old series from my childhood and introduced her to them. It was fun to watch her enjoy what I'd loved growing up.

"I don't understand why my church was so against television. It's funny, and some of the shows even have a decent moral lesson. And it's educational." Rilla was sitting against me, her legs draped over my lap and my arms around her. We were still moving slow. I'd found Rilla loved kissing, and she let me touch her back, her legs, her arms . . . I was dying to slide my hands under her shirt, and maybe even unzip her jeans, but I didn't want to spook her. Not until I was sure she was ready.

"Well, honey, I haven't shown you everything that's on here. There's just as much smut and violence and nastiness as your pastor probably said. You just have to be choosy about you watch." I ran my finger along the outer seam of her jeans where they clung to her thigh. "Plus, sometimes watching television can lead to activities some people consider wrong."

She tilted her head so that her hair tickled my neck. "Like . . . making out for hours? Kissing . . ." She touched her lips to a spot just under my jaw. "Touching . . ." She ran her hand over my chest. " . . . inappropriately?"

I caught her hand and held it tight. "I was thinking more about eating junk food and not exercising enough, but I like how your mind works, Mrs. Wallace."

Rilla giggled, and I watched for the soft glow that always covered her face when I referred to her as my wife or called her by her married name. It was, I mused, an amazing thing to watch her bloom. To blossom from the scared, shy little thing I'd met only a few months ago into a woman with confidence and spunk.

She'd had a few visits with Boomer and his family. The whole clan had come over for dinner one Sunday, much to Rilla's delight. She'd made a big fried chicken dinner and gotten to know her cousins, her aunt Tammie and Boomer's wife Millie. I'd loved watching her show off Piper to her family, and Piper drank up every minute of it, being fussed over and spoiled by a whole new crowd of people.

Sadly, Rilla still hadn't heard a word from her father or her grandmother. I wasn't surprised about Emmett Grant, but I'd expected more of his mother, from what Rilla had said about her. I was tempted at times to take a ride by their farm and have a little chat, but something held me back. Part of me wondered if Rilla didn't need this time to heal and grow, without any interference from two people who'd both loved her and bound her for the first two decades of her life.

I teased her that she had a busier social schedule than I did, and it was true. I'd given her my mom's car to drive for the time being, since Mom wasn't using it. She and Piper made frequent visits to the farm to hang out with Meghan and Sam. Piper even went along whenever Rilla wanted to work at the stand and I wasn't home. They'd had a lovely tea out with Mrs. Nelson when Rilla took Piper to see the Nelson horses again.

She continued to implement her promotion plan for the club, but she wouldn't let me pay her any more. When I'd protested, she'd stood up with her hands on her hips.

"Mason, I'm your wife, right?"

"Seems that way."

"And what's yours is mine?"

I smirked. "You want half ownership of the bar, baby? The bar you're still afraid to actually come visit after four o'clock in the afternoon?"

"You're getting off topic. Answer my question."

I groaned. "Okay, yes. Technically, you're an owner of the bar."

"So I don't get paid for doing work for *our* business."

I couldn't argue with her logic, so I just laughed and kissed her until she stopped fussing at me.

She'd taken on Boomer as a client, too, and I'd heard the mechanic bragging to anyone who'd listen that his niece had made him a website. I wasn't sure how much business it brought the auto repair shop, but it made both Boomer and Rilla happy.

And of course, as long as everyone was healthy, Rilla and Piper went to see my mom in the hospital as often as they could. It was where they'd been planning to go one Friday afternoon after Rilla and I had been married for about a month. I was finishing up at the bar, going over some deliveries and receipts before I left for the evening.

"I think that's it, boss." Rocky set down a case of beer. "I've got it here. You can head on home to that pretty wife." He winked at me. Rocky never failed to tease me about my abrupt marriage, crowing his I-told-you-sos until I threatened to fire him.

"Yeah, I'm heading out. Rilla and Piper went to see my mom today, and I want to hear how it went."

"How's she doing? Any good news?"

I shrugged. "She's had a few set-backs, but nothing the doctors didn't expect, I guess. They haven't given us a date for her release yet. Her immune system has to recover, but the doctors can't rush it, or she could have problems with rejecting my stem cells."

"I still think that's freaky, man. So you gave your mother

your stem cells . . . and it's going to heal her?"

I laughed. "Yeah, the marvels of modern medicine, huh? You know, once the new marrow takes over, her blood type will actually change to what mine is. The doctors even said they've known cases where the person getting the new stem cells has all new food likes and dislikes. Crazy, isn't it?"

"No shit. So did it hurt when you gave it?" Rocky eyed me with interest.

I shrugged. "Nope. No more than giving blood. They just set me up with one set of tubes taking blood and another giving it back. The blood went through a machine that separated the stem cells from the rest of the blood."

"Pretty amazing that you could do that for your mom, huh? She gave you life. Now you gave it back." He clapped me on the back.

"That's right." I stepped out from behind the bar. "Now cross your fingers it takes and she doesn't reject it. That's the battle now."

Rocky nodded. "I got her on my church's prayer chain. Our pastor always says, you need prayer, you get the old ladies on it. And we got lots of old ladies on our prayer chain."

"Every little bit helps." I paused. "Rocky, where do y'all go to church?"

"Ah, First Methodist on Barnam Street."

"Can I ask you something? At your church, do they let the kids date? And are y'all allowed to watch TV?"

Rocky squinted at me. "Yeah. The kids date, and man, they better not tell me I can't watch baseball. Why?'

I shook my head. "Nothing. Just the church Rilla grew up going to—it's really strict. I think she'd like to find some place to go in town, but I don't want her getting mixed up in another bad situation, you know?"

Rocky nodded. "Burton Community, right? Yeah, we hear things. We get people coming to our church who left that one, saying it was a little too much." He lifted one shoulder. "Hey, listen, to each his own. But if Rilla ever wants to come with us, just have her call my wife. We'd love to have her." He winked at me. "You too, boss. If they let a guy like me in, they might even bend the rules enough for a dude like you."

I laughed. "That's true enough. Okay, I'm out of here. See you tomorrow."

Driving home, I considered what Rocky had said. It didn't surprise me that Burton Community Church had a reputation. It blew my mind that in this day and age, Rilla had grown up so protected and sheltered. As a father, I understood the desire to keep my daughter safe at any cost, but I couldn't imagine stunting her emotional growth like that. It was almost miraculous that Rilla had turned out as well as she had.

I turned into the driveway and climbed out of the truck. It had been a long day—a long week—and I was ready to eat dinner, put my daughter to bed, and have a little necking session with my wife. Maybe tonight I'd get my hands under her shirt. The thought of touching her breasts, maybe making her moan under me while I covered them with my lips, put a smile on my face, even if it made my jeans a little less comfortable.

I opened the kitchen door, sniffing in appreciation. Meatloaf. But although dinner was clearly underway, Rilla and Piper were nowhere to be seen. I was about to call their names when I heard music coming from down the hall.

Following the sound, I headed for my mother's room, where the unmistakable lyrics and tune of *Come on, Eileen* were blasting. I glanced into the room and then did a double take.

Rilla was dancing. She had the music turned up loud, and she was swinging her hips in time with it. Those jeans that had been making me hot and bothered for quite a while clung to her ass as she shook it. And she was singing along.

I was a musician, and even more, I had the gift of recognizing musical talent. It had been my job in Nashville, and I was damned good at it. I'd heard the magic in Lu's voice the first time we met. It had been a big part of falling in love with her.

Rilla didn't have talent. She didn't sing badly, but she was barely on key. She wasn't going to win any talent contests, and she'd never be signing a recording contract. But all the same, the sound of her belting out those words, some of which she got horribly wrong, was one of the most beautiful sounds I'd ever heard.

She was singing with such joy and abandon. And she was dancing with the same freedom. My pretty girl had never looked more beautiful to me.

I didn't want to stop her, but neither did I want to startle her. I was about to turn around and sneak away, wait in the kitchen until the song was over, when she turned in mid-dance and spotted me.

My goal to not startle her went out the window, as her hand flew to her chest and her eyes grew wide. She recovered quickly and moved toward the music blaster where she hit a button to turn off the song.

"Oh my gosh, you scared me to death. How long were you standing there?"

I shrugged. "Not long. I just got home." I let my eyes wander up from her jeans to the green shirt that gave me a tantalizing hint of the boobs beneath. "Come here." But before she could move, I took two long steps forward and pulled her against me. The difference in our height didn't come into play during our evenings on the sofa, but now it did. Her face, turned up to mine, barely skimmed my chest. To kiss her I'd have to hunch over. I solved that problem by hooking my arms beneath hers and lifting her to me.

Almost as though she'd done this a million times, Rilla wrapped her legs around my waist, clasped her hands behind my neck and pulled my face down to hers. She kissed me, open-mouthed and eager, and I wanted her more than I wanted my next breath.

I threaded my fingers through her hair and moved my head, frantic to get even closer. I consumed her mouth, swallowing the moans that were coming out of her, and letting my tongue cover every part of her I could reach. The hand that wasn't buried in her hair skimmed down her back to cup her ass, finally getting to massage what had been tempting me for so long.

I walked blindly out of the room, down the hall and into the living room, where I pushed Rilla against the wall and slid my hand out of her hair and down over her ribs. I wanted to get to her tits, but she was pressed so hard against me, I couldn't get my hand between us.

She was still kissing me, but now she was moving against me, too, rubbing her core into my abs. I was just considering—in the small part of my brain still capable of thought—whether I should try to make it upstairs to my bedroom or just fall onto the sofa on top of her—when Rilla lifted her head.

"Mason—phone. Your phone is ringing."

She was right. I could hear it as though from a distance, and I swore under my breath. "Ignore it."

"But—" She placed an open-mouthed kiss on my neck. "Your mom. You have to answer it. Could . . . be . . . the hospital."

"Shit." I stepped back and dug into my pocket for my phone. I answered without even looking at the caller ID. "What?"

"Mason?" Rocky's voice sounded strained.

"Yeah, Rocky, what's up?" I tried not to sound like I could've murdered him for interrupting.

"I'm at the hospital. Lacey—my oldest—started getting really sick, and we brought her to the ER. They think it's her appendix. They're prepping her for surgery."

"Oh my God, Rocky. You okay?"

"You know how it is with your kids. Scary stuff. I'm so

damned sorry to do this to you, but I can't cover tonight. I can't leave Carey here to handle it herself, and I want to be with Lacey when she comes out."

"Of course. No worries, Rocky. I got this." I struggled to get my mind back into the game. "Listen, you need anything? What can we do?"

"Just prayers. I got to go now, but I'll text you as soon as we have news, okay?"

"Absolutely." I ended the call and blew out a breath.

"What's wrong?" Rilla touched my arm. "Something with Rocky?"

"Yeah." I swallowed down frustration. "His daughter's in the hospital. They think appendix."

"Oh, no. Is she okay? What can we do?"

"Sounds like they have it under control, but I have to go in tonight and cover Rocky's hours at the bar. I'm sorry, honey."

"It's okay." I saw the disappointment in her eyes before she hid it, and it gave me a burst of gladness to know I wasn't the only one feeling that way. I kissed her lightly on the lips. "I need to get moving. Hey, where's the rugrat? I was on my way to look for the two of you when a certain vixen lured me into kissing her against the wall."

Rilla flushed, but there was a smile on her face. "She fell asleep on our way home from the hospital, and I carried her upstairs. Then I thought I'd clean up Naomi's room. Meghan's been giving me songs to check out, since I'm clueless about any music that wasn't played in church. So I turned on the playlist she gave me, and then you were there . . . I'm sorry, Mason, I didn't think. She could've walked in on us."

I laughed. "Honey, first of all, I started that, not you. Second, it doesn't hurt a kid to walk in and see her parents making out. Kissing. And third, she didn't wake up, so don't worry." I brushed the backs of my fingers over her cheek. "My only question is, why were you listening to that song and not some good old country music?"

Rilla rolled her eyes. "I knew you were going to say that. Meghan says I need to stretch my boundaries, and that you'll only expose me to country." She held up one hand. "I know, I know. According to you, that's the only good music around. But don't you want me to be well-rounded?" She widened her eyes, trying to look innocent, and I couldn't help laughing.

"I'm pretty sure I just gave you a taste of how much I appreciate your, uh, well-roundedness." I reached around to pinch her lightly on the ass, making her squeal as her face went even redder. She was so fucking adorable sometimes. I tugged her toward me again, brushing my lips across hers. "Hey, I have an idea. Why don't you come over to the club tonight? It's Friday, so it'll be busy but not insane—no band tonight. You can dance, or you can just sit up at the bar and hang out with me."

Interest warred with worry in her eyes. "What about Piper?"

"Well, you could call one of Boomer's daughters to babysit, or see if Meghan might want to come over for a little while. I don't know, it was just a thought." I kissed her again. "I might be late, though. So I'll see you in the morning if you don't make it over." I headed for the door. "Oh, and Rilla? Even if Piper had walked in on us . . . it was totally worth it."

I winked at her and left, whistling.

Chapter Thirteen

Rilla

PIPER WOKE UP, CRANKY and disoriented after her late nap. I soothed her, gave her time and space to adjust and then made her macaroni and cheese for dinner.

While she ate, I called Meghan.

"Hey, Rilla! How's it going?"

"I'm good. Are you eating dinner?"

"Nah. Sam had a special Guild meeting tonight, so I'm just sitting at home. What's up?"

I chewed the corner of my lip. "Mason had to go into the club to work tonight at the last minute—Rocky's daughter is getting her appendix removed. He asked me to stop in for a little while." I paused. "I was thinking about it."

"You need a babysitter? Sure, I can either drive into town or you can bring her in to spend the night on the farm. You could have a romantic evening. If you're thinking about a romantic evening, that is."

I grinned. Meghan had become a good friend indeed. She hadn't even blinked last month, when I'd announced that Mason and I were getting married. She'd been nothing but supportive ever since.

"I'm not saying I don't want a romantic evening, but actually, I have a babysitter. My cousin Jenna's coming over to sit with her. I was going to ask you to come with me."

"On your date?" Meghan sounded amused. "With your husband?"

"I was thinking, Mason's going to be working, and I don't want him to have to worry about me. If you were there with me, he could relax." I hesitated. "I've never done anything like this before, Meghan. I went to The Road Block once, during lunch hours, and even then I was a nervous wreck. I need some support."

"Then you came to the right girl. I've got history at that club, you know. Get dressed, sweetie. I'll be by to pick you up in an hour."

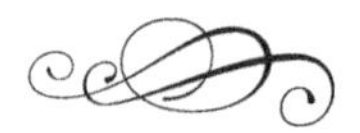

"Rilla Grant—uh, Wallace, you look hot, girl!" Meghan stood in the kitchen with her hands on her hip. "Wait a second, I promised Ali I'd take a picture of you. She called me on the way over here." Meghan held up her phone. "Strike a pose, lady."

I laughed and stood with one hip jutting out, a serious expression on my face, and then crossed my eyes and stuck out my tongue. Meghan snapped away.

I hadn't been sure what to wear tonight, but then I remembered a dress Meghan had insisted I buy during our shopping trip. I'd argued that I wouldn't have any place to wear it, but Meghan had been adamant. Now I was glad I'd listened.

The dress was a deep blue, a shade that matched my eyes. It was made of a light material that hung on my body, accenting curves I'd been hiding my whole life. The hemline hit just above my knees, showing enough of my leg to make me nervous at the time we'd bought it, but I was more used to the idea now.

And the skirt of the dress was the reason I loved it. It swirled, dancing around my body when I moved. It made me feel glamorous and pretty, and as soon as I'd opened my closet tonight, I'd known it was the perfect dancing dress.

"Okay, let's get moving. I can't wait to see the expression on Mason's face when he gets a look at you."

I rolled my eyes at Meghan and turned to kiss Piper's cheek, smoothing her hair. "Okay, sweetie, I'm going to go see Daddy for a little bit. Be good for Jenna."

"Aw, don't worry about us." Jenna, Boomer's youngest daughter, was a senior in high school and apparently one of the most in-demand babysitters in town. I'd been lucky to get her for this last minute job. "We're going to be fine."

"Have fun, Mama!" Piper leaned over Jenna's phone, absorbed in the game she was playing, oblivious to the fact that she'd just made my heart stop.

I bent over, brushing her hair out of the way, and kissed her cheek. "I love you, baby girl."

"Love you, too."

I followed Meghan to her car. Once we were on the road, she cleared her throat.

"Well, that's one way to turn on the water works, huh? Since when does Piper call you mama?"

"That was the first time." I was too shocked to cry.

"God, kids. They can just wrap you up, can't they?" She sniffled. "Rilla, you know, I look at you and I just can't believe everything that's changed since I first saw you at the stand last spring. You're a different person. You're not timid anymore. You're not closed off. It's a beautiful thing."

I flushed. "I'd still be that same person if it wasn't for you and Sam. And Ali. You all gave me a chance, and if you hadn't, I'd still be living with my father, miserable and alone."

"Rilla, we gave you an opening, but you did the hard work. You made the tough decisions. You made some choices that made the difference. Sam and I are proud of you." She reached across to squeeze my hand. "And we're so happy for you and Mason."

I sighed. "I'm not sure exactly what Mason and I are." I'd been honest with Meghan from the beginning about why we'd gotten married. "Sometimes I think he might really care for me, and then others, I remember what he said about Lu."

"Sweetie, you might be a little bit older than me, but let me give you some advice. Men are idiots. They don't know what they mean. Sometimes they don't know what they want. When Sam met me the first time, he hated me. When he met me the second time, he yelled at me."

My eyes got wide. "Sam did that?" The man worshipped not only the ground Meghan walked on, but also the flowers that grew there. "What happened the third time he met you?"

She smiled. "I moved into his house, and we fell in love. Well, not just like that. First he had to tell me how he was too old for me, how he had no time for a relationship, how we couldn't ever be serious. But finally, once I left town, he came to his senses and realized the truth of the matter. That he was an idiot and he loved me."

"So romantic," I murmured.

"Yeah, he's lucky I loved his idiotic ass right back. But I'm just saying, Mason might have himself convinced that he can never love another woman after Lu. That doesn't mean it's the truth. Rilla, the way he looks at you—sometimes I'm afraid you're going to burst into flames, it's so hot. Like he could unwrap you and devour you in one sitting."

"I hope you're right." I shifted in the seat and took a deep breath. "Because Meghan, I'm pretty sure I'm in love with him.

And I don't know what I'll do if he doesn't love me back, at least a little."

Meghan didn't appear the least bit surprised by my revelation. "Of course you're in love with him. I've seen it on your face almost since the beginning. Don't worry so much. It's all going to be all right."

I rubbed my hand down the skirt of my dress and prayed she was right. I figured praying for my husband to fall in love with me was something God could get behind.

The Road Block was lit up and full when we pulled into the lot. Meghan maneuvered around until we lucked upon someone leaving a spot in the front. She parked the car, and we joined the groups of people heading inside.

My stomach turned over. I was about to go into a club. A bar. A place where they served alcohol and encouraged men and women who weren't related to dance with each other. If my father knew, he'd flip out.

Pull it together, Rilla. I spoke to myself sternly. *You've done so much in the past months. You're grown-up. A married woman. Piper called you mama tonight. You're old enough to go into a bar—one that your husband owns, for criminey's sake—and hold your head up high. You're not doing anything wrong. Be the woman Mason and Meghan think you are. Be brave.*

I took a deep breath and determined to do just that.

The Road Block looked completely different after dark. The lights were low, and the entire place was chock fill with people. They surrounded the bar, two and three deep. On the other side of the huge room were the tables where I'd sat with Mason that first day here, and beyond that, a huge dance floor. A man was set up at a table with equipment, playing music, and on the floor, everyone was dancing.

Meghan held onto my arm. "Let's go to the bar first, so you can say hello to Mason. Then we can get a table if you want."

She had to shout so that I could hear her.

I nodded, and together we pushed our way through to the oak bar. I spotted Mason right away, pouring drinks and leaning over to hear customers. Darcy was covering the other end and looked just as busy. She caught sight of me first, and a broad smile spread over her face. She tugged on Mason's sleeve and pointed toward Meghan and me as we made it the last few feet to the barstools.

Mason's eyes searched the crowd, and when he found me, his face lit up. I always thought that was a figure of speech, but with Mason, it was literal. His eyes brightened and his mouth curled into a grin. His expression lit a fire deep within me, and I felt like I glowed, too.

I managed to wedge my small body between two stools where both occupants were facing opposite directions. Mason met me there, folding himself over the polished oak and taking my face in his hands. His kiss was hard and hot. I was pretty sure I would've melted right there if I didn't have the crush of other bodies holding me upright.

"Hey, baby." He rubbed his thumbs over my cheeks. "You came."

I nodded. My heart was still pounding too hard to speak coherently.

"And you brought a partner in crime. Hey, Miss Meghan. You going to give me your credit card up front so you can get hammered?"

Meghan threw back her head and howled with laughter. "I can't believe you remember that, Mason. Yeah, I thought I'd come to a backwater bar that night to get wasted and forget my troubles. Didn't think I'd ever come back to this place again." She held up her left hand, where Sam's diamond sparkled. "And look at me now. Stuck here but good."

Mason chuckled and shook his head. Down the line, people were shouting for his attention. I watched his chest rise and fall in a sigh. "You okay, darlin,' while I work?"

"Yes." I shouted the word, cupping my hands around my mouth. "That's why I brought Meghan." I pointed to the other side of the room. "I think we're going to try to find a table."

Mason followed my gesture and nodded. "If you can't find an empty one, tell one of the wait staff. They'll set something up for you." He glanced at the crowd. "I'll try to come over and see you in a little bit."

I shook my head. "You work. I'll be fine." I summoned up my bravery and blew him a kiss. He raised one eyebrow and shot me the smolder.

Oh, Lord. I was a goner.

Meghan and I pushed and shoved our way through to the other side of the room. I didn't know how Mason did it, but as soon as we got to the edge of the dance floor, which was surrounded by round tables of various sizes, a girl in a wait staff uniform tapped me on the arm.

"Are you Rilla?"

When I nodded, she motioned. "Hi, I'm Andrea. Come this way. We have a table for you."

I glanced at Meghan who waggled her brows at me as we followed the waitress to a table for two, right off the dance floor. When we were seated, Andrea leaned over to speak to us again.

"Mason says you should stay here so you don't lose the table. And I should get you whatever you want to drink. What'll it be?"

Meghan grinned. "I'm designated driver, so I'll have one beer and then switch to ice tea. Tell Mason the stout he made me try last week, okay?"

Andrea nodded and looked at me. I shook my head and shrugged helplessly, looking at Meghan. My friend laughed.

"Bring Rilla a margarita. Tell her husband to go easy on the tequila."

When Andrea had vanished into the crowd, Meghan leaned

to speak to me. “You’ll like that. It’s light and refreshing.”

I nibbled on the edge of my thumb. “Meghan, I’ve never had anything alcoholic. Will I get drunk?”

She smirked. “Not on just one, sweetie. And not if you drink it slow.”

I shifted in my chair to see the dance floor. I’d expected writhing bodies, not unlike the woodcarving depicting Hell that I’d seen in one of my father’s books. But this was nothing like that. There were couples of all ages dancing to the slow song. I smiled as a woman with snow white hair gazed up into the eyes of her partner. What shone on her face was the same thing I’d seen between Meghan and Sam, and Ali and Flynn. And heck, I’d even seen it between Alex and his boyfriend Cal, though I was still trying to work out exactly how I felt about that relationship.

Andrea returned with our drinks and a red card on a long silver stand. Black letters on the paper spelled out *VIP Reserved.*

“Mason says to leave this on your table, so you can get up to dance if you want.”

I smiled my thanks as the waitress hurried off again. Meghan lifted her bottle in my direction, and I raised my glass. It was filled a pretty yellow-green liquid, rimmed with salt and topped with a lime.

“To the idiocy and adorableness of the men we love. Cheers!” We clinked, and while Meghan tipped back the bottle, I took a cautious sip of my drink.

It was good. A little sour, but not so much that I didn’t like it. I took a longer drink.

“Remember what I said. Take it slow.” Meghan put her hand on my arm, and I set down the glass. The coolness of the liquid trickled down my throat, and I waited to feel drunk. When nothing happened right away, I began to relax.

The music changed from a ballad to something faster that had the crowd roaring.

"Ooooh, I love this one! Let's dance." Meghan grabbed my hand. I would've protested, but she was already dragging me out onto the dance floor and begun moving in time with the music.

For the space of several heartbeats, I panicked. Self-conscious doubt attacked me. *I couldn't dance, not in front of people. Not where everyone could see.*

Meghan took both my hands in hers and pulled me a little closer. "It's okay, Rilla. Everyone's here to have fun. No one's going to judge you. C'mon. This song is so much fun." She started to dance, keeping hold of my hands as she turned and twisted, and slowly, the panic dissolved. I even managed to smile as I tried to follow her lead, laughing when we ended up stepping on each other or on other dancers.

Within a few minutes, the music had seeped under my last bit of doubt, and I was dancing as though I'd been born on the dance floor. The music was bright and upbeat, and I loved how happy everyone seemed. Some sang along, others just danced, but they were all having a good time. This didn't feel wrong. It didn't feel like sin.

After five or six fast songs, the DJ announced he was slowing us down for the next number. Meghan pointed back to the table, and I nodded. I was hot and thirsty, more than ready to enjoy a little more of my margarita.

Before I made it back to our seats, a tall, thin guy in a black cowboy hat stepped in front of me. He smiled down into my face and laid his hand on my bare arm. I frowned.

He bent over to speak into my ear. "Hey. Want to dance?"

I opened my mouth to say no. I didn't want to dance with anyone but Mason, and I knew he was too busy. I hesitated, only because I wasn't sure how to turn down the cowboy without being rude.

"Um, actually, I was just going back to my table with my friend." I fanned my hand in front of my face and forced a laugh. “Dancing’s hot work.”

“Yeah.” He let his gaze slide down my body. I’d caught Mason doing this to me often, and it always made me feel beautiful, but this time, with this man . . . I felt ashamed. I wanted to cross my arms over my chest and tug down the skirt of my dress so that it covered more of my legs.

“Excuse me.” A warm, familiar hand closed over my hip and pulled me back against a hard body. “I’m going to dance with my wife.”

The cowboy’s eyes widened, and he backed up, holding his hands before him. “Aw, no problem here, man. Mason. Sorry, I didn’t know. Didn’t know she was yours.” He melted back into the crowd.

I lifted my head to look up at Mason. “Thanks for the rescue. I was doing okay, though. I just didn’t want to be rude to him.”

“Sometimes with guys like that, rude is all they understand.” Mason growled the words into my ear, and I shivered. The hand on my hip moved, rubbing gently over the soft material of my dress, while his other hand drew a line down the goose-bumped skin on my arm.

“As long as I’m out here, will you dance with me?” He touched his lips to a spot just below my earlobe.

I turned in his arms to face him. “I’ve never slow danced before, Mason.”

He smiled down, bringing his hands to cup my face. “There’s nothing to it, darlin.’ All you have to do is let me hold you, and follow my lead. Trust me?”

I let my lips curve upwards. “Well, you haven’t steered me wrong yet. I guess I’ll give it a try.”

Mason skimmed his fingers down my arms to grip my wrists and bring my hands to the back of his neck. He linked his hands together at my lower back, pulling so close that I could feel every inch of his body.

"I didn't get a chance to tell you before, Rilla, but you look gorgeous tonight. I was watching you dance out here with Meghan. You're the most beautiful woman here."

I bowed my head into his chest, happy that I'd let Meghan talk me into the heels I was wearing. They brought me up so that my head at least reached Mason's chin.

The music surrounded us, singing soft and gentle words about staying forever, and swaying on the dance floor, with Mason's arms tight around me, staying forever sounded like a mighty fine idea.

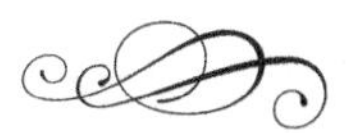

Meghan left The Road Block around eleven-thirty. Sam was on his way home, and she wanted to be there when he arrived. I planned to leave with her, but when I told Mason I was going, he took my hand.

"Why don't you stay just a little bit? I'm not too far from wrapping up here. Darcy's going to cover closing for me, and the crowd's thinned out quite a bit." It was true; the room was not nearly as full now as it had been even an hour ago. "You can ride home with me. Is Jenna okay staying a little longer?"

I nodded and held up my cell phone. "I texted her a few minutes ago. Piper's in bed, and Jenna said not to rush."

"There you go then." Mason had come out from behind the bar and was leaning against it. He winked at Meghan and gave her a quick hug. "Thanks for bringing my girl over. I'm glad you two had fun."

"Hey, any time I get treated like a VIP at a dance club, I have no complaints." Meghan laughed. "It's good to have friends in high places."

"You're always a VIP in my book." Mason patted her back. "Tell that man of yours he better get his ass in here for a beer soon. I haven't seen him in too long."

"That's 'cause he's got something good at home." Meghan grinned. "But we'll try to stop in on one of your slower nights." She turned and hugged me. "Night, Rilla. See you this week."

I boosted myself up on a barstool and settled down to watch Mason work. He and Darcy were huddled in a far corner of the bar, discussing the schedule. Next to me, two women who looked to be a couple of years older than me made themselves at home, leaning on the bar. The taller of the two wore a shirt so tight and low-cut that I could see most of her breasts. It made me very uncomfortable, and I looked away.

"Is that him? The hot bartender?" The shorter woman spoke in a low voice. "God, he's yummy. I'd let him do me."

"You know it. Seven ways to Sunday." Tall and low-cut sighed. "Wonder if we can get his attention." She straightened a little. "Hey! Bartender!"

Mason looked up from the form he'd been showing Darcy. He gave the two women a barely-there glance before returning to his conversation.

"Well, hell. Why's he so stand-offish?" The short woman pouted.

I wanted to be anywhere but here, listening to these two women talking about Mason. I was torn between keeping my mouth shut and saying something. I didn't want to embarrass them or me. Then again, I'd want to know if I were making a fool of myself over some man while his wife sat next to me.

"Excuse me." I kept my tone pleasant. "Were you trying to get my husband's attention? Did you need a drink?"

Both of their faces went utterly blank. Short girl's mouth dropped open.

Before they could answer me, Mason finished what he was doing and ambled down the bar to me. I smiled up at him.

"Mason, I think these two ladies were hoping to get something to drink." I hesitated just the slightest bit over the word "ladies." He raised one eyebrow and grinned.

"Sorry about that . . . ladies. I was just wrapping things up so I can take my wife home, but I'm sure Darcy can help you with a drink order." He came around to my side of the bar and lifted me from the barstool, letting his hands linger on my ribs just a little longer than necessary. "You ready to go home, Rilla?"

We both called good night to Darcy as we left. I held it together until we cleared the doors, but once we were outside, I couldn't help laughing. "I'm sorry, Mason. I probably should've kept my mouth shut, but they were just being so . . ." I shuddered. "So crass in how they talked about you. Why do women do that?"

Mason shrugged. "Too many reasons to think about tonight. Don't worry about it, darlin.' I've been fending off women since I was sixteen years old. But I do appreciate you taking up for me."

"Hmmm." I let him take my hand and lead me around the side of the building toward the back. His truck was parked in a dark section, away from the other cars.

"You know what I was thinking inside, Rilla?" Mason brought our joined hands to his mouth and kissed the back of my fingers. "I was thinking that I've shown you my sofa moves so far. But you haven't seen my car moves yet."

"Car moves?" I stood to the side as he unlocked the passenger door of the truck.

"Yup. Well, in this case, they're truck moves. But same principle." He opened my door and offered his hand again. "May I help you in?"

I glanced at him. Mason always helped me into the truck. I wondered why he would be asking about it now. "Why, certainly you may, kind sir." I placed my hand in his and took a step toward the seat. Before I could raise my foot to the running board, Mason tugged my hand, bringing me flush against him. He blocked me in, so that my back was against the side of the seat and he covered my front. Slowly, he released my hand, rubbing up my arm to hold my face and lowering his mouth to mine.

His kiss was soft but insistent, and it made my heart skip a beat. His fingers spread out to cover my cheek, and his tongue urged my lips open. When I parted them, he made one thorough stroke within my mouth and sucked on my bottom lip.

While I was preoccupied with the magic his mouth was working, he brought his hands down to cup my backside, rubbing me there for a few seconds before he gripped me and lifted. I landed on the seat, with Mason standing between my legs.

"Those are some moves, mister." I took advantage of my rare height advantage to comb my fingers through his soft brown hair. "I'm impressed."

"Oh, baby, you haven't even begun to be impressed yet." He moved back, helping me swing my legs around to face front, and then shut my door behind me.

I was just reaching for my seatbelt when Mason slammed his own door. "Uh, uh, uh. Not yet." He crooked his finger at me. "Come here."

I turned my body to face him, hesitating. "Come where?"

Mason smirked, and I had a feeling I was missing a joke. "Crawl over here onto my lap."

I remembered driving home from our wedding, wanting to do just that but not understand why or how. I eased my skirt up a little higher so it wouldn't catch and rose up on my knees. Mason held my hips.

"Swing that leg over me. So we're facing each other. Good."

And then I was sitting on his lap, my back to the steering wheel and my front . . . well, it was touching Mason Wallace in some very intimate places. Between his legs, for example, where a hard ridge rubbed against the forbidden place between my legs. And the tips of my breasts were pressed into his chest.

"Don't get tense, Rilla. Trust me." Mason circled his hands around to knead my butt again before he ran them up my back, to the spot where the sleeves of my dress rested on my shoulders. Watching my face, he lowered the straps down my arms, baring my bra to his sight.

I'd known this was coming. I was sheltered, yes, but I'd also grown up with a pragmatic grandmother, who'd decided the human reproductive chapter in our homeschool science course wasn't thorough enough. She'd taught the rudiments of what went on between a man and a woman.

Plus I'd seen Mason staring at my breasts enough that I figured he was going to get around to wanting a better look sooner rather than later. I'd just never guessed it would be in the front seat of his pickup truck.

He skimmed his fingers over my ribs first, with each pass drawing closer and closer to the edge of my bra. Finally he palmed both breasts, exhaling a shaky breath when he did.

"You're beautiful, Rilla. Beautiful and perfect." He moved his thumbs so that they brushed over my nipples, and a shot fire erupted low within me. I heard a small, almost desperate sound and realized it was coming out of my own throat.

That noise seemed to unleash something in Mason. He half-growled, half-moaned and curled his fingers under the cup of my bra, pulling down so that I was exposed. Without waiting, he lowered his mouth to capture one aching tip.

I'd seen babies nursing before. For all the modesty enforced at church, mothers were encouraged to breastfeed, since it was the natural way to feed a child. I'd watch women holding conversations, each with a baby attached to a breast, and I'd wondered how they could do it. It looked painful.

But Mason's mouth on my nipple was anything but painful. It was the most exquisite form of pleasure I'd ever felt. Without thinking about it, I held his head to my breast, my breath coming in soft pants as he suckled and rolled the nipple between his tongue and the roof of his mouth. Meanwhile, his hand played with the other side, drawing it to a hard point.

When he lifted his head, Mason kissed me as he had earlier, hard and with intent. This was not the gentle, tentative touch of his lips. This one meant business. I returned his passion with my own, letting my tongue playing against his, sucking it into my mouth and tangling them together once again.

He broke off from my mouth and lowered his head to draw my other nipple between his lips. I arched my back, trying to give him more, and the movement rubbed the juncture of my legs to the ridge beneath Mason's fly. A bolt of pure and addictive pleasure made me cry out, and I couldn't help rocking again when I found that the movement only made me crave more.

"That's it, darlin.' Just like that. Does it feel good?" Mason spoke with my nipple still at his lips and the vibration only added to the building intensity. I gasped a terse answer to his question.

"Yes."

Mason laughed, but I was too intent to pay him any mind. He kept his mouth at my breasts, but he dropped his hands back to my hips, helping me find the rhythm my body needed. I gripped his shoulder, rubbing with more speed, racing toward something I didn't quite understand.

Mason groaned and bucked his hips up to mine, and the change in position pushed me over the edge of precipice I hadn't known I'd been climbing. I tensed as waves of ecstasy rolled through me. Between my legs, something pulsed and throbbed, gripping me in pleasure. I fell onto Mason, panting and covered in perspiration.

When I could speak again, I raised my eyes to Mason. "That was what they call a climax, right?" I remembered the word from Gram's basic teaching.

Mason's chest shook with laughter. "Oh, honey, I hope so."

He brushed a kiss over my tangled hair. "Because that was most beautiful, erotic thing I've ever seen."

"Was it okay? I'm sorry. I don't know what you wanted. I didn't know . . ." I kept my eyes on the buttons of his shirt. "I thought you could only do that during, you know . . . intercourse."

Mason rubbed small circles on my back. "No. You can come without having sex. I mean, without having full intercourse."

"Come?" I ventured a glance at him, my eyebrows raised.

"Yeah, it's slang, I guess. When you climax or have an orgasm, we say you come. And don't ask me why. I have no idea."

"Hmmm. Is it different for a man and a woman? When they . . . come?"

"In some ways, yes. I mean, in some obvious physiological differences, sure. As far as feeling, I couldn't tell you. I've never had an orgasm as a woman."

I giggled against his chest. "I guess not."

"Rilla?"

"Hmmm?"

"Did you like my truck moves?"

My lips curved into a smile. "I think I did. But I do have a question. Do truck moves only happen in the truck, or do they translate to the sofa, as well?"

"Well, that's a very good question." Mason pretended to ponder it. "I'd say they do. They might be even better on the sofa."

"I guess the only way to find out is to try it and see." I nuzzled his neck.

Mason sighed. "The things I'm willing to do for research. Okay, I guess if I must, I must. But not tonight. Tonight, I'm going to buckle you into your seat, drive home and we're both going to sleep. All experiments will have to wait until later." He lifted my face to his and kissed me. "But I promise, they'll all be worth the wait."

Chapter Fourteen

Mason

IT'D BEEN A BITCH of a day.

The first problem was that the day had begun too damn early. Four-thirty this morning, my cell phone, which I kept next to the bed with the ringer on while Mom was in the hospital, rang loud and shrill. I sprang awake and fumbled to hit the answer button.

It was the nurse at the hospital, telling me that my mother was running a fever and there was some concern that she'd either contracted some kind of infection or was rejecting the stem cells. Either way, they strongly suggested that I come in as soon as I could.

I jumped out of bed and took a fast shower before heading out. Pausing in the hallway, I opened the door to Rilla's room as quietly as I could. Still, she turned over in a rustle of sheets and comforter and sat up, blinking in the dim light from the hall.

"Mason?" she whispered. "Is everything okay? Piper—"

"She's fine. Still asleep. Hospital just called. Something's going on with Mom, so I'm going to run over there and see what's happened."

"Okay." She tugged the sheet a little higher over her breasts, which made me smile since by now, I was intimately familiar with that particular set of ta-tas. And they were magnificent. Not too big, which would've looked funny on her slim body, but enough to fill my hands, and God, were they responsive . . .

I gave my head a little shake. *Not the time, dude. Pull it together.* I couldn't stop myself from walking the rest of the way into the room and bending to frame her face in my hands, kissing those sweet lips. "I'll call you when I leave the hospital. Or I'll text you if I'm going to be there for a while. If it gets too late, I might just go right over to the club from the hospital."

"All right. Just keep me updated, okay?" Her voice was still husky with sleep, but I heard the worry. "And give Naomi my love. If you need me to come in with you, I can get Millie to watch Piper."

"I'll let you know." I smoothed my hand over her hair. "Go back to sleep now. You can probably get in another hour or two before the pip squeak wakes up."

With no little difficulty, I left her snuggled in bed and drove out of town, preoccupied with what I might find when I got to the hospital. My mother had sailed through the transplant process with relative ease, but the doctors had warned us that for several months after the procedure, she'd be at risk for infection, for picking up viruses and for the issues that accompanied rejection.

Mom was sitting up in bed eating toast when I arrived. She glanced at me with her eyebrow raised. "Well, good morning, son. What brings you in so bright and early?"

I sank into the ugly brown formaldehyde chair. "A nurse called this morning and said you were running a temp. They didn't know what was causing it, but they thought I should come in."

Mom waved one hand. "Oh, goodness. Yes, when they did their normal wake-me-up-to-check-me-out at three this morning, I had a slightly elevated temperature. The doctor's keeping his eye on it, but they don't think it's anything serious. They ran tests, and all my counts look good. Well, for a woman who's been through what I have, anyway."

"Good." I leaned over and snagged a corner of her wheat toast. "Well, since I'm here, I might as well have breakfast with you."

I enjoyed my time with Mom, catching her up on everything at The Road Block and making her laugh with some new Piper stories. She raved about how much she appreciated Rilla's frequent visits.

"She's just the sweetest thing, Mason. I know I was a little concerned about you marrying her, but things seem to be going well." She paused. "They are, aren't they? Rilla's seemed very content the last few weeks."

I nodded. "Yeah, Mom. It's all good. I wish she could settle things with her dad and her grandmother, but between us . . ." I couldn't help the smile that spread over my face as I thought about Rilla. "I'm happy. I think she is, too."

"That does my heart good, Mason. I've worried about you, since Lu. You're young, and you know the last thing she would've wanted was for you to mourn her forever. You deserve happiness. And love."

I was about to answer her when my phone went off again. This time, the number was unfamiliar.

"Hello, Mr. Wallace. This is Safety First Alarm Company, and we wanted to alert you to the fact that we received notice of a break-in at your place of business this morning."

I frowned. "A break in? Are the police there?"

"Sir, as a matter of course, we contact the police first and send them to the scene. They should be arriving shortly, if you'd like to meet them there."

Shit. All I wanted to do was go home and catch another hour of sleep. Maybe give in to temptation and climb into bed with Rilla. Just for a snuggle or two; things were still moving slowly during our evening television make-out sessions, but we hadn't been in bed together yet. Rilla was surprisingly adventurous for someone so inexperienced. I knew it was only a matter of time before neither of us could hold back anymore. But clearly that wasn't going to happen this morning.

When I arrived at the club, two police cars were in the lot, and an officer stood outside the front door. I slammed the door of my truck and stalked over to meet him.

"Hey, Mason." The cop, who I vaguely recognized as the brother of one of our waitresses, stuck out his hand. "Sorry to get you out of bed so early."

I didn't tell him he hadn't been the one to have that honor this morning. "No problem. What's going on?"

He smirked. "Well, it seems like your intruder triggered the motion detector. When we got here, we couldn't find any evidence of a break-in. However, we were able to apprehend the suspect red-handed. He was wearing a mask, which should count in the evidence against him."

I drew my brows together. "What the hell? Who broke in? What was he stealing?"

The door opened, nearly hitting me, and I stepped back out of the way. Another uniformed officer came out, followed by a man in coverall carrying some kind of cage.

"Mr. Wallace, meet your intruder." He lifted the cage, and the bright eyes of a huge raccoon stared out at me. "We caught him digging into your pretzel supply. I did a little poking around, and I didn't see any holes, anywhere he might've chewed his way in. Do you open the door to the supply room after dark?"

I nodded. "Yeah, it's been known to happen. And last

night, we had a late delivery. Truck had gotten held up out on 95, didn't get here until after seven. I know they had the door propped while they were unloading."

The first officer grinned. "That's likely what happened. Good news is, it didn't look like he got into the beer."

"Good to know. Last thing we need is a drunk raccoon running around." I glanced into the trap again. "What're you going to do with him?"

"Eh, he doesn't appear to be rabid. We'll test him just in case, but if he's clean, we'll release back into the wild." The second cop winked at me. "With a stern warning to change his ways, of course."

Once the police had left, along with animal control and the masked perp, I went into the club and got to work, cleaning up the mess the little fellow had made. He'd gone to town in the supply room, and it took a while to sweep up all the food and note what we needed to replace. By the time I was finished, it was after nine. I sighed, rubbing the back of my neck; I could go home, but I had to be right back here in about an hour to gear up for the lunch crowd. The early cooking crew would be arriving by then. It didn't make sense to make that drive.

Rocky was still on limited hours, since his daughter had had some complications and was having a slow recovery. I'd told him to take today and catch up on his rest, so that he could start back fresh tomorrow. Now I was regretting my generosity.

My phone buzzed in my pocket, and I gritted my teeth. "What now?" When I saw Rilla's pretty smile looking at me on the caller ID screen, I relaxed.

"Hey, darlin.' I'm sorry I didn't call or text. It's been a shit storm of a morning."

"Why? What happened? Is Naomi okay?"

I felt a stab of guilt for not updating her sooner. "Yeah, she's actually fine. I think it was a false alarm. But then, speaking of false alarms, I got called to the club because of a break-in. Turned out to just be a raccoon, but I've been here cleaning up after it. I just finished, but I don't think it makes sense to drive home."

"Yeah, I agree. Anything I can do to help?"

I smiled. I loved that no matter what, Rilla offered to lend a hand. "Nah, I'm good. I'm going to be late tonight, though." I paused. "I'll miss you. I'll miss our time on the sofa."

"Me, too. But you're off tomorrow, right? We're taking Piper out to the Nelson's."

"You know it, honey. Can't wait. Everything all right on the home front?"

"We're all good here. Do what you need to. Call me if I can do anything to help. I'll see you in the morning, I guess."

There was something so sweetly intimate about these meaningless little conversations between us. Nothing important or earth shattering; just mundane stuff that made the world go 'round. I'd forgotten how much I missed that. Rilla had a peace about her that centered me, calmed me. All the other shit going down in my life lost its importance when I was with her. I wasn't exactly ready to tackle what that might mean. For now, I was just happy to let it be.

My day continued much the way it'd begun. Half the wait staff called in sick, thanks to some bug going around. Our beer delivery was delayed. The band who was scheduled to play the next night was dealing with a broken down bus outside Charlotte and wasn't sure they'd make it in time for the show.

"When it rains, it pours." Darcy slid her tray onto the bar. "Got two kids over there trying to pass phony IDs. I turned them down, but do you want to call the parents?"

I sighed. We didn't get a lot of phony IDs here, unless they were kids from out of town. Burton was too small to get away with it. "Confiscate and threaten. If they give you any lip, send them over here to me and I'll put the fear of God into them."

"Yeah, they're morons. One of the dickheads is in my

daughter's class. He didn't think I'd recognize him? I'll take care of it."

I closed the doors at midnight and worked for another hour before I did one more walk-through to make sure we hadn't let in any unwanted guests. It was just after one when I set the alarms and locked up.

I'd been up for nearly twenty-one hours. My eyes were gritty with the need for sleep, and I rolled down the windows and blared the radio to stay awake until I got into town.

My house was quiet, but Rilla had left on the light over the kitchen door. Another burned in the hallway, giving me just enough light to stumble up the steps and into my room. I didn't even stop to check on Piper, or open Rilla's door. I didn't want to disturb her sleep, knowing she'd be up early to keep my daughter from waking me up.

With a twinge of lust-filled regret, I closed my bedroom door behind me. Our make-out sessions were leaving me with a perennial case of blue balls; Rilla hadn't moved to touching me yet, and I didn't want to push the issue. But God, I wanted her. I was holding onto sanity with the tips of my fingers.

I took a quick shower, just to get rid of the day, and pulled on a pair of boxers. I missed the days of sleeping nude, but with a daughter who liked to wake me up early in the mornings, I needed to be decent.

I was about to crawl between the sheets when I heard a sound at my bedroom door. It was a knock, just one quiet rap, but definitely a knock. I smothered a sigh of frustration and turned toward the door, expecting . . . I didn't know what. After today? Probably a puking kid who'd keep me up all night.

Except Piper didn't knock. It had to be Rilla. I frowned and opened the door.

She stood before me in a long white cotton nightgown. Her blonde hair streamed down her back, and her feet were bare. She looked five years younger than she was. Large blue eyes shone at me in the glow of my bedside lamp.

"Rilla? What's wrong?" I reached out to touch her cheek, running my fingertip over her soft skin.

"I . . . can I come in?" She brought her thumb to the corner of her mouth and bit down on it, which I knew meant she was nervous about something. Inwardly, I groaned. *Had she wrecked the car and wanted to confess? Or had something else happened today, something I didn't really want to know about at nearly two in the morning?*

"Of course." I stood back and she stepped inside, pausing as I closed the door behind her. "What's up, darlin'?"

She drew in a deep breath, her breasts swelling beneath the thin material of her nightie. I could see the outline of her nipples, and my cock stirred between my legs.

"I heard you come in. I was lying in bed, and I was thinking about you. I wanted to tell you . . . I missed you tonight. On the sofa. It wasn't the same without you."

"I should hope not." I took her hand in both of mine.

"Anyway, I was laying there, and I couldn't sleep. I realized . . ." She lifted her eyes to stare into mine. "I don't want to wait anymore, Mason. We're married. We, um, like each other. If you . . . if you want me, I want to be with you. I want you to, um, make love to me."

Suddenly, I wasn't tired anymore.

But my gentleman training couldn't be shut off. I cupped her cheek and moved my thumb over her lips. "Rilla, are you sure? I don't want you to feel pressured. I promised you we'd move slow."

"I think we have, Mason. We've been married three months, and we haven't had a wedding night yet. That's got to be some kind of record."

Her humor was what sunk me. I could hear certainty in her voice, and it was all I needed to give me the big flashing green light I'd been waiting for.

Without saying another word, I bent and swept her into my arms, cradling her head on my chest. I bent to cover her lips with mine, sealing our mouths together in a kiss that was a promise I couldn't quite speak yet.

Laying her on my bed, I stretched out next to her and propped my head on my hand. I could feel Rilla's nerves buzzing, vibrating; she didn't know what came next, and it scared her.

I skimmed one hand down her body, from her neck to just below her ribs. "Rilla. Darlin.' It's okay. It's just you and me. Same as . . . same as on the love seat. Same as in the front seat of my truck. It's you." I kissed her forehead. "And me. Nothing to be scared about. I promise. And if you feel like you need to slow us down, stop, you tell me. You're in charge."

She nodded, her head rubbing against the pillow. "I don't want to stop. But I don't know what to do. I want to make you feel as good as you make me feel."

I grinned. "Just do what comes naturally. Whatever feels right. If it's a problem, I'll tell you. But I can pretty much promise that as long as it's your hands on my body, I'm not going to complain."

She smiled. "Will you kiss me?"

"Baby, you can bet on it." I slid my hand behind her neck and held her head up. My lips brushed over hers, and then I bent my head to take her mouth more fully. I sucked her bottom lip between mine, teasing it with my tongue until she made that small noise in her throat that drove me wild.

I rained kisses down her neck, to her collarbone, and then brought my hand up to palm her breast. Taking a minute to appreciate the weight of it in my hand, I lowered my mouth to surround her nipple, wetting the cloth that covered it.

Rilla cried out, combing her fingers through my hair and arching her back to bring me closer. Rampant desire pounded between my legs, and my dick ached with the need to take her.

I raised my head and took in a deep breath, trying to calm myself again. *Slow, buddy. Slow but sure.*

I reached for the hem of her nightgown and tugged it up, revealing the perfect pale skin of her legs. When I got to her hips, Rilla raised herself to free the material. My heart thudded as I saw her simple white underwear. I'd seen some sexy lingerie in my day. Maybe more than my share. But nothing had ever affected me like the sight of the white cotton that covered Rilla.

She pushed up on her elbows to sit, and I peeled off her nightgown the rest of the way, leaving her bare but for the panties. I nuzzled her tits, using my fingers on her nipples the way I knew drove her absolutely crazy. When I took one between my teeth, she made a sound almost like a growl. Her breath was coming in short bursts, and her hips had begun to rock against me.

I kept my mouth on her nipple as I lazily moved my hand down to cover the wet heat between her legs. At my touch there, she inhaled sharply and bucked to meet my fingers.

"Shh, honey. I'm going to make you feel good. Just relax." I teased her with one finger over the cotton. It was saturated with the evidence of her desire, and it took every bit of tattered control within me not to push aside the material and drive myself into her.

I rubbed over the underwear for a few seconds, until I couldn't take it any longer. I slipped my finger underneath, into her slippery folds. When I touched her clit, she went off like a rocket.

Her hands clutched my shoulders, and her upper body reared off the mattress. "Mason! Oh my God, oh my God, oh my God . . . ohhhh." She moaned, her body jerking as I kept stroking her, bringing her back down from her climax.

When her breath had calmed a little, she turned her head to look at me, eyes still soft. "Mason . . . that was . . . incredible." She ran her hand down my chest, faltering when her fingers reached the elastic waistband of my shorts. “Can I make you feel the same way?”

I kissed her cheek and kept going down her throat. “Honey, I want you to. Believe me. But if you touch me right now, I won’t be able to finish what we both want.” Even as I spoke the words, my cock twitched, ready for action. Against my better judgment, I covered her hand with mine and slowly lowered it so that she could feel me through the nylon.

Her eyes widened. “You feel . . . big. Are you sure this is going to work?”

I chuckled. “Yeah, I’m sure.” I paused. “Are you sure, still?”

She nodded. “Very sure. Completely sure. Absolutely sure. Totally—”

“Okay, you had me at very sure.” I kissed her again, just to shut her up. “Hold on a minute.”

I rolled away from her to reach into the drawer of my nightstand. Retrieving a condom, I glanced at Rilla, smiling a little when I saw her watching me. Keeping my eyes on hers, I slid off my shorts.

She let her gaze wander down, and when she reached my dick, she licked her lips and swallowed hard. If it was possible, I got even harder.

But she didn’t look away. I tore open the wrapper and slid the condom over me before I crawled back over to hold myself above her.

She was nervous. I could tell by the thumb that had made its way to the edge of her mouth. I lowered my face to take that thumb between my own lips, sucking it into my mouth and letting my tongue circle it a few times.

“Did you know, when you’re worried, or nervous, you bite your thumb?”

Surprise showed in her eyes, more that I’d noticed than that she had this tell.

"And did you further know, that every time you do that, I'm dying to suck that thumb into my own mouth and do exactly what I'm doing now?" I swirled my tongue around it a few more times and then bit it gently. Rilla closed her eyes as pleasure filled her face.

"Remember that every time you do it, from now on." I dropped my knees to the bed between her legs, nudging them a little wider. My dick was poised at her entrance, but I stopped, holding myself in check one more time.

"You're ready, Rilla?"

She nodded. "It's going to hurt, isn't it?"

I exhaled. "I wish it didn't. I'm going to do whatever I can to make it . . . not. But it'll get better. I promise."

I took my cock in my hand and rubbed the head over her wetness, over her clit, and then finally slid into her, just barely.

She tensed. I knew that was going to make it worse for her, but I couldn't do anything about it right now. My body knew heaven was inches away, and there was no holding back. I pushed in a little further.

Rilla sucked in a gasp, closed her eyes again and bit down on her lip.

"You okay, baby? Want me . . . want me to pull out?" *Oh God, please say no, please say no, please say no . . .*

"No. It's—I'm okay. Just feels . . . like I'm stretching. Burning a little." She gripped the straining muscles of my arms. "Don't stop."

As if my cock took that as a mandate, I thrust into her all the way. *God, she was tight. Tight like the best thing in the world I've ever felt, bar none and I never wanted to leave this spot or this moment.*

I wanted to stop, give her a moment to adjust, but my control was shattered. Gone. I moved, rocking into her and then withdrawing, trying to keep the thrusts gentle but failing miserably as nature took over. Weeks of wanting this, dreaming of it, waiting for it meant that release came fast and hard. I emptied myself inside her, my entire body one huge, hard muscle as I growled out her name.

I had enough presence of mind not to land on her when I fell onto the bed. For the space of several moments, we both caught our breath, hearts pounding.

When I could move again, I lifted my head. Rilla's eyes were closed, but she looked . . . happy. Peaceful. Sated.

And thank the good Lord, so was I, at long last.

"You okay, darlin'?" I brushed hair from her face, wrapping a strand around my finger. "Do you hurt?"

She shook her head, keeping her eyes closed, but a smile curved her lips. "I'm a little . . . not quite sore, but aware that I might be sore. You know?" She turned her head, meeting my gaze. "But totally worth it. Mason, was that as beautiful for you as it was for me? And is it always like that?"

I gathered her close, drawing her body onto mine so that her head rested on my chest. "Rilla, that was . . . beyond any words I have for it." I tipped her chin up with one finger so that she was looking at me. "You gave me a gift tonight, and I don't take that lightly. Your first time, and the trust you have in me . . . that's sacred. Thank you." I crunched up to reach her lips and kissed her gently. "And no, it's not always like that. There's all kinds of sex. There's fast and intense, and slow and lazy, and there's friendly sex, and then there's making love." I purposely didn't mention the fucking kind of sex. It wasn't applicable to this situation, and if I had my way, Rilla would never know that kind.

"Mason, thank you for tonight. I can't imagine having my first time with anyone but you." Her eyes shone at me, and her passion-swollen lips curved into a lazy smile.

I pinched her arm lightly. "I should hope not. As your husband, I am definitely against you doing this with anyone but me."

She turned her head so that her chin rested on my chest and her eyes bore into mine. "Really? That matters to you?"

I frowned. "Of course it matters to me. It matters a hell of a lot. You're my wife, Rilla. What we just shared is something that's only between us. For always."

She nodded, her chin digging into my muscles. "I just thought . . . I know what you said, Mason. About Lu. How she's the only woman you'll ever love. And I just thought . . . if you can't feel that way about me, this . . . sex . . . might not make any difference to you. Not like it does to me."

I gripped her upper arms and hauled her up until her face was level with mine, taking her by surprise. Her eyes were huge and her mouth a small O. "It matters, Rilla. What we just did was more than sex. I made love to you. You made love to me. It's important, and you're the only one I want to experience this with. Do you understand what I'm saying?"

"Yes." She kept her gaze on me. "I only ever want you, Mason. I only ever want you to touch me. I only ever want you . . . inside me."

"Good." I crushed her lips with a kiss. "Now that we've got that straight, all I want is to go to sleep with you in my arms. I've had a long-ass day. It ended on a high note, for sure." I mock-leered at her. "But the rest of it was kind of crap, so I want to sleep until our daughter makes us wake up. And I want you close to me." I rolled so that we lay on our sides. Wrapping my arms around Rilla, I hauled her against me, buried my face in her neck and fell into oblivion.

Chapter Fifteen

Rilla

THE NEXT FOUR WEEKS were the most perfect of my life.

Nothing had really changed, except that one thing had, and that one thing changed everything. Mason had made love to me, and a whole new world had opened up.

He hadn't said he loved me, but every touch, every time he brought me pleasure, every time I made him moan . . . we were saying it to each other. I was sure of it.

I'd moved into his bedroom, which we now both referred to as our room. I slept in his bed every night, tangled in his arms. Piper jumped on us every morning, and if Mason hadn't been out too late the night before, we all cuddled and played until she demanded that we get up for breakfast.

I loved every minute of it.

There were a few things I tried not to think about. I pushed aside any hurt that my grandmother still hadn't tried to contact me. I missed her with an ache that never went away, but I knew I couldn't go back to the farm, not even to visit. Not yet. The pain was still too fresh and raw.

I tried to ignore the nagging voice inside that said I needed to go back to church. Not Burton Community, but somewhere. Over the last months, I'd had time to examine my feelings about the church, as well as my own relationship with God. I realized that the resentments and anger I felt were toward some of the people in the church, most notably Pastor Shand and my father. My dad at least had the excuse of my mother and how she'd abandoned both of us, but Pastor Shand . . . the more I thought about it, the more it repulsed me that he'd led a group of people who trusted him down a road that was downright wrong.

I shared some of my mad with Mason as we lay in bed one night. My head was on his chest, listening to the slow beating of his heart. His fingers traced small circles over the bare skin of my back as I spoke.

"The thing is, I don't think there's anything wrong with wanting to be holy. But the Bible says we can't ever be perfect, and that God accepts us and loves us in our imperfection. Pastor Shand didn't teach that. He told us that God couldn't stand us if we weren't holy. So he convinced a bunch of people to focus on trying to reach some impossible ideal. The more I look at it, the more I believe God wants us to focus on love, not on trying to make sure everyone else is behaving."

"How can you see the splinter in your brother's eye before you remove the plank in your own?" Mason's words were muffled against my hair.

I twisted to look at him. "Why, Mason Wallace, did you just quote Scripture?"

He winked at me. "My talents are endless, darlin.' And don't sound so surprised. I went to Sunday school, remember."

"Yeah." I laid my head back on his chest. "Do you think . . . can you ever forgive God? Would you go to church with me, if

I found a place for us? Could I take Piper?"

"Of course you can take Piper. As for me . . ." He sighed. "I don't know, Rilla. I'm still not sure. I mean, how can I believe in a God who took away my wife? The woman I loved more than anything else in the world?"

An ache grew around my heart. I swallowed. "What about believing in a God who gave you Piper? Who gave you a wonderful mother?" Every ounce of me wanted to add, "*Can't you believe in a God who gave me to you? Who gave you a second chance at love?*" But I was too afraid of what Mason might answer. As long as I didn't come right out and ask him if he loved me, I could pretend that he did. I could find all the evidence and build a case for it. If I asked and he said no, I wasn't sure I could handle it.

"So you're saying I should focus on what God has given me instead of what he's taken away?" Mason mused. "I guess I see what you mean."

"I'm not pressuring you. I just . . . I just want you to be okay. Not bitter." I kissed his shoulder.

"Speaking of God . . ." Mason rolled over, pinning me to the bed. "Did you notice that you, Miss I-Never-Cuss-Or-Swear, take the Lord's name in vain each time I make you come?"

My face heated, and I covered my eyes with one hand. "I know! I can't help it. It's just . . ." I shrugged. "I tell myself it's because it's like a prayer. We say God's name when we pray, and when you're inside me, it's almost like a holy experience."

"What God has joined, let no man put asunder." Mason nodded, putting on a serious look until I poked him in the ribs. "What? I was quoting scripture again." He rubbed his lips over my throat. "How about we join together and see if I can make you break the second commandment?"

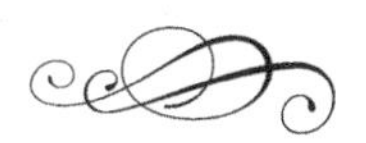

After a few setbacks and delays, Naomi finally came home from the hospital. I'd spent days cleaning the house, since we still had to careful of exposing her to germs. Piper and I made a big welcome home sign, and when Mason led her into the kitchen, seeing Naomi's bright eyes made my heart sing.

"Oh, it's so good to be home! Oh, my, look at how nice everything looks. Rilla, the house is sparkling. Piper, my sign is beautiful!"

"Are you all better now, Nan?" Piper cocked her head.

"Not quite, sweetie, but I'm on the road. I just need to rest up and stay away from sick people for a while."

Mason helped me settle his mom in her room. We both fussed over her until she ordered us out.

"I need my rest. And you two have things to do. Mason, shouldn't you go to work? Don't you have a club to run? And Rilla, Piper's been asking you to come play with her for ten minutes. Off you go."

It was good to have Naomi home again. I liked being able to pop into her room and chat whenever I wanted.

"I have to say, honey, that I'm pleased as punch to see you and Mason together. Just tickled." She beamed at me.

"I'm glad you're happy about it. I wasn't sure—we didn't exactly have a promising start. I know Mason only proposed to protect my reputation. But he's been so good to me, and I think . . . I think we're getting along all right."

"Getting along all right? Rilla, my son is besotted with you. And I know you've been in love with him for a long time. It's mighty nice when that works out, isn't it?"

I nodded, but some of my worry must've shown in my eyes. Naomi frowned. "What's wrong, sweetheart?"

I took a deep breath. "Naomi, I do love him. I'm in love with Mason. But I haven't told him. And I'm not sure he loves me." I bit my lip. "I mean, I think he loves me, but maybe not the same way I love him. He told me Lu was the only woman he could ever love like that."

"Hogwash." Naomi's pronouncement was succinct. "My son's an idiot, Rilla. He might not have told you—heavens, he might not've admitted it to himself—but he is head over heels in love with you. Trust me. Be patient."

It was easier to believe Naomi was right at night, when Mason held me, kissing me until I was breathless. He was a patient teacher, letting me set the speed at which we moved, and I'd discovered the heady power I possessed to drive him crazy, just with my touch.

"Darlin'. . ." His voice sounded strangled. "Rilla. Oh, God, baby. . ."

I lay between his legs, with my mouth on his cock. Cock. It was a funny word, I thought, but it was the one he used when we were in bed. This was my first experimentation with taking him in my mouth, but since I knew I loved when Mason used his lips and tongue on me, I was happy to return the favor.

"Like this?" I moved my head, testing.

"Oh, God, yes." His hands were tangled in my hair.

I sucked a little harder, swirling my tongue around the pulsing shaft. Gram's lessons had never talked about this, but I'd come to believe that anything that happened in our marriage bed was beyond reproach. After all, God had created us man and woman and declared it was good. I couldn't accept that in his wisdom, he hadn't wished us pleasure in each other.

"Rilla." Mason's hands moved to my shoulders as he panted. "Come here, baby. I want to be inside you when I come."

I crawled up his gorgeous, hard body, rubbing myself against him as I went. He groaned and hauled my face to his before flipping us over. Nudging my legs apart, he coaxed my knees to bend before he thrust into me.

I arched up to meet him, swept into the need to get as close as I could while he picked up speed, plunging over and over until I cried out, my fingers digging in his back.

Mason growled out something I didn't understand and then slid into me once more, his body tensing into solid muscle as he spilled himself inside me.

It wasn't until my breath had slowed to almost normal that I realized that for the first time, Mason hadn't used a condom. He was always careful about rolling it on, but I sensed tonight, urgency had been too much. I didn't know whether I should mention it or not. We hadn't discussed matters of birth control or whether Mason wanted more children. I was almost afraid to ask him that question.

"I know." His words were muffled under my shoulder. "I'm sorry, baby. I never forget to—well, I just wasn't thinking, I guess." He pushed up onto his elbows to look down at me. "I promise, I'm clean. I've never had sex without protection since Lu."

I nodded and swallowed. "Mason . . . do you think . . .we never talked about it. Do you want more children?"

He didn't answer right away, and I decided that was a good sign. Lowering his body next to mine, he skimmed one hand over my ribs to cover my stomach.

"Darlin', there's a big part of me that says, hell yeah. I want babies with you. I want to see you carrying my child, and I want the world to know that you are." He ran his lips down my neck, kissing the pulse at the base. "But I'm not sure I want to risk you that way. Or whether I have it in me to love another child. I worry about Piper so much, about everything that could go wrong. Another one . . ." He shook his head. "I need to think about it. I need some time."

I turned my head to touch my lips to his jaw. "We have plenty of that." Running one fingertip down his arm to his fingers, I decided a change of subject was in order. "Mason, would you sing to me?"

He stiffened. "Sing to you?"

"Your mom says you have a gift. And I've seen your guitar in the closet. I mean, if it's too painful, I understand." I sat up, pulling the comforter around me. "But I'd love to hear it."

He studied me for a few minutes. "Okay." Before I could say anything else, he swung his legs off the mattress and stalked over to the closet. I watched him walk, muscles flexing in his backside and legs. I'd never really understood what lust was until I'd seen my husband naked. Now, it was practically my constant state of being.

He picked up the guitar and came back to the bed, piling the pillows up so he could lean against them. I crossed my legs and sat quietly, watching him tune it.

I thought he might ask me what I wanted to hear, but instead he began singing. The melody was soft and so beautiful that tears filled my eyes. I didn't recognize the song—not surprising, considering how little popular music was familiar to me—but the words were deep and simple. Love me tender . . .

I didn't move until his voice was silent and his fingers had stopped moving. When I lifted my eyes to Mason's, his were cautious, tentative.

"Mason, thank you. That was the most . . . you have such talent." I bit my lip. "I know that wasn't easy. I'm sure you used to sing to Lu—"

"Nope." He held the guitar by its neck and stood to put it away. "I never sang to her. She—she sang to me, sometimes. But it was so much a part of our professional life that she didn't even do that often. It would've felt like bringing business to the bedroom. And I never sang to her because I wasn't good enough."

"How can you say that? Mason, you might not've wanted to be a professional musician, but still, you are so gifted." I scooted up to the pillows as he came back to bed. "Thank you. That was the most beautiful song I've ever heard."

He sat next to me, the bed dipping. "Only for you, Rilla.

There are parts of me . . . from when I was young, that will always belong to Lu. They died with her. But this was only for you. I've never sung for a woman before." He kissed me, his lips firm and seeking. "Only for my wife."

I sank back into the bed, pulling him with me, and as his body covered mine again, in that moment his love was more real and certain than anything I'd known.

Even if he hadn't said the words.

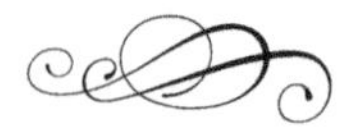

My perfect four weeks came to a screeching end a few days after Naomi came home. I'd made dinner that evening, cleaned up and put Piper to bed. Mason was working late, so I helped Naomi settle in for the night as well, closing the door to her room so he didn't wake her when he came home.

I was in the living room, watching reruns of one of Mason's favorite series when I heard a knock at the kitchen door. It was late, after nine o'clock, and I wasn't expecting anyone. Mason had his keys. I couldn't think of who might be here.

I pushed aside the sheer curtain to peer outside and nearly fell over from shock when I saw who was standing on the kitchen stoop. I stood back, unlocking the deadbolt and opening the door.

"Jonathan." My voice was flat. "What're you doing here?"

He looked the same as always, the same colorless, wide-eyed pious man, although the expression on his face was cautious. He glanced around before stepping over the threshold. "Rilla. I'm glad I had the right house. I wasn't sure."

"Yeah, you got the right house. Why are you–what do you want?"

He frowned and glanced over my shoulder. "Maybe we could sit down. Are you here alone?"

Irritation nearly made me roll my eyes. He was still worried over the impropriety of being in a house with me and no chaperone in sight. "Jonathan, whatever you have to say, you can tell me standing here. And no, we're not alone. My mother-in-law is in her room, and Piper is upstairs sleeping. Mason's still at work." I hesitated and then added, "In case you hadn't heard, I'm married now."

"I did hear it. The whole church heard it. You humiliated your father, and broke your grandmother's heart. And you can imagine what people were saying about me."

I raised one eyebrow. "Actually, I can't. Why would anyone think anything about you, just because I got married?"

Jonathan shook his head. "Because everyone knew I was courting you." He spoke as though it were the most obvious answer in the world.

"Courting me? Really? All I ever heard from you were excuses about why you couldn't commit. But I have to thank you. If you'd been even the least bit appealing to me, I might not have met Mason. And the truth is, he changed my life." I huffed out a breath. "So why're you here?"

He fiddled with the buttons on his sleeve. "I came, Rilla, because I feel that you've had sufficient days to come to your senses. You've wallowed in sin long enough. It's time for you to repent, and I'm here to assure you that you can come back to the fold. If you admit your wrongdoing, give up your sin, and take up your home with your father again, the church is ready to receive you."

I stared at him, incredulous. "What're you talking about? I'm not coming back, Jonathan. I don't have any desire to be part of that life anymore. I've moved beyond it." I crossed my arms over my chest. "I've found freedom. And I'm not giving it up."

"But you have to. Your father and your grandmother need you." He paused. "I need you."

That actually made me laugh. "You need me? I'll remind

you that you had your chance with me, Jonathan. And now those chance are gone."

"I know we had a misunderstanding, Rilla. I might not have been clear enough at the time, but I'm willing to overlook your deliberate flouting of Pastor Shand's teaching and even your stumble here." He took a step toward me, and instinctively I moved back. "I've looked into it. We can have this sham of a marriage annulled, and once you've come back to full fellowship in the body, we can be married. An opportunity has come up for me to take over a church near Macon, and I'll need the help of a wife."

"And you think I'm your best candidate?" I saw the conflict crossing over his face, and the truth dawned on me. "Ohhh. I see what's happening here." He began to speak, and I held up my hand. "No, no. Let me see if I've guessed right. Pastor Shand—and possibly my father, too—know you've been jonesing for your own parish. I bet they dangled this church in Macon in front of you, like a worm before a fish. The only catch, of course, is that you need a wife, and since both my dad and the good pastor hate that I'm finally living my own life and happy, they decided to make marrying me a condition of you getting the church. We'd be far enough away that gossip wouldn't necessarily follow us, and I'd get the fresh start they think I need. Am I close? Did I nail it?"

He had the good grace to blush. "Rilla, your father and Pastor Shand care about you, and they want you back on the straight and narrow. Yes, they felt that you and I taking a church a little distance from Burton would be a good idea."

"But did they tell you that the church and I are a package deal? If you come back tonight empty-handed, do you still get the pulpit?"

Jonathan looked down at his hands and shrugged. "I always thought you were a nice person, Rilla. And that you'd be a good and faithful wife. If you'd been patient . . . waiting for me a little bit . . .”

“I’d still be waiting, and so would you. Besides, Jonathan, it might interest you to know that I didn’t leave home because I was tired of waiting for you to make your move. I left because my father kicked me out, after calling me some very un-Christian-like names, and he did that because I’d taken a job with a man who desperately needed help with his child and his sick mother. There was nothing wrong between us. And if my dad had been reasonable, I’d probably still be living at home, working here and for my own company, and I might even be thinking about marrying you. But he wasn’t, and I’m not. And now, I want you to get the hell out of my kitchen.” I didn’t swear often, still. It felt odd and awkward coming out of my mouth, but in this situation, I decided, it was entirely warranted.

“Rilla, don’t do this. Don’t endanger the fate of your immortal soul in exchange for something worldly and wrong. We’ll talk to your father together. We can still be married. You’ll see, it’ll all work out.”

“What the hell is going on here?”

I jumped, startled. Mason stood in the doorway of the kitchen, fury and incredulity on his face. He glanced from Jonathan to me, and I saw the tic in his cheek that meant he was close to the edge.

I drew in a deep breath. “Mason, this is Jonathan. He’s a youth pastor at my father’s church.” I was careful to make the distinction. “Jonathan, this is my husband.”

Mason came inside the kitchen, towering over Jonathan and moving to stand behind me. “Uh huh. And why is he here talking about marrying you?”

I shrugged. “I have no idea.” I’d tell him my theory about the church and Rilla package deal later, when we were alone. There wasn’t any need to humiliate Jonathan further, no matter how much fun it might be.

Jonathan’s face went tomato red. “We all know that you

only married this man in order to live here after your father . . . after your misunderstanding. We understand that it is not a real marriage. That's why it can be annulled. It'll be like it never happened."

"Oh, really?" Mason slid his arm around me, circling my ribs and resting his hands just below my breasts. "You know, Jonathan, I just met you, but I'm going to have to say, I don't much care for you. Kind of ballsy to come into a man's house and say his marriage isn't real." He tightened his arms and bent his head to my hair. "Feels real to me. Do you want to tell him, Rilla, how real our marriage is?"

Mason's voice was deceptively calm, but I could feel the buzz of his anger beneath it. "Jonathan, you've made some grave errors and assumptions. I'm not coming back to the church. I'm not repenting of sins I never committed. I'm sure as hell not marrying you." I covered Mason's hands with mine. "And my marriage is about the most real thing I've ever known."

I had the momentary satisfaction of seeing the shock and distaste on Jonathan's face before he managed to speak again. "Rilla, you will regret this day. You've been given the blessing of a second chance, and you're turning it aside. You won't be invited back again."

"Hope springs eternal." I pointed to the door. "I think you need to leave, Jonathan."

He turned, still sputtering words, and disappeared into the dark. I breathed out a long sigh and turned in Mason's arms.

"I'm so sorry, I had no idea he was going to—"

My words were cut off by the crush of Mason's lips on mine. Before I could catch my breath, he'd lifted me up so that my face was near his and my feet dangled. He gripped my backside, grinding my center against him, and I wrapped my legs around his hips, my cotton skirt hiking up to my thighs.

"Mason . . ." I tore my mouth away. "What're you doing?"

"Claiming what's mine." He covered my mouth again,

kissing me with swift possessiveness. His tongue plunged between my lips, stroking and branding me. I opened my mouth wide, letting him in, tangling my tongue with his.

Never breaking the kiss, Mason strode down the hall and up the stairs, not stopping until we were in our bedroom. He shut the door behind us with his foot and dropped me on the bed, not roughly but not with the same gentle care he usually showed me. Not that I was complaining. I found this side of my husband exhilarating.

"Mason . . ." I tried to speak again, but my words faded away as I saw him unbutton his jeans. He stripped them off along with his boxers, kicking both away from his feet. His erection strained toward me.

I gasped as he pushed up my skirt. His fingers found my underwear and tore them away from me, the sound of ripping fabric loud in the silent room. As soon as they were out of the way, he was touching me, rubbing insistently between my legs until I was panting and begging.

"Please . . . please . . . oh, God." I clutched him, trying to bring him down to me. "Please, Mason."

"You want this, Rilla? You want me? You want to feel me inside you?" He was growling the words as he stared intently into my eyes, his blazing with passion and need.

"Yes! Now. Please now." I arched up toward him, needing to feel him as much as he needed to brand me as his. "Please."

With a groan I was certain could be heard throughout the house, Mason thrust into me. He lifted my hips, angling me as he plunged, watching our bodies join.

"You're mine, Rilla. Mine. See this? Feel me inside you? You're only mine."

"Only . . . ever . . . yours." I ground out the words, and then I was flying, flying and falling into the pleasure that convulsed between my legs. As my body pulsed around him, Mason gave one last deep thrust and grunted, spilling himself into me.

He let of my hips, holding onto me until I was flat on the mattress again. Lifting me gently, he tugged until we both lay with our heads on the pillows.

I rolled over to my side, brushing my hand over Mason's face. His eyes were closed, but they twitched at my touch. His chest was still moving up and down rapidly, as though he hadn't quite recovered. With one finger, I traced his cheekbone, down to his jaw.

What had just passed between us was so different from his usual gentle, almost reverent touch. The intensity, the way Mason had taken me . . . it should have been frightening. But it wasn't. Instead, the fact that he'd needed to make sure I was his and his alone made me feel powerful. And loved. And brave enough to say what had been on the tip of my tongue for so long.

"I love you, Mason." I whispered the words that I couldn't hold back any longer.

His eyes fluttered open, and he stared at me, his expression unreadable. I drew in another breath and repeated what I'd said.

"I love you."

"You love me." Mason pushed up off the bed and stalked to his clothes, pulling on his jeans. "God, Rilla. How can you . . . after what I just did? And now you say you love me? What the hell?"

A lump rose in my throat. "But . . . I do, Mason. I have for a long time."

"Goddammit, Rilla. I told you from the beginning that I could never . . . offer you that." He rubbed his hand over his face. "I was always honest with you."

I nodded, but numbness, centered in my chest, was spreading throughout my limbs.

"You deserve more. But I can't give it to you. I never said I could. This was supposed to be something that worked for both of us, going in with our eyes open. And you know what?

You only think you love me, because I'm the first man you had sex with. I thought I could . . . give you a life. Better than what you had. Even if I couldn't be your prince charming, I could be your knight in shining armor." He sighed. "I tried, Rilla. I tried my damnedest to be who you needed. But turns out it didn't matter how much I tried, right? Because I ended up fucking you anyway."

"You didn't hurt me tonight, Mason. At least, not when we were making—having sex. You didn't hurt me until you opened your mouth just now." I wrapped my skirt tight over my legs. "You said . . . when we were . . . you said I was yours. Why would you say that if you didn't have some feelings for me?"

"Of course I have feelings for you. I like you. I've always liked you. On some level, I even love you, but not the way you want. What you've done for me, with my mom and Piper—I can't ever thank you enough for that. I could pretend, you know. Just now I could've told you I loved you, and you wouldn't have known any difference. Ignorance is bliss, right?" He leaned over me, his face close to mine. "But then we'd both be living a lie."

The numbness had taken over. Everything I'd come to treasure over the past few months was unraveling here in front of me, and I couldn't stay in the same room with Mason another moment. I'd gone from feeling safe, wanted and loved to feeling . . . dirty and stupid.

I stood up, forcing him to move away from me. "Mason . . . I need some space. I'm going to sleep in the guest room tonight." I turned to leave.

"Rilla." He spoke my name as though it'd been ground out of his chest. "What're you going to do?"

I didn't face him again. "I made a commitment. To Piper, to Naomi, and to you. I just need some time to figure out how I'm going to make it work."

As I reached the door, he whispered one more time. "I'm

Chapter Sixteen

Mason

I WOKE UP THE next morning to a cold and empty bed. My arms reached for Rilla before I was fully conscious, and when I remembered why she wasn't there, the lump of pain in my chest expanded just a little more.

It was still early. Piper wasn't even awake yet. I'd gotten into the habit of lingering at home in the mornings, enjoying the time with my wife and my daughter, but today, I couldn't get out of the house fast enough. I showered, dressed and headed for the club.

Images from the night before flashed across my mind as I drove. Rilla's face as she confronted that spineless dick Jonathan. Her eyes when I lifted her into my arms and carried her upstairs. Her body as I took her, intent on making sure she was mine. It had been primal, that need; my wife's body belonged to me alone, and I was driven to prove that to her. But when she'd offered me her heart, too, I'd tossed it back in her face.

Nice move there, moron.

I'd known, even as I'd spoken the words, that what I was doing was wrong. The truth was, I'd been ashamed of how I'd taken her. After I'd promised myself that I'd always treat her with gentleness and care, I'd pounded into her small body without holding back. I'd hated what I did. I'd wanted her to be angry at me, to punish me, so I could push her away.

But no. She'd chosen that moment to tell me that she loved me.

It wasn't a shock. Rilla didn't have a poker face, and I'd known for a long time that her feelings were . . . deep. Intense. But if I didn't admit it to myself, I didn't have to deal with it. Denial was a beautiful thing.

I buried myself in work that morning. Thanks to Rilla's plans and hard work, our lunch time hours were a huge success, and we'd had to begin taking reservations. Rilla'd had the idea to have live music on some days, too; not dance bands, but local musicians who didn't mind playing for cheap. We'd had the local music teacher in with her harp, the woman who played the piano at the Lutheran church, and even a performance from the town's barbershop quartet. They'd all been wildly popular, and I was working out a schedule to bring them back as well adding new performers to the lineup.

Right before lunch, my phone buzzed with a text. I glanced at it and snatched it up fast when I saw Rilla's name. My heart pounded; although she'd said she wasn't going anywhere, part of me didn't believe it.

Taking Piper out to the farm. Be back in time for dinner. Mom's fine.

Relief eased into me. If she was telling me their day's plans, it didn't sound as though she was taking off. Not yet, anyway. I needed to figure out my shit and talk to her. Smooth things over. See if we could get back to where we'd been before.

We had a full house for lunch, and enough lingering guests

that we had to rush to get everything set up for the evening. I was helping haul cases of liquor from the storeroom when Rocky yelled out my name.

"Hey, boss! Your phone's ringing."

I gritted my teeth, struggling to keep hold of the crates I carried. "Who is it?"

"Unknown caller."

"Ignore it." I maneuvered behind the bar and set down the boxes with a huff of breath. Pulling the box cutter from my pocket, I sliced them open as Rocky helped me unload.

We'd gotten through two crates when I heard my phone again. Muttering a curse under my breath, I picked it up, checking the readout. Unknown caller again . . . but now there was a voicemail, too.

Frowning, I hit the button to listen to my messages. The voice on the other end was unfamiliar.

Mr. Wallace, this is Elinor Robinson, and I'm a nurse at Bryan County Hospital. Please call me as soon as possible. There was an accident, and your wife and daughter are here—

Horror, fear and an unspeakable sense of déjà vu overwhelmed me. Other words from another time echoed in my head.

We're so sorry, Mr. Wallace . . . nothing more we could do . . . injuries were too extensive . . .

"Hey, boss, you okay? You look like you seen a ghost." Rocky straightened, frowning at me.

I stared at him as if I didn't understand what he'd said. "I—I gotta go. Hospital—Rilla and Piper were in an accident."

Rocky's face fell into lines of concern. "Okay. Come on, I'll drive you." He yelled over his shoulder even as he grabbed my shoulder and steered me around the bar. "Darcy, take over. We gotta go—emergency."

Without waiting for a response, he pushed me ahead of him, out the door and into the waning sunshine of late afternoon. I stopped at the bottom of the steps and turned to him, gripping his arms.

"I can't lose them. Rocky—I can't do it again. I can't lose them."

"It's gonna be okay, Mason. Come on. Let's get out there and see what's going on. It's gonna be fine."

Rilla

"Mama, why are you in here? And Daddy's not in his bed." Piper climbed up with me, cuddling her small body alongside mine.

I glanced around the guest room, confused. And then it all crashed down onto me, and I swallowed hard before putting on a bright smile.

"Oh, I wasn't feeling well last night, so I slept in here so I didn't keep Daddy awake. He had to go to work early this morning." I tickled her neck. "So Miss Thing, what'll be for breakfast? Pancakes? Waffles? Fried possum?"

She giggled, and I scooped her up to nuzzle her neck. I loved this child with every ounce of my being. Sometimes I watched her and knew, without a doubt, that she couldn't be more precious to me even if she'd come from my own body. I could never leave her. No matter how painful my relationship with her father might be.

We made breakfast together, both of us clapping when Naomi joined us at the table. Her diet was still restricted, thanks to her immune suppression, but she enjoyed the pancakes I made. We lingered around the table, chatting and listening to Piper's funny little stories. I watched Naomi's face, loving the joy I saw there, despite the gauntness of her body and the pain in her eyes. She too was dear to me, and I couldn't leave her, either.

I was just finishing the breakfast dishes when my phone rang. I saw Meghan's name on the caller ID.

"Rilla! I hope you don't have any plans today, girl. Guess who just came back into town for a surprise visit?" In the background, I heard laughter and a familiar voice called my name.

"Rilla, come play with us! Bring Piper, I've got Bridget with me, too."

"Ali's here?" Despite my own aching heart, I managed a smile. "I thought she wasn't supposed to come home for another month."

"Flynn's sister Iona had her baby, and they decided to fly down and meet the new nephew. They're only here for two days, but we want you to come out and catch up. Can you make it?"

I glanced around the window. Part of me wanted to burrow at home and wallow in my misery. But I knew it'd be good for me to see Ali, and Piper would love playing with her daughter Bridget, even though Bridge was older.

"Okay. I'm in. Let me make sure Naomi's okay, and then we'll head out."

"Yay! We'll see you in a little bit."

I closed the dishwasher and pushed the start button. "Hey, Piper, want to go for a ride?"

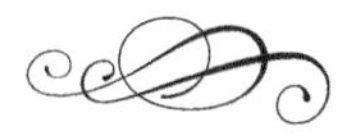

"Okay, so I leave for New York, and you're our quiet little Rilla Grant, working at the stand, jumping at her own shadow, wearing clothes two sizes too big, trying to make her PR business work . . . and I come back home and you're Rilla Wallace, wife, mother and seriously smokin' hottie. Wearing jeans. Married to Mason Wallace, for God's sake. Meghan says you even went to a bar."

When Ali put it that way, it really hit home how much my life had changed. I shrugged. "I didn't plan any of it. It just kind of happened."

"And you should see the two of them together, Ali." Meghan grinned. "They might've gotten married for very practical reasons, but Mason is head over heels for her. I mean, like, it's like scorched earth when he looks her way."

Ali laughed, but when I didn't join in, both girls narrowed their eyes. "All right, Rilla. Come clean. Something's wrong. You've got shadows under your eyes, and you're just going through the motions here today. What's going on?"

I hadn't intended to tell them anyway, but I heard the words erupting from my mouth anyway. "Mason doesn't love me. Last night . . . I told him I loved him, and he said he'd never feel the same way."

"Bullshit." Meghan didn't even blink. "He loves you, Rilla. He's lying to himself and he's lying to you. I don't know why, except maybe he's scared shitless, but I'm telling you, sweetie. He loves you, he's hot for you and he is crazy in love with you."

"He might just need some time." Ali reached across the table and laid her hand on my arm. "He's probably afraid of what happens if he gives in to loving you. I can't imagine what he went through after his first wife died."

"Maybe." I traced the grain on the wooded table with my finger.

"The question is, can you be patient that long? Let him get there in his own time? It might not be easy."

I thought about Piper and Naomi. And I remembered Mason the first night he'd made love to me, his face and the way he'd touched me. Could I hold onto all of that and have faith that Mason would come around?

"It all comes down to faith, doesn't it?" I glanced at Meghan. "That was drilled into me my whole life. It'd be a little ironic if I couldn't manage to hold onto it now."

"Now faith is the substance of things hoped for, the evidence of things not seen." Ali smiled as Meghan quirked an eyebrow. "What? I paid attention in church." She gnawed on the side of her lip. "Rilla, I wish someone had told me eight years ago to have faith in Flynn. To believe in him, even after he left. I wish I'd believed in him enough to tell him the truth about Bridget right away. But even after he came back this year, and we fell in love again—or realized we'd never stopped being in love—it still took some doing to believe we could make this work. But we can. We are." She winked at me. "So can you."

By the time Piper and I left the Reynolds' farm, it was late afternoon. I was anxious to get home to check on Naomi, and my mind kept darting back to Mason, and to my talk with Ali and Meghan. A small nugget of hope had begun to grow within me again. I could do this. I could bide my time, wait until Mason realized that he was in love with me. Until he worked up the courage to admit it.

I turned onto the highway that led into town past The Road Block. I could stop in and see him, just bring Piper in to say hello, kiss my husband and remind him that no matter how much he tried to fight it, I loved him. I smiled a little. That was a perfect plan. It wouldn't take more than five minutes, and Naomi would be okay for a little while more—

The crash was loud, sudden and shocking. My arm was pinned against me, and I screamed.

Everything went black.

Chapter Seventeen

Mason

"WHERE ARE THEY? WHERE the hell are my wife and daughter?" I towered over the woman at the nurses' station, my hands planted in front of me. I was probably scaring the shit out of her, but I didn't care.

"Sir, I can help you. But you need to calm down and tell me their names." On the other hand, maybe I wasn't scaring her so much. She seemed pretty calm, and that infuriated me.

"Wallace. Rilla and Piper Wallace." I glowered at her as she punched some keys on her computer.

"Okay, they're in room ten. Here in the ER. Go down to the end of this hall and make a left."

I turned to leave, but I heard Rocky behind me thanking the woman. I forced myself to stop and look back.

"Yeah. Thank you. Sorry about—" I waved my hand vaguely.

"No problem. You're not the first one to get worked up here, you know."

I nodded and wheeled around again, almost running down the hall. When I reached room ten, I came to a halt and paused before going in.

Was I ready for this? What if . . . what if . . .

"Mason?" Rilla's voice, sweet and clear as ever, jerked me aware. She was standing in the doorway, holding Piper in one arm.

Relief flooded over me, and my knees nearly buckled. If she was standing, she was okay. I took a closer look. Her hair was a mess, and she had a bandage on her head and another on the arm that didn't hold our daughter. But she was whole and unbloodied and so blessedly alive.

"What happened?" I couldn't make myself move yet, no matter how much I wanted to take them both into my arms.

Rilla shook her head. "We were on our way home, and some guy ran the stop sign and hit us. But we're okay." She seemed to know I needed to hear it. "The airbags went off, and my arm's a little burned. And I bumped my head, but not bad. Piper's absolutely fine, just a little scared."

As if on cue, Piper burst into tears. "Daddy!" she wailed, holding her arms out to me. I took her, holding her tight against me. My baby, whole and healthy and untouched. I sent a mental thank-you to the inventor of the child safety seat.

"We're just waiting for them to discharge us. I came out to see if I could find the nurse." Rilla leaned against the doorway. "I'm so sorry, Mason. I know you must've been terrified. I tried to call you from here, but you didn't pick up." I heard the slight edge of hurt to her voice. Had she thought I was ignoring her because of last night?

I patted my pocket. "I think I left my phone at the bar after I got the call from the hospital."

Rilla nodded. "The car got banged up pretty badly. I guess

they towed it to Boomer's."

"I don't care about the car." I half-growled the words. "As long as you're both okay . . ."

"And they are." A woman in scrubs breezed over to us. "Here's the paperwork, Mrs. Wallace, and the discharge instructions. We recommend you see your primary physician for a follow-up, but you shouldn't have any problems. If you show any signs of concussion, like vomiting, not being able to be woken, dizziness, call us. Otherwise, you're good to go."

Rilla thanked the nurse, and the three of us made our way to the lobby, where Rocky was waiting. When he saw us, his face blossomed into a huge grin.

"Oh, thank God." He gave Rilla a gentle hug and patted Piper's back. "See, boss, all's well. Didn't I tell you?"

"Yeah, you did." I clapped him on the shoulder. "Thanks, man, for getting me here."

"Hey, I'm your ride back to the bar, too, right? C'mon. I even have a car seat for the little lady. Lucky the wife and I both keep one in our cars." Rocky led us outside, glancing back at Rilla as we walked. "Rilla, you should've seen this guy. Never seen a man so freaked out. You ever doubt your husband loves you, just come to me. I'll remind you about how he acted today."

I slid Rilla a sideways look, but she didn't say anything. As a matter of fact, she was quiet all the way to the bar and then during the ride home, when I'd moved them from Rocky's car to my truck. Piper kept up a running commentary on everything that had happened that day—playing with Bridget on the Reynolds' farm had made as much of an impression as the accident had—but Rilla didn't speak beyond the bare necessities.

When we got home, we had to explain everything all over again to my mom. Halfway through the story, Rilla excused herself.

"I'm tired. If you don't mind, I'm going upstairs." She

pressed a kiss to Piper's head. "Be good, sweet girl."

I watched her moving gingerly. The impact of the crash must've been catching up with her. I thought of how close I'd come to losing her today . . . yes, she was fine, but if that car had been going a little faster, if he'd hit her in a different spot . . . it could've been so different. A cold hand of fear squeezed my heart.

I kept busy for the next few hours, feeding Piper and my mom and getting everyone ready for bed. It was after nine by the time I finally opened my bedroom door.

I wasn't sure if Rilla would be in there, or if she'd stayed in the guest room. But there she was, curled on her side, tiny in our big bed. Thinking she might be asleep, I tried to be quiet as I closed the door behind me and began to undress.

"Mason." She spoke, and there was weariness in her voice that went beyond exhaustion. "We need to talk."

"Are you feeling okay?" I went to stand next to her, shoving my hands into my pockets.

"I'm fine." She pushed to sit up, curling her legs beneath her. "I want to talk about last night." She bit her thumb, seemed to realize what she was doing and slid her hands under her legs. "About what you said."

I nodded. "Okay."

"Today, I was thinking . . . maybe you just need time. Maybe once you see that I'm not going anywhere, that you're not going to lose me, you'll feel like it's safe to love me." She smiled a little, shaking her head. "I was even on my way to see you when we got hit."

"Rilla, I—"

"Let me finish, please." There was steel in her tone, and I shut my mouth.

"I thought if I just had a little faith—" She broke a little. "I thought with faith and time, we could make it work. But then we were at the hospital, and you thought we were really hurt.

And you held Piper. I saw you hold her, close your eyes over her head, and just hug her tight. But you never touched me. You never held me."

I closed my eyes and breathed out.

"Mason, you're right. We didn't go into this promising each other anything but companionship and help. We weren't looking for love. And maybe it makes me unreasonable, but I changed my mind. I want love. I want the whole package. I love you, Mason, and I'm not going to apologize for it. I want what I see between Meghan and Sam, where he can't help touching her and she lights up when she sees him. I want what Ali and Flynn have, where they'd both give up everything to make the other happy.

"And I deserve that. I might not have thought I did before, but I do now. I love you, and if you can't love me, if you're truly sure you can't and you never will, then it's not fair to either of us." Tears streamed down her face, but she didn't wipe them away.

I wanted to tell her that I loved her. I wanted to give her the answers she craved, but that same hand of fear that had clutched me earlier wouldn't give up its grip. It wouldn't let me risk hurt again.

"I'm sorry," I whispered. "I can't do it again. When I was driving to the hospital today, and I thought—I didn't know how bad things were. And all I thought was *I can't fucking do this again.* I'm sorry."

Rilla nodded slowly. "I know." She uncurled her legs and stood up. "Boomer dropped off a loaner car for me to use while your mom's is being fixed. It should be out in the driveway. I'm going out to Meghan's, for tonight at least. I'll figure out what comes next, but for tonight, she said I can sleep in Ali's room, since Ali and Flynn are staying with his mom."

I stepped back as she skirted around me. That same agony I'd felt earlier had overtaken me, and I couldn't do or say anything.

Rilla picked up her handbag and a sweater. "I'll be back later to pack up my things, I guess. I—" She choked out a sob and turned to leave. I heard her going down the steps, and a few minutes later, the sound of the back door closing.

She was gone.

Rilla

I didn't have any place to go.

The thought occurred to me as I drove out of town, my stomach still roiling and my hands trembling. For tonight, sure, I knew Meghan and Sam would welcome me. But long-term? They were about to be married. They didn't need a third wheel living in the spare bedroom. I couldn't go to my father's farm. It was no longer home. I couldn't go to Boomer's house; they didn't have room for anyone else in their small home.

For a moment, I wavered. I could go back. The brick house on the quiet street in Burton was always going to be home for me, no matter what, because it was there that for a brief period, I'd loved and lived.

But I couldn't live a lie, and staying there would be just that. I headed out into the country, focusing only on getting to the farm and not letting myself think of anything else. When I arrived, I pulled around to the back, and for a minute, I just sat there in the dark, in the silent car with the driver's door open. Resting my head against the steering wheel, I waited for the tears to come. For the pain to drag me under.

"Rilla?"

I jerked upright. Meghan stood next to the car, concern knit all over her face. "Are you okay?"

I nodded and then shook my head. "I don't know, Meghan. I'm sorry. I know I'm imposing . . . but I just–"

"Would you shut up? We're family, Rilla. We might not be blood, but it's true all the same." She pulled me into a tight hug and slung her arm around me. "Come on inside." She slammed the car door and glanced at it curiously. "Where'd you get the wheels?"

"Oh, it's a loaner from my uncle Boomer."

"Huh." Meghan patted the roof of the old Chevette. "Imagine that. I have a little history with this car myself. Some time I'll tell you that story." She steered me into the house, and we sat down at her kitchen table. It was hard to believe that just that afternoon, we'd sat here with Ali, and I'd let myself feel hope.

"Do you want to talk?"

I shrugged. "It's nothing new. I just saw it with clearer eyes tonight." I ran my tongue over my lips. "I think I've been lying to myself. I thought Mason loved me. Even though he didn't say it, I thought . . . and after he told me last night, when he said he could never love me like he loved Lu, I was devastated. But then I listened to you and Ali, and I thought I could wait. I could keep the faith."

"And what changed?"

I'd already told Meghan about the accident. "He was so relieved about Piper. I saw it wash over him. But he didn't touch me. Didn't even really ask if I were okay. Just . . . nothing. I realized Mason's right. He can't do it. And I can't pretend that it's okay."

"Oh, sweetie." Meghan took my hand.

"How could I have been so blind? So stupid? I married him, Meghan. I married him, and I pretended it was because of what people were saying about me, but it was because I loved him even then. And I thought I could make him love me, too. Even though he told me . . ."

My throat closed, and finally the tears I hadn't been shedding overwhelmed me. I laid my head down on the table and cried, my shoulders shaking and my chest heaving.

"Rilla, shhhh. It's okay." Meghan sounded on the verge of crying herself. "It's going to work out. He's being an idiotic jackass, but I've known my share of them. He has a good heart, and there is not the slightest doubt in my mind that he loves you."

I wiped at the wetness on my face. "He broke my heart, Meghan. I don't know what to do. I don't want to lose Piper, but I can't live there and make believe something that isn't true. I can't be with him when he doesn't really love me."

She sighed. "Rilla, listen. It's late. Why don't you sleep on it before you make any decisions? And in the morning, let's see how you feel about everything."

I doubted I'd ever be able to close my eyes, but once I was alone in Ali's room in the dark, tears still pouring down my face, exhaustion overtook me and I fell into oblivion.

The sun still rose the next day. Even though it felt like my world was ending, it turned out the earth would continue to spin.

Meghan had to go to work, but she'd left coffee for me and a note telling me to make myself at home. I knew Sam was probably somewhere else on the farm. I sipped my coffee without tasting it and thought of Piper waking up without me. Of Mason having to juggle his mother's care today, along with work hours. And I cried again.

Something I'd said to Meghan last night echoed in my brain. *I don't want to lose Piper, but I can't live there and make believe something that isn't true.* I remembered how often I'd wondered how my mother could've left me. If she loved me . . . had it broken her heart to leave me behind? Had she cried as she drove away from the farm? And now I wondered if I were like her. I'd left Piper because of my own heartache. I was as selfish as my mother.

With that condemnation ringing in my ears, I showered and changed in an old pair of jeans Ali had left. They were huge on me, but I rolled the waist and the legs, and I found a shirt that almost fit me. Picking up my purse, I got into the car and headed down the road, until I came to a familiar driveway. I avoided the potholes and stopped at the front of the house.

Climbing the porch steps, I glanced around. Nothing had changed in the months I'd been gone. But then again, I wasn't sure much had changed in the last fifty years, so it wasn't surprising my departure wouldn't affect the house.

Before I could knock on the door, it opened. Gram stood behind the screen, looking at me with tear-filled eyes.

"Rilla," she breathed. "Thank you, Jesus." She pushed open the screen door and pulled me into a tight hug, rocking back and forth a little.

"Hi, Gram." I spoke into her neck, my voice muffled.

"Come in, come in, child. I'll get you something to eat."

I hesitated. "Gram, can we sit on the porch? I'd rather not go inside. Not right now."

She narrowed her eyes, nodding. "Of course. Sit down."

I took the old wicker rocker, and Gram sat in the chair that always been hers. She leaned forward, looking me up and down as if she couldn't get enough of me.

"Gram, first of all, I want to say I'm sorry that I put you in the position of having to choose between my father and me. He's your son, and I understand that you have to respect his wishes. I'm not sorry that I stood up for myself, or that I took the job. I didn't do anything wrong. I'm sorry Dad couldn't trust that you and he'd raised me to have good judgment. I'm sorry that he felt he had to make me leave home. And I've missed you, Gram."

She sighed. "You have no idea how I've missed you. How

many times I came close to just getting in the car and going to see you. But your father asked me not to. He said if you were going to come to repentance, we had to leave you strictly alone. I didn't agree, but Rilla, I live with him. He is my son. I hoped that this would blow over, or be resolved. But I know now that it's going to take an act of God to change him."

"Gram, I didn't come out here to blame you for anything or to dredge up old arguments. I wanted to talk to you about my mother."

She frowned. "Your mother? Why?"

I didn't want to tell my grandmother everything that was going on between Mason and me. I hadn't confided in her for a long time now, and it was going to take time to renew that trust. I spoke carefully, around the truth.

"I have . . . well, I'm helping to raise Mason's daughter Piper. She's my step-daughter. I love her so much, Gram. You'd adore her. But I worry . . . what if I'm too much like my mother? What if I don't know how to be a mother, since I never had one?"

"Oh, Rilla. Honey, you couldn't be more unlike your mother if you tried."

I bit my thumb. "I've gotten to know her family since I've been living in town. All that time, Gram, and you didn't tell me that I had an uncle and aunts, and cousins. Two more grandparents for part of my life. And I never knew."

"Your father didn't want you to have anything to do with them. He was afraid they'd spoil you, like they did Joely."

I nodded. "Boomer told me that. But he couldn't really tell me why my mother left. You lived here with her and my dad. Why did she leave him? Why did she leave me?"

Gram cast her eyes up. "It was so long ago, Rilla. And she was young. Too young. I told your father to wait. I said they should date a while longer before they got married. But they were both bent on doing it, no matter what anyone said. And then I told them to be careful and wait on having children. Joely needed time to adjust to being married and living out here. But they didn't listen then, either.

"I think she always figured she could convince your dad into leaving the farm and moving somewhere else. She had a wandering foot. She'd pour over magazines and show me pictures and tell me how she couldn't wait to see this or that. She'd plan these vacations and then pitch a fit when your father couldn't leave the farm.

"It seemed like she left in pieces. She stopped laughing so much, she stopped helping me with the cooking and the house. She didn't go into town to see her family like she always had. She'd just sit and look out toward the road. She'd hold you close and cry. And then one day, she just left."

I stared past Gram, into the vegetable garden. It was bare and empty this time of year. "Did she stop loving my dad? Is that why, do you think?"

Gram shrugged. "Hard to tell. Did she ever love him, or was it just fun to have all the fuss and attention of getting married, and then having a baby? I always suspected your mother was one who liked the high points in life and couldn't live through the mundane days. She didn't understand that the real joy came from those boring days."

"Okay." I rocked a little. "Thanks, Gram. Thanks for telling me."

"You're welcome. But honey, don't worry about being like her. You're not. Your heart is good, and you're going to be a wonderful mother."

"I think . . . I think I might've messed it up already, Gram." Tears filled my eyes. "I think I ruined it."

"Sweetie. Come here." Gram stood up and took me in her arms, hugging me close. "Don't cry, child. We'll work it out. It's going to be all right."

Chapter Eighteen

MASON

RILLA HAD BEEN GONE for less than twenty-four hours, and my life had already gone to hell.

Piper had cried for fifteen minutes this morning when Rilla wasn't there to fix her breakfast. I'd had to explain her absence to my mother, who frowned at me and asked what I'd done to upset that poor girl.

"She'll be back," I told them both grimly. "She just needed a little break. The accident . . . and everything. It was just stressful."

Mom narrowed her eyes at me. "What did you do, Mason?"

"Why do you assume *I* did something?" I scowled.

"Because she's been so happy, and so clearly in love with you. You must've done something to make her leave in the middle of the night." Her sparse brows drew together. "If you broke that girl's heart and threw her love back in her face . . . I'm going to be real unhappy, son."

I rolled my eyes, but before I could answer, there was a knock at the kitchen door.

Ali Reynolds Evans stood on my stoop with her daughter. "We're here to take care of Piper. Meghan said you might need some help while Rilla . . ." Her eyes slid to the side. "Recovers."

"Bless you, Ali." I could've kissed her.

"I'm not doing this for you." She shot me the stink-eye. "I'm doing this for Rilla. And for Piper."

Why she did it didn't matter, so long as I could get to the club. I arrived around ten and buried myself in work. The less I thought about Rilla, the better.

The lunch crowd was just beginning to die down when a familiar face made his way to the bar.

"Hey, Mason."

I forced a grin. "Flynn. Long time and all that. I heard you were in town."

"Yeah, and I heard you got married. Congratulations, dude. Rilla's a great girl."

I nodded. "Yeah."

"Also heard you fucked it up."

"News travels fast." I wadded up the bar rag and tossed it into a barrel. "What can I do for you, Flynn?"

"Nothing, but I can do something for you. I'm here to tell you to man up."

"Oh, really? What the hell's that supposed to mean?"

"Means you love the girl. That's what everyone tells me, anyway. But you've convinced her you don't. Now, Mason, I'm not saying you don't have issues. You've got cause to be cautious. Life fucked you over and took your wife, and that sucks beyond the telling. But now you're getting another shot. Why in the world would you turn that down?"

"You don't know what it's like to lose someone you love."

I spoke through gritted teeth. “I can’t do it again.”

“I get that. Believe me, dude. I know you don’t think it’s the same, but when I left town without Ali all those years ago, I thought my life was over. I didn’t want to love anyone ever again. And when I got back here and found myself falling for the same damn girl? You don’t think that made me stop and think? But I finally came to one conclusion. I love Ali. I’m not going to stop. So I can be miserable and think I’m protecting my heart, or I can take a chance and be happy. Call me crazy, but I chose the happy.”

“I’d die if I lost her.” I couldn’t look him in the eye, for fear I’d break down and bawl like a wuss. “I know what that pain feels like. I can’t deal, not again.”

“Oh, okay. I get it. So you’d rather go ahead and embrace the hurt right away than admit you’re already in love with the chick. See, Mason, what you’re not seeing is that by pushing her away, you’re getting what you think you can’t handle. You already love her. That’s not going to change. Odds are better for you if you grow a pair and tell her the truth.” He leaned forward. “Grab your happily-ever-after, man. They don’t hand them out like candy. Take it and run.”

A glimmer of hope began to burn in me. I thought of Rilla’s eyes, trusting and filled with love, and something that might have been peace started to edge out the fear, melting its grip on my heart.

Flynn stood up. “All right, I’ve said my piece. I’m outta here. My wife and daughter need to leave your house in about two hours, so make sure you’re home by then. We’re catching a late plane back to New York tonight.” He winked at me. “See, I got my happy ending. Turns out it was only the beginning.”

Rilla

"I need to see her. Meghan, so help me . . . you know how I feel about you, but if you don't step aside—"

Loud voices woke me. I blinked into the sunlight that streamed through the window, confused for a moment until everything from the last few days came tumbling back down on me. I was still at Meghan and Sam's house. But why was I hearing Mason's voice?

"Mason, calm down. She's sleeping. She needed rest. Just sit here and have a cup of coffee, and when she wakes up, and you can say whatever you think you need to tell her. But I'm telling you, buddy, if you're here to try to convince her you don't love her again, you can just turn yourself right around and get out of my house. Because that's bullshit."

I climbed out of bed, careful to avoid any creaking floorboards. I opened the door just enough to ease into the hall above the steps.

"Of course that's not why I'm here. I'm an asshole. I'm an idiotic, stupid dick. I almost threw away the best thing that's ever happened to me. But I'm here to correct that now."

"Oh, yeah? What happened, Mason? Were you haunted by three ghosts last night?"

I heard his sigh. "No, more like my mother, Flynn and my own stupidity." There was a scrape that sounded like a boots against hard wood. "Meghan, I just freaked. The other night, when she said she loved me—God, I've known I loved her for months. But I kept pushing it away. And then the accident—it was like a warning. Don't dare love her. She'll be taken away. I got a taste what losing her would feel like. And it scared the shit out of me.

"I swore I wouldn't love her, because I couldn't take that pain again. But dammit to hell if I haven't gone and done it.

I love her. I love Rilla. I'm in love with her, and I can't live without her. And that scares me beyond anything I know. When I loved Lu . . . I was young. I thought we had lifetimes ahead of us. Then in just one night, it was gone, and it almost killed me. If I hadn't had Piper, I might've let it. But now I know what it's like to lose. I know that pain. I thought I could protect myself from it, but . . . it's too late. And if I've fucked it up, lost her because I was afraid to lose her? No. I can't accept that. I'll do anything. I'll beg. I'll grovel. I'll spend the rest of my life proving how much I love her."

Tears spilled out of my eyes again. His pain was anguishing, and I could feel it to my very soul. But taking a step . . . letting him love me . . . letting myself love him . . . it was risky. It was a gamble. What if he changed his mind again and decided I wasn't worth the pain?

I closed my eyes, breathing a prayer for guidance, and in that instant, I was filled with something more beautiful and real than anything I'd ever known. It had nothing to do with the fire and brimstone of my childhood. It was an assurance, a promise and a fulfillment. I whispered the words to myself.

"The substance of things hoped for, the evidence of things not seen."

Before I realized what I was doing, I walked downstairs, halting two steps from the landing.

Meghan heard me first. She glanced up, and within seconds, Mason followed her gaze.

He looked like hell. There was no other way to describe it. He hadn't shaved, and his jaw was covered with dark stubble. His eyes were bloodshot, and he was wearing rumpled clothes that he'd probably slept in them.

I'd never seen anything or anyone look so wonderful.

I curled my toes over the edge of the step and leaned over the banister. "Mason, did you have something to say to me?"

His Adam's apple bobbed as he swallowed. "Rilla, I love

you. I'm in love with you. I've loved you since the day you wore that ugly funeral dress into my bar, and I've only loved you more every day since. I didn't marry you to save you. I married you because I love you. I don't ever want to lose you, in any way. But I'm not going to miss out on our life together because I'm too afraid of what could happen."

My voice trembled. "Love is scary and risky, Mason. I'm not looking for a prince charming or a knight in armor. And we both know you're no saint."

Meghan snorted, reminding both of us that she was still in the room, and I grinned as I continued.

"I can't promise you I'll never leave you, because none of us can control what happens in life. But I promise you as much as it's in my power, I'll be with you forever."

"That's a start."

He took a step toward me. As I stood on the stairs, we were about the same height. Without looking away from my eyes, Mason knelt at my feet and wrapped his arms around my legs.

"I'll never make you want to leave again. Come home with me, Rilla. Come be my wife and let me be your husband. Let me be in love with you, as long as we both shall live." He smiled. "Let's claim our happily-ever-after."

The vows we spoke in that old farmhouse, in the early morning light, were more binding and real than any words we'd spoken before the judge in Savannah. The room was alive with love that was bigger than either of us, transcending time and space and loss and fear.

Mason stood up and lifted me into his arms. His lips covered mine, both possessing and giving. Surrendering.

"Take me home." I whispered the request against his throat.

"Darlin,' those are the most beautiful words I've ever heard." Mason held me closer and carried me into the light of the rising sun.

The End

Epilogue

"THERE'S NOTHING LIKE A beach wedding." Emmy Carter sighed as she shifted in her wooden slatted chair.

"And they've got the perfect day." Abby Donavan adjusted the straw hat she wore to protect her pale skin. "I can't believe how many people are here."

"Well, pretty much the whole Cove's turned out for today, and then you have all the folks who drove down from Georgia. Oh, look, here come the bridesmaids."

Four women in lilac dresses of varying styles made their way across the narrow walkway to the tent. The first carried a pretty baby girl dressed in the same shade and held the hand of a little boy in a tuxedo.

"Lindsay looks wonderful, doesn't she? And how sweet are those babies? I swear, DJ looks more like Joseph every day."

Emmy nodded. "You didn't know Daniel, but DJ resembles him, too. And Lindsay and Joseph are doing a wonderful job running the Tide."

"Who's the next bridesmaid?" Abby squinted in the sun.

"Oh, that's Meghan's college roommate, Laura. She's married to a Marine. They flew in from California for the wedding."

"She's lovely. And the other two?"

Emmy smiled. "Rilla Wallace. She's one of Meghan's friends from Burton. Look at how she's holding her flowers over her stomach. She's just beginning to show, and I think she's a little self-conscious about it. See that big guy over on the side of the tent? The one holding the little girl? That's her husband, Mason. They're the sweetest couple. The way he looks at her . . . it makes me believe in true love again."

Abby put her hand to her heart. "Emmy Carter, are you getting soft in your old age?"

Emmy snorted. "Hardly. And shut up, I'm not old. Just older than you. But thirty-five is *not* ancient."

"I'm just teasing you. Oh, that's Sam's sister bringing up the rear, right?"

"Yes, and her daughter's with her. Her husband is Sam's best man. See, here they come."

The back door of The Rip Tide opened, and three men emerged. "Wow, they grow 'em sexy up there in Georgia, don't they? Makes me think I might have to look into relocating."

"Don't you dare. First of all, Jude and Logan need you to run the bed and breakfast. And second, I don't want to lose my best friend."

"You mean your only single friend." Abby elbowed her. "Don't worry. I don't have any plans to move. Oh my gosh, here comes Jude with Joseph. She looks so beautiful."

Joseph Hawthorne escorted his mother to her seat before stopping to kiss his baby and his wife, patting his son on the head as he passed. He greeted Sam, Flynn and the minister and joined them to stand in the front.

The music from the trio in the front changed from the soft classical notes to something decidedly more country.

"What's this song?" Abby whispered. "You're the country music expert."

"It's called *It's Your Love.* Tim McGraw and Faith Hill sang it. It's the perfect wedding song." Emmy sniffled and touched a tissue to her eyes beneath the sunglasses.

"Emmy, are you crying?" Abby's voice sounded a little teary.

"Of course not. I'm just—I got something in my eye. Oh. Oh, Abby, look. She's just breathtaking. Have you ever seen such a gorgeous bride?"

Meghan walked toward the tent, holding tight to Logan's arm. At the sight, half of the guests dug for tissues or hankies. Although no one spoke his name, there was not a doubt that Daniel Hawthorne was in every Cove heart as his best friend escorted his daughter down the aisle.

Emmy turned a little. Two rows back, Cooper Davis glanced at her, holding her gaze for a beat before she dropped her eyes.

Sam Reynolds' face shone with a transcendent happiness when his bride reached his side, and now it was time for the guests from Burton to wipe away a few tears.

"If only Joe and Elizabeth could be here to see this day . . ." Ellen Nelson squeezed her husband's hand. "Wouldn't they be proud of Sam?"

"They'd be busting their buttons at both their kids." Fred patted his wife's shoulder. "They're here, don't you doubt it."

The minister spoke the opening words of the ceremony, welcoming family and friends to this celebration of love and life.

When it was time to speak vows, Sam took Meghan's hands in his. "Meghan, you were the last one I expected to meet. You were the last one I wanted to love. You are my heart, my soul and my life, and I never want to spend another day apart from you. I promise you laughter at the dinner table, evening swims at the river and love every day of your life. You are my last, my first, my only."

Meghan smiled through shining eyes. "Sam, you taught me love. You gave me your heart, even when you didn't want to do it. You've given me a life I never dreamed I could have. I promise you art lessons at dawn, dancing whenever I can talk you into it, and love every day of your life. You are my last, my first, my only."

Two other couples in the tent sought out each other's eyes. At the front, Ali smiled at Flynn around the bride and groom. Rilla gazed into the congregation until she found Mason.

My last, my first, my only.

If you loved Rilla and Mason, don't miss the first and second books in The One Trilogy.

THE LAST ONE is Meghan and Sam's story.
THE FIRST ONE is about Ali and Flynn.
The best way to show how much you love a book is by leaving a review on your favorite venue. Please leave some love for THE ONLY ONE. Thank you!

Want to make sure you don't miss any new releases, special content and giveaways? Sign up for Tawdra Kandle's newsletter here (http://eepurl.com/isWKs).

Those Crazy Christians Brad Paisley
On The Verge Collin Raye
Without You Keith Urban
Limes Brad Paisley
Stay Forever Hal Ketchum
If I Didn't Have You Thompson Squared
If You Leave Me Now Suzy Bogguss
Long, Long Time Mindy McCready
Me and Jesus Brad Paisley
I Always Get Lucky With You Suzy Bogguss

Acknowledgements

Well, here we are, at the end of *The One* Trilogy. And what a way to go out.

When I decided to write Meghan's story, after *The Posse,* I had no idea that it would stretch into three books. But the longer I hung around Burton, Georgia, the more at home I felt. I've lived in that world for so long now that I could walk you down Central Street, stop in to say hey to Boomer, visit at the hardware store and then maybe swing into Kenny's Diner for a slice of pie. I can tell you all about The Colonel's Last Stand, and what the horses on Fred Nelson's farm look like.

So leaving that place and those people hurts more than a little. The good news is that we'll still get pieces of them in the Crystal Cove books. I expect Meghan and Sam will pop down to visit her mom and Logan. It's even possible Alex and Cal might go check out the beach scene. Who can say?

First thanks must go to my wonderful readers who have fallen in love with Burton alongside of me. Thank you for loving the people inside my head. You make every bit worthwhile.

Appreciation to my amazing team: Laura Hidalgo at Book-Fabulous Design for the gorgeous cover, Brad Olson Photography for the photo, Stacey Blake at Champagne Formats for the beautiful interior, Kelly Baker for being picky and sneaking in Oxford Commas everywhere and Olivia Hardin for beta reading, sanity patrol and rockin' the rock.

More gratitude to Jade Eby and Maria Clark, who have begun the process of keeping me organized, on task and productive. Good luck, ladies.

To my Naughty Temptresses—I seriously <3 you all.

Of course, my family is my source of inspiration and love always, and big hugs to each and every one.

A few quick notes: Mason's mother Naomi is fighting leukemia in this book. I didn't know the nature of her illness right away, although I knew it was a vague form of cancer. But leukemia is a monster I know too well. I lost my mother to it in 2007, after a stem cell transplant and a brave, well-fought battle. And a friend of mine, Pam, is fighting that war right now, with more grace, dignity and humor than is fair to the rest of the world. I urge you to do two things: first, register with the bone marrow registry http://www.deletebloodcancer.org/). You may have the key to saving a life within your body, and I promise, you won't regret it. Second: please support The Leukemia and Lymphoma Society (https://donate.lls.org). As many of you know, my purple hair is in support of this organization, and they do so much good.

My last note is about some delicate issues of faith and belief touched on in Rilla's story. If you read some of it and thought that it would never happen in this day and age . . . I promise you, each part of Rilla's story before Mason happened to different people I knew. I don't stand in judgment of any person's beliefs. Our walks are between each of us and God. This was simply part of who Rilla is and why she made choices she did.

Thank you for spending a season with me in Burton. I'll see you in Crystal Cove.

Photo by Heather Batchelder

Tawdra Kandle writes romance, in just about all its forms. She loves unlikely pairings, strong women, sexy guys, hot love scenes and just enough conflict to make it interesting. Her books run from YA paranormal romance (THE KING SERIES), through NA paranormal and contemporary romance (THE SERENDIPITY DUET, PERFECT DISH DUO, THE ONE TRILOGY) to adult contemporary and paramystery romance (CRYSTAL COVE BOOKS and RECIPE FOR DEATH SERIES). She lives in central Florida with a husband, kids, sweet pup and too many cats. And yeah, she rocks purple hair.

Follow Tawdra on Facebook, Twitter, Tsu, Instagram, Pinterest and Tumblr.

Keep up with her releases and events on her website and her newsletter.

Other Books by the Author

The King Series
Fearless
Breathless
Restless
Endless

Crystal Cove Books
The Posse
The Plan
The Path

The Perfect Dish Series
Best Served Cold
Just Desserts
I Choose You

The One Trilogy
The Last One
The First One
The Only One

The Always Love Trilogy
Always for You
Always My Own

The Seredipity Duet
Undeniable
Unquenchable

Recipe for Death Series
Death Fricassee
Death A La Mode

CPSIA information can be obtained
at www.ICGtesting.com
Printed in the USA
BVHW031154011119
562694BV00001B/195/P